# Second Fiddle (An Anthony Carrick Mystery)

by

Jason Blacker

PUBLISHED BY:
Lemon Tree Publishing
Copyright © 2013
Jason Blacker

Visit **www.JasonBlacker.com** on the web to stay up to date

Editing: Andrea Anesi

ISBN: 9781927623534

*For my father who always encouraged from the sidelines*

# Table of Contents

SECOND FIDDLE (AN ANTHONY CARRICK MYSTERY)

# One

I'd just finished another show at an art gallery in LA called Worthington's Fine Art. It had gone better than I'd expected. What that means is I'd sold three paintings. Three paintings at five grand a piece. My take is half of that. If I was really careful I could make that money last three, maybe four months. All depended on how much art supplies I had to buy.

It was breathing room but I could use a new gig too. It had been a few months since I'd actually been hired independently of the LAPD and my good friend Roberts. Not that I wasn't grateful for his help. I was. But a private gig paid twice as much. Five Bennies was better than two and a half. I didn't need high school math to figure that out.

And can you imagine my surprise when I got a call? It was like my lips to God's ears and he responded. I was sitting on a park bench just up from the beach and not far from the pier when the call came in. Sometimes when I'm looking for inspiration for a painting I'll waste my time watching little old ladies with their leathery faces walk up and down the path along the beach with their little white trolleys dragged behind them, like stubborn dogs, filled with a brown bag of groceries.

On this particular occasion there weren't too many old ladies out. But there were tourists walking arm in arm. Couples kissing and holding hands. Ain't love grand? None of that earned me any money. It's the killing and the pillaging that puts food on my table. Though if you asked me after a few drinks, I'd sooner starve than live off the dead. But human nature being what it is, there's an abundance of work in my field.

It was getting towards dinnertime and I was thinking of something to eat when my phone rang. I looked at the number and I didn't recognize it. I don't usually answer it if I don't recognize it. It was a two one two number. I had no idea where that was from. But I felt like taking a chance.

"Hello," I said.

"Is this Anthony Carrick?" the voice on the other end asked. It was a man's voice. I'd put him middle-aged and polite. He had a generic accent, not something I could pinpoint.

"Who's asking?"

"Frank Moody," he said.

"I don't know a Frank Moody."

"I'm sorry to have bothered you, I must have the wrong number."

I had a feeling he was about to hang up.

"I didn't say you had the wrong number. I am Anthony Carrick."

"Are you always this careful, Mr. Carrick?"

"In my line of work you can't be careful enough, Frank. How can I help you?"

"I heard you're a private investigator, Mr. Carrick."

"My father's Mr. Carrick, I'm Anthony. Yeah, I help grannies get their cats out of trees."

There was a pause on the other end. It was probably a frown but I couldn't see it.

"I don't understand."

10

"Yes, I'm a private investigator. Where're you calling from anyway?"

"I'm in New York, Mr... Anthony."

"Right. You know I'm in California?"

"Yes I do, but I was asked to call you."

"I see. And what is it you'd like me to do?"

"Well, perhaps it's a bit premature but we're very concerned about our concertmaster."

"I see."

"He didn't show up for practice today and our show starts in five minutes and he's still not here."

"So you want me to ring him up and scold him?"

There was a frustrated sigh on the other end.

"No, that's not why I'm calling. We've tried that, but he's not answering."

"Have you sent anyone around?"

"Yes, and he's not answering. Mrs. Sonia Varnier, one of our benefactors is deeply troubled by this. It simply isn't like him to miss a practice or not call."

"I'm not sure how I can help. Missing persons cases are often solved within a few days. If not, the likelihood of finding them alive diminishes. You're better off calling the police."

"We've thought of that, but we don't want to burden the police unnecessarily. It has only been one day."

"Then I'm not sure why you're so worried."

"Because Paul Klee, he's our missing concertmaster, was worried for his safety recently."

"How so?"

"He had started to become paranoid that he was being followed and that nasty sorts were after him."

"And did he have any proof of this?"

"No. But honestly, Anthony, his behavior had changed in the last week and something must have been bothering him. It was quite the change."

"I understand. Did he give you any idea about who was threatening or what they might have been after?"

"Not to me specifically. He said it was a private matter but that he might need to take some time away. That was the last I heard from him. Will you come to New York, Anthony, and help us look for him?"

"I think it'll be a waste of my time and your money. He'll likely show up in the next day or two."

"That doesn't matter. We're happy to pay for you to come out. At the worst, it might just end up being a short holiday for you in our lovely city. We'll even throw in complimentary tickets to Vivaldi's Four Seasons."

That was mighty tempting.

"My fees are five hundred a day with a twenty-five hundred minimum. Plus expenses."

"That won't be a problem."

"Alright then," I said. "Transfer the money over, send me a ticket to New York, business class, and I'll see you tomorrow."

"Thank you, Anthony. We're very grateful."

"You might not be when he shows up tomorrow having just been on a bender for a day."

"Mrs. Varnier is not certain about that. Though I certainly hope that's what happens. I'll send the money and the ticket information right away. We'll have someone pick you up at the airport too."

"That'd be swell."

I hung up and got up from the bench. It was definitely dinner time. I was hungry enough to eat a horse, but horse is not what I wanted.

I got into my car and drove around until I found a restaurant that looked like my kind of place. Big steaks for small bills. I sat down and thought about this concertmaster. These artsy types could be flaky. He'd probably holed himself up in a hotel with some hooker and a bag of blow. I figured he'd beat me to the Philharmonic tomorrow with egg on his face, and I'd end up taking a week to tour the Big Apple.

It could've been worse. I could be stuck here painting portraits of tourists down by the pier for twenty five bucks a pop. If Moody wanted to be a sucker. I'd take his money. There's a reason police didn't take missing persons seriously, and it's because usually people go missing for a reason. Not kids of course, that's different. But a grown man in a big city. He's missing because he wants to be.

## Two

At just after ten the next morning, that was a Saturday, the plane touched down at JFK. As promised, as I got out of the terminal and into the public greeting area there was a chauffeur waiting for me. He was dressed in a well-fitted black suit with a black cap and black gloves. My name was written in block capital letters.

He was a tall thin man with sallow complexion and heavy jowls. He was all business and no vacation when I greeted him. I shook his hand and he offered his begrudgingly.

"Anthony Carrick," I said.

"Terrence Smith," he replied in a monotone that could have been mistaken for a sigh.

His hand was warm through the glove and soft as overcooked fish that hadn't been filleted. Regardless of his manner, I was nevertheless pleased that I was being chauffeured around. Though I also found it surprising that the New York Philharmonic would go to such expense for a PI. I was even more unnerved when he opened the door for me to the Maybach.

"The Philharmonic sure treats their guest in style," I said to him, grinning.

"I work for Madam Varnier," he said, dryly.

He closed the door behind me and walked around to the driver's seat. When he was in he started up the car and started to drive towards town.

"There are soft drinks and bottled water in the middle compartment next to you if you wish, Mr. Carrick," he said without looking back at me.

I opened up the armrest and took out a cream soda. They had always been my favorite ever since I was allowed my first soda.

"Where are you taking me?" I asked him.

"To your hotel to sign in and then I'll take you straight to the Philharmonic's offices."

"And which hotel am I staying at?"

"The Ritz-Carlton, Mr. Carrick."

Indeed, I thought to myself. These people didn't have any idea of the kind of man I was. But if they were footing the bill they could put me up in a tent in Central Park for all I cared.

Terry drove slowly and carefully towards Central Park and I took in the surrounding views as we drove by. The whole trip took around thirty minutes for us to get to the Ritz.

Terry got out, but by the time he got to my door it was open and I was out. He shut it for me nevertheless. He got my single piece of luggage out of the car and placed it next to me.

"I'll wait right here for you, if you don't mind not being too long," he said.

"I was thinking of a lap around the pool and a massage first," I said.

His face drooped like a wilting flower.

"I'm kidding," I said. "I'll be just a few minutes. Am I supposed to tip you?"

"No, sir, that would be inappropriate."

"Very well. I'll see you in a short while."

I put on my fedora, picked up my bag and walked into the main reception area. I signed in and received the card for my room. I felt like a fish out of water. Like a bum being offered a cigarette holder for his rolled up stub of a cigarette. My room was on the thirteenth floor and I declined any help with my single bag. I needed all the money I could save from this gig for myself.

The room was opulent. Almost bigger than my apartment in Santa Monica. I didn't know if Sonia Varnier was trying to impress me or ridicule me. The room had an attached suite and it looked right over Central Park. I was looking north over The Pond. I didn't understand how people afforded hotels like this. But then I'd never been around much money.

I unpacked quickly and closed the door after I left. I made it back down within five minutes. I was pretty sure of that. As much as the room was nice, it was a lonely place. The only thing I could figure it was good for was making me maudlin about the one percent and the rest of us.

Eagle eyes Terry saw me coming and hopped out of the driver's seat and had my door open by the time I reached the car.

"Just under five minutes, I reckon," I said to him.

"Very good, sir," he said. "I'll now take you to the Philharmonic which shouldn't take us long."

Because I'm a keen student, I knew that the Philharmonic was at Lincoln Center Plaza, less than a mile away. I could have walked it, but the soft leather of the Maybach was more comfortable than the hard leather on the soles of my shoes. I also figured that folks this foolish with the amount of money they were spending on a missing man who would likely be arriving as soon as I was wouldn't mind if I made use of their extravagance.

So I enjoyed the ride to the Philharmonic in comfort and ease and almost half a million dollar luxury. In a world that had gone down the economic toilet, this was pure lunacy. Such are those with extraneous cash and dimmed empathy.

Terry dropped me off by the main entrance. The Lincoln Center reminded me of Stalinist era communist building creativity. It wasn't bad, but it wasn't inspiring either. From some angles it looked like the architect had tried for some Greco-Roman inspiration but then got tired and gave up. In other words, I wasn't a fan. And I appreciate the arts, but too much of it has become pretentious.

Nevertheless, I wasn't about to look a gift horse in the mouth. I walked into the main administration area. A woman in a dark blue suit was seated behind the main reception desk and looked up at me with her blue eyes. Her black hair was tied behind her in a pony tale. She was attractive in an odd sort of way.

"May I help you?" she asked.

"I'm here to see Frank Moody," I said.

"Can I tell him who's here?"

"Anthony Carrick."

"Oh good. We've been expecting you, Mr. Carrick."

She had a slight accent that I couldn't put my finger on. It was sexy and it sounded a little French, a little Italian and maybe a little Greek. It also gave me a warm feeling to be expected. The last time I'd been expected somewhere I got my clock cleaned. She stood up and walked around the front of her desk.

"I'm Christina Tedder," she said. "Assistant to Mr. Moody."

I shook her hand which was the color of light caramel cream and just as soft. I told her how much of a pleasure it was to meet her, and I wasn't lying. She lowered her gaze from me and withdrew her hand.

"Where you from?" I asked.

"Why do you ask?"

It was a non-threatening curious question.

"I can't quite pinpoint your accent. If I was to guess, I might say Greek, maybe even Italian?"

She smiled and shook her head.

18

"Close, but no. I'm from Israel."

I nodded.

"It's unusual, and sexy," I said, feeling a little bit like a chump. She blushed again.

"Mr. Moody is right this way, if you'll follow me."

And follow her I did. She had an hourglass figure that I would have followed to the ends of time. But our journey was quicker than that. Through frosted glass doors and left down a hallway we made our way to a corner office that looked out over an outdoor water feature with a sculpture in it that looked to me like a broken leg.

Christina knocked on the wooden door and walked in. I was right behind her enjoying the view, and not the one of the outdoor water feature. We were on the third floor. A man in a big leather chair finished his conversation on the phone and looked up at us. He stood up and came around the front of his desk. He was tall and thin and gray. His skin, eyes and hair almost the same color gray. His thin hair was brushed fore to aft but it fell in little wisps at the sides of his temple. The first image that came to mind was of Dr. Schweitzer, but Moody wasn't as handsome or as healthy. He looked the worse for wear and he was clean shaven.

"Frank Moody," the tall man said, offering me a thin bony hand.

I took it and shook it gently, afraid I might snap his fingers like dry kindling.

"Anthony Carrick," I said.

"You're younger than I imagined," he said.

"So are you."

That was a bald faced lie, but the only thing that came to mind.

"Please sit down, Mr. Carrick."

"Anthony," I said.

Frank nodded and smiled at himself.

"Yes, you said so last night. It might take me a while, Anthony." He looked over at Christina. "That'll be all for now."

She bowed and walked out of the room, closing the door softly behind her, like a lover might. I watched after her.

"You must excuse me," said Frank. "I've forgotten my manners. Can I offer you anything to drink?"

I shook my head.

"I had a soda in the car from the airport."

"Ah yes," said Frank. "Mrs. Varnier was adamant that she pick you up personally. Just as well, as we don't have a chauffeur service as you might imagine."

"I had wondered about that," I said. "I wasn't sure how well funded the performing arts were here in the Big Apple."

"The best thing we have going for us, Anthony, is our benefactors and the large population. That's what keeps us going. But with that comes more competition as you can imagine."

I nodded.

"How was your flight?"

"It was fine, thanks. Business class allows a certain more discretionary room which is most welcome."

I wasn't sure if he was being polite or if he was stalling. Perhaps he had heard from Paul and was now feeling a little embarrassed and not sure how to tell me.

"Have you heard from your concertmaster yet?" I asked, deciding to get down to business.

Frank looked down at his lap and then slowly shook his head.

"No, I'm afraid not. I've rung him up several times at home and on his cellphone. No answer from either."

"I see."

This was not what I had expected. And the longer it went without hearing from Paul the less likely it would be that he'd just gone for a short personal break.

"I think now is the time to get the police involved," I said.

Frank looked up at me, his face a squiggled map of worry.

"I was hoping you wouldn't say that."

"People sometimes go missing for a day or two just for personal reasons. However, beyond that, we usually get a little more concerned."

Frank nodded, and picked up the phone.

"Can you make a missing person's report with the police, Christina," he said. "Thank you."

"Christina will get on that right away. You know, this is very unlike Paul. He loved the orchestra. He loved music and he loved being concertmaster."

"How long has he been in that position?"

"Only three years. He was the youngest concertmaster in the history of this orchestra. But such a rare talent."

"Do you have a picture of him?" I asked.

Frank looked around his desk and then looked in a drawer. He pulled out a program for the upcoming concert of Vivaldi's Four Seasons.

"I have this," he said, turning through the program pages until he got to the photograph of Paul Klee. He handed the program to me. "Christina can print you out a larger one if you need."

I looked at the thumbnail color image of Paul. He didn't look like a concertmaster. I imagined an older man, perhaps with a double chin, graying, balding hair with wire rimmed glasses. Paul was a handsome man. Probably in his early to mid forties, with jet black hair and a clear complexion. He wore no glasses but had an English mustache and soul patch, the same deep black as his hair. It gave him a roguish look. He had an intensity about him as he looked at the camera. His mouth formed a knowing smile. As if he were looking at an attractive woman.

I had no idea as to why a young, handsome man like Paul would go missing. Unless you wanted to.

"Tell me about him," I said.

"What do you want to know?"

"Anything you feel is important."

Frank looked down at his hands. He rubbed one over the other and picked at the corner of a nail. Then he looked up at me.

"Paul was well liked and charismatic. He had been playing violin since he was three years old. He turned forty three just a few months ago, and we made him concertmaster just after his fortieth. He's been with the New York Philharmonic since he was twenty two when he finished his music degree at Juilliard, and we snapped him up right away."

"He didn't want to take an advanced degree or go into teaching?" I asked.

"I don't think he knew what he wanted to do. However, we made him an offer that he found hard to refuse."

"Tell me about that."

"Mrs. Varnier and her late husband, may he rest in peace, have been strong patrons of the arts and especially the Philharmonic for over thirty years. Mrs. Varnier promised to provide for Paul in quite an extravagant manner if he took our offer as second violinist straight after graduation."

"I would have thought an opportunity like that would be snapped up by any number of students."

Frank looked at me and smiled wistfully, as if I'd just come in on the turnip truck.

"And you'd be right. We had, how should I put it, any number of eager students practically prostrating themselves for the opportunity to perform. We only had three positions. A second violinist, an oboe and a trumpet."

"I might not know much about classical music but why would he choose a second violin position?"

"There's usually a hierarchy, Anthony, in the orchestra. As much as everyone pretends to get along and play together, it is much more competitive than most laymen suppose. One usually starts as a second violinist and moves up from there."

"I don't understand. Earlier you said he was a rare talent. Are you saying that no one else offered him something better?"

Frank smiled at me again like a doddering uncle.

"You're quite right. Chicago as well as the Boston orchestras were both offering first violin positions."

"And he didn't take it?"

"No. We had a secret weapon."

"Which was?"

"Mrs. Varnier. She promised him the world and luxuries beyond measure. If there was a fault in Paul it was that he had been pampered and spoiled his whole life. An only child who, in the eyes of his parents, could do no wrong. And we didn't help it either. If I must be candid with you, Anthony..."

"That would help," I said, feeling the rim of my fedora for any rough edges while looking at the old and wrinkled Moody with a sharp eye.

"Well, we promised him a first violin position within a year."

"And did you fulfill your promise?"

"We did."

Frank leaned forward and interlocked his hands together and lay them upon his empty desk. He looked at me from kind eyes. The kind of eyes a fox bats at you before it goes for your neck.

"What do you think, Anthony?" he asked.

I thought he was getting very comfortable with my first name.

"I think you've exhaled a lot of air mixed with some noise. Most of it not interesting to me."

He frowned at me. I figured he wasn't used to hearing these sorts of things from people. But then he wasn't used to speaking with private dicks either.

"What do you mean?" he asked, genuinely insulted.

"You've told me a lot of things, none of which are any good for a man in my position. You've told me he's a rare talent. That you bribed him to come over to the New York Phil. You've told me he's spoiled and that he's been with you since he got out of diapers. I knew all of that just looking at his smarmy mug."

"You asked me to tell you what I thought was important."

"Yes I did, and you've told me nothing at all. A man doesn't go missing, and I don't get called by his handlers for nothing. You're not being completely honest with me, Frank, are you?"

"I don't know what you could mean?"

"Let me give you a little help. I look at Paul, and I see a young man with a roving eye. A man who's had everything handed to him on a silver platter. He gets whatever he wants and he's never refused. But he's soft. There's no hard corners to him. What I mean is that he could get into trouble with the wrong sort and not be able to extricate himself. I imagine you and Sonia have spent a few bucks getting him out of a few jams. Am I getting warm?"

Frank leaned back again and folded his hands in his lap. He smiled at me again. I was getting tired of his smiles. Any minute I was going to knock it off his face.

"They said you're the best, and I might have doubted them before now, but not anymore."

"If you brought me here and paid me good money just for a dance, you've wasted my time and yours. I'll gladly take my leave."

I stood up and started to put on my hat. No wonder artists get such a bad reputation. Frank stood up like someone had stuck a hot golden rod up his ass.

"Please, Mr. Carrick, this is a difficult situation and we could really use your help."

He'd found my last name again. It sounded better on him than my first name did. I sat back down but kept my hat on.

"Then we need to get down to brass tacks, Frank, if you're really after my help."

Frank nodded his head vigorously. It went on for a long time like he'd got a spring in his neck stuck.

"Yes, we really need your help. What do you want to know?"

"I want to know what he was really like. Let's imagine that he's been kidnapped or worse..."

"What do you mean worse?"

"We'll leave that up to the imaginations of horror writers. But imagine he's been kidnapped or hurt. Who and why would somebody want to do that to him?"

Frank pushed his hands to his face and wiped them with his palms. When he looked back at me he looked older and tireder.

"This is all rather unpleasant to think about, Mr. Carrick."

I'd let him hang his hat on my last name. Respect might get me closer to the truth.

"My business specializes in the unpleasant, Frank. If you really do want to help your concertmaster you'll start living up to your name."

He was so morbid that it didn't even get a smirk out of him. Frank sighed and slouched back into his couch.

"Well, you're right about one thing, Paul did have a roving eye. He's had affairs with two women in the orchestra that we know of and we had to let one of our assistants go because of him."

"What happened?"

"He got her pregnant. We paid for the abortion and we paid her a sum of money to go quietly. Quite a nasty ordeal."

"You didn't pay her the money, did you?"

"No."

Frank shook his head and his chin sagged against his upper chest.

"Who did?"

"You know who did."

He looked at me and I nodded.

"How much did she pay?"

"Two hundred and fifty thousand dollars."

"Right, and what else?"

"Well, there were quite a few upset violinists when Paul came on board."

"Why is that?"

"Because we gave him a first violin position after just a year. There have been second violinists waiting patiently for over a decade for their chance. Being of artistic inclinations, many of our musicians are somewhat moody."

I smiled at that. Here I was speaking to a man who until recently had not been frank and still hadn't seemed moody. He looked at me with a frown.

"Carry on," I said.

"Anyway, three years ago, when we made Paul the concertmaster, that pretty much divided our house. Half of the musicians were quite upset with our choice of him and the other half were quite pleased."

"And I don't have to ask which half had more women on the team."

"No you don't, Mr. Carrick, no you don't."

"And are most of these musicians still around?"

"I should think so, yes. It's difficult to become mobile in our business. Musicians will wait years and decades to go from second violin to first violin for instance. Only the exceptionally rare talents are able to jump the ranks rather quickly. There aren't a lot of open positions at the top orchestras in the major centers. And where there are, you'll also find intense competition."

"Now we're getting somewhere," I said. "These are some of the reasons why people get hurt."

"I hope not," said Frank, his smile thinning much quicker than his hair.

"I hope for peace amongst men. Hasn't happened yet."

Frank looked at me with his smile hanging precariously from one corner of his mouth like a defunct sign on a bankrupt business.

"You don't believe in the best in people do you, Mr. Carrick?"

"I believe that after twenty odd years in this line of work, a man who goes missing for more than a day or two is usually in trouble."

Frank inhaled deeply and let out a slow, sad sigh.

"I'll need to speak to other members of the orchestra," I said. "I'd like to start with the two women he had affairs with, and I'd also like to speak with the assistant you let go."

Frank nodded his head.

"Those two women from the orchestra. Were they single?"

I had a suspicion that at least one of them might have had a lover or husband. That's just the way these things generally turn out. Frank looked at me and raised his eyebrows just above his nose.

"They were both married," he said. "Actually, I believe they still are. We had an incident a few months back."

"What kind of incident?"

"Lauren's husband came in quite upset and he and Paul got into it. They had a bit of a scuffle. He said he'd kill Paul if he didn't stop sleeping with his wife."

"And did he?"

Frank pinched his mouth closed into two blistered rolls of skin.

"No, I don't think he did. Like I said before, some of these musicians are quite temperamental, Paul being one of them."

"I'll need their names. I'd also like to speak with any of the musicians who were friendly with your concertmaster."

Frank nodded.

"I'll get Christina to give you that information," said Frank.

"I assume they'll be here today?"

"They should all be in shortly after lunch. Practice starts at two and we have the concert at six tonight. If you'd like to come back then, I can arrange a room for you to interview them if you'd like."

"That won't be necessary, I'll just take them aside."

"As you wish."

I stood up to leave. Frank got up and came around to the other side of the desk. He walked me out to the reception area and asked Christina to get me a list of the names I needed and a forwarding address for the assistant they let go.

"I've put in a police report on Paul," she said to Frank, "they'll be sending someone around shortly to take the information down and then pay a visit to his apartment."

Christina looked at me through her blue eyes. Looked to me about as deep as the shallow end of a pool. You could get hurt jumping into them if you weren't careful.

I left them at the reception desk. I was off to roam the mean streets of Manhattan. More truthfully, I found myself cocooned in the soft leather of the Maybach on my way back to the hotel for a rest and some lunch.

# Three

I decided to walk back to the Philharmonic. Terry had given me a card with his private number on it. He'd said he was at my disposal for the rest of the day. I told him thanks and left it at that. But I felt like a walk. I wanted to clear my head, start thinking about all the ways a guy like Paul Klee could get lost, abducted or worse.

I decided to walk through Central Park up to West 63rd Street. The park was nice. Busier than I thought it would be, but then New York is a big city. The views were great. It was late summer and the trees were in full foliage and the women were fit and sparse of clothes.

I figured that after I'd had a talk with some of the artsy, moody musicians, I'd see if I couldn't get a key to Paul's place. If Sonia Varnier had wanted me here, I was certain she'd have a key for me to get into his apartment. Which dollars to donuts she most likely paid for. I had a bad feeling about this whole thing.

I was starting to think Paul might be dead. He'd gone missing at least a day and a half now and there'd been no ransom demands. That only meant one thing. He hadn't been kidnapped. And I couldn't swallow the idea that he'd just taken some personal time. As much as I chewed it it wouldn't go down. He'd been in New York for a long time. He'd spent over twenty years with the Phil. A guy like that didn't seem to me to be a guy that just got up and left one day because he had an itch on the soles of his shoes.

I left the Ritz at just around two and I arrived at the Phil just before twenty after. I made my way up to the third floor where I was greeted by Christina. She was very pleasant and very flirty. I got to thinking I should talk to her about Paul. I was pretty sure he'd plowed those fields before.

But instead she led me back to Frank's office. When I arrived, Frank was looking out the window over a shallow pool with two black sculptures that looked like turds dropped in and called art. Maybe I was being unkind, but I was in no mood for art appreciation.

Frank turned and looked at me. He wore a tired smile, almost as tired as the tie around his neck which hung limply a couple of inches too low.

"That's Henry Moore's Reclining Figure," he said, following my gaze out of his window.

"One of several reclining figures," I said.

"You know his work."

"I studied art," I said. "Though it seems to me that Moore either went blind or crazy in his latter years. Being generous I'd say he went blind."

Franks face drooped like a wilted lily. You might have suspected me of stealing his childhood teddy bear.

"Yes, well, I suppose we're all entitled to our opinions. Though I'll have you know that that sculpture is worth millions."

"I won't doubt it," I said, "seems to me that here in the Big Apple a fool and his money are easily parted."

"Have you always been so acerbic, Mr. Carrick?" asked Frank.

"Only when I'm in a good mood," I said.

"Alright then. If you don't have a kind word to say, perhaps you'd rather speak with the musicians. I'm sure they'd be rather entertained with your disconsolate outlook on life."

He came around and walked out of his office. I followed him into the reception area where he told Christina he was taking me to Avery Hall. What I didn't realize was that Avery Hall was part of the building we were already in. The one that looked like a leftover Stalinist building with more lights and windows.

We had to go around the building on the northwest side and enter from the south side. The hall looked very much like any other orchestral hall you might find yourself in. Lots of warm, soft yellow woods and three tiers of balcony. The orchestra of course being at the far end. I couldn't help but think how quickly a place like this would burn down with all that dry, parched wood.

But that thought was short lived. My attention was caught by the musicians at the far end. They were in casual dress and making a cacophony of sound that was best described as a collection of feral cats screaming at varied states of duress.

Two women were bickering about something when we came up and walked onto the stage. They shut up when they noticed Frank amongst them.

"As you know," said Frank, once he'd got everyone's attention. "Paul has been missing for about two days now. We've put in a police report and New York's finest is looking into it. In the meantime, we've brought in a private investigator from LA, Mr. Anthony Carrick."

He gestured towards me with open arms as if I was about to step up as the lead baritone in The Marriage of Figaro. One of the women who had been bickering looked me up and down as if she were at the butchers. I couldn't tell if she wanted my flanks or my loins.

"You mean there was nobody in New York qualified to look in on our very own dilettante?" asked a man holding a trumpet.

"No one with Mr. Carrick's qualifications. Mrs. Varnier would personally consider it a kindness if you'd treat Mr. Carrick with the respect and candidness that he deserves. Mr. Carrick, would you like to say a few words?"

I hadn't come prepared with a speech as I hadn't realized this was a wedding. But I'm pretty good off the cuff. I stepped forward and drifted my gaze upon all of them. I paused here and there, mostly on the more attractive women. I was buying time.

"No," I said, and waited. All the long faces looked at me with blank stares. "I'm kidding." That got a few snorts and chuckles. "I have a few of you I want to speak with personally, but I'd also like any of you to speak with me afterwards if you have any information, however trivial, that you think I might like to hear. I'm especially fond of gossip."

A hand shot up from the back. It was a woman's hand. Somewhat chubby like boiled chicken sausages.

"Yes," I said.

"Do you know what's happened to our dear Paul?" she asked.

There were a few eye rolls around the room that started to make me dizzy.

"No, we don't," I said, and paused, thinking how much I should tell them at this stage. "However, in my experience, if you haven't heard about a ransom within forty-eight hours, you're usually not dealing with kidnappers."

"He probably just went on a bender again like he did before," piped up a grumpy young man.

I looked at him and nodded.

"That's exactly the sort of thing I'd like to hear," I said. "Come and speak with me afterwards if I don't call you up."

He raised his eyebrow and nodded as if I was wasting his time. He was a small thin man who for some reason reminded me of a court jester. His hair was an unruly mess of brown thatch and his nose was beaked. His lips were razor thin and the teeth I did see were small and sharp.

"I'd like to see Lauren Alcantara first. Lauren?"

I looked around at the faces and the women with cellos. There were only three of them. I fancied the slim blonde woman. The most attractive of them, and I was right. She stood up.

"I'm Lauren," she said.

"Would you mind coming and speaking with me?" I asked, as I led her down the stairs of the stage and about half a dozen rows into the orchestra seating. I stepped in first, and took the second last seat from the exit. Lauren sat next to me. She smelled like spring rain and flowers. Her long blonde hair was done up in a clump behind her, highlighting her long, creamy neck. She was a delicious morsel. I could see how Paul might like her. She had green eyes and a small upturned nose. Her mouth was full and her teeth were straight and white like piano keys. She smiled at me shyly and I felt a tickle in my lower abdomen.

"I understand you knew Paul quite well," I said.

She nodded.

"He was an exceptional talent."

That's what everyone kept telling me. I couldn't tell if she was talking about his violin playing or his flute. I thought I'd ask.

"Do you mean his musicianship?" I asked.

She blushed and lowered her eyes. She was a tease and she knew it. She looked back up at me coyly.

"Of course, whatever else do you think I might have meant?"

She bit her lip and in heaven I could hear angels weep.

"I thought you might have been speaking about his intimate powers."

I gave her a roguish grin. She looked at me hotly, her eyes aflame with anger.

"You are a coarse man, Mr. Carrick," she said, faking concern.

"And you are an adulterer," I said. "In some parts they stone beautiful women like you."

She looked up at me and squinted. I wasn't sure if she was trying to see through me or look angry. When she slapped me across the face I realized what that look meant. At least we were getting somewhere.

"How dare you," she said, hissing like a viper.

"I've only spoken the truth, Lauren. And as Frank said, I'd sure appreciate you offering the same. Now you knew Paul in the biblical way, didn't you?"

She nodded.

"I don't know what that's got to do with you."

"Nothing interesting," I said, "I don't like seconds. But it might mean the world of difference for Paul."

Her hand came up for another quick feel of my cheek. I stopped her this time. I was still stinging from the first smack.

"The first one might have been free, but you'll have to earn another," I said.

"I think I'm done here, Mr. Carrick," she said, standing up.

I grabbed her arm and held it firmly. She winced and tried to wriggle out of it.

"Let go of me!" she said. "You're hurting me."

"If you sit down and behave like a good girl I'll let you go."

She thought about it for a moment and sat down. I let her arm go and she rubbed it gingerly.

"When did you start seeing Paul?" I asked.

She looked down at her wrist, pouting like a spoiled child.

"We've been seeing each other on and off for years."

"Did your husband know?"

"He's suspected for awhile but he confronted me about it a few months ago. I told him the truth. He told me to end it and he went to speak with Paul and tell him to back off."

"I heard about it," I said. "I heard it was a nice and friendly hands-on conversation."

She looked up at me and I could tell she was still angry. She didn't look as attractive when she was angry.

"It wasn't like that."

"That's not what I heard."

"Perry went and spoke to Paul. They had a shoving match and Paul told him that he would end it."

"But you didn't, did you?"

"No, but I don't think Perry knew."

"You certain about that?"

"Yes, I'm certain. Perry would have said something if he didn't think I'd called off the relationship. There's something you have to understand, Mr. Carrick, it's not like Paul and I were exclusive..."

"Clearly."

Lauren huffed and blew air up at her bangs. That was cute, but it didn't derail me.

"What I mean is, Paul wasn't the sort of man that would be happy with just one woman. What we had was an on again off again fling. He was a lot of fun to be around."

"And your husband isn't?"

More huffing and blowing of air. She was beginning to remind me of the three little pigs.

"No, not like that. If you ever meet him you'll understand. Paul knows how to treat a woman special. He makes you feel special."

"Help me understand something. If you're not really in love with your husband, and it sounds like you're not, then why did you even marry him?"

"Perry is a good provider and I thought I loved him once. An orchestral musician, especially one that plays cello, and not first cello either, doesn't make a lot of money."

"And how much isn't a lot of money?" I asked.

"Forty-eight thousand a year. I spent four years in college getting my music degree and ten years before that practicing everyday. That kind of money isn't a lot to live on in New York, Mr. Carrick."

"I suppose it isn't. What does your husband do?"

"He owns his own construction company."

"So he's with the mafia," I said, cavalierly.

She was about to blow my house down with her huffing and puffing.

"No, he's an honest, hardworking businessman."

"With a spendthrift, adulterer of a wife. He must think he's got the nuts."

"I don't get your meaning, Perry is a good man."

"It's a poker thing."

"He plays poker," she said.

"Badly, I bet," I answered.

I was eager to meet this man who couldn't read his own wife. I wouldn't mind playing him in a high stakes poker game. But that was just crazy thinking.

"I'd like to talk to him," I said.

"You can find him at the job site everyday."

"Even on the Sabbath?"

"Even tomorrow. We're not particularly religious," she said with a straight face.

"I hadn't mistaken you for a nun, darling."

"Are we done?"

"Hardly," I said, "I'm just getting through the foreplay. Where is Paul?"

"I don't know."

"You don't know or you don't care?"

"I said I don't know. I tried calling him this morning and yesterday. I left a message for him yesterday but this morning his mailbox is full and I couldn't leave a message."

"When was the last time you saw him?"

In the background, the musicians were still strangling cats and making all sorts of awful sounds. I couldn't believe people paid for this. Yeah, I know, I'm being facetious. I've been to a concert or two.

"I saw Paul on Thursday for rehearsal. Before that, we spent some time on Wednesday night."

"How did he seem at rehearsal?"

"He seemed agitated, he said there were some people out to get him."

"Did he tell you who?"

"No he didn't. I didn't give it much thought, you see he often got paranoid if he'd been on a bender."

"So if he's been on benders before, why is everybody so worried about him this time."

"Well, he's never gone missing. He's always come in to practice even if he was sent home. But he's never missed a practice yet."

"When you say he's been on benders, what are you talking about. Booze or drugs?"

"Both, Paul likes to party. He likes his alcohol and his cocaine."

"And where does he get it from?"

"We all go to Gary, Gary Johnson, when we need a pick me up," she said. "I mean, I don't, but those who need it find he's very helpful. Gary and Paul were quite close."

"And where can I find this Gary Johnson?" I asked.

She turned around and looked towards the stage.

"He's the tall, thin one playing on the trombone."

I followed her eyes and saw him right away. He looked like a doctor who took his own medicine. Only these weren't prescriptions. He was tall, and thin like she said. He had mousy brown hair, and he looked old. Even from this distance I could see his complexion was sallow and unhealthy. He might be the drug dealer but he could also be his own best client.

"Did Paul seem worried about Gary at all?"

"No, I don't think so. I've never seen Gary and Paul get into a fight. But Patrick Francis is not a fan of Paul. They've never liked each other, not since Paul got that first violin position just a year after he got here."

"And who's Patrick?" I asked, looking out at the orchestra.

"He's the one who spoke to you. He told you Paul was probably on a bender."

I nodded my head. Yeah, I wanted to speak to him. And now I'd make sure I did just that.

"You said earlier that Paul had a roving eye. Other than Rosanna, was there anyone else here who he was having an affair with?"

"No, Paul was settling down more in his older age. At least he seemed more content with me taking care of his needs than the other woman. I think he was calling it off with Rosanna. He had tried to bed a couple of the other women here but unsuccessfully. Not everyone finds him as attractive as I do."

"Right."

"How was Rosanna taking it?"

"Not well. I had a feeling she was willing to leave her husband for him, but he wouldn't hear of it."

"Her husband or Paul?"

"Both, but her husband especially. She came in with a black eye once."

"How did she get it?"

"She said she walked into a door, but we all suspected it was thanks to her husband. She acknowledged that he had found out about her and Paul and got really mad over it. That same week, Paul came in pretty beat up too. They had to give him a few days off just so that he didn't appear on stage in the shape he was."

"What kind of shape was he in?"

"He had a black eye and a swollen cheek."

"And did he say what happened?"

"No, he just said he got involved with a couple of thugs on his way home. But the rumor was that Kieran, Rosanna's husband, had waited for him after a concert a while back and given him a licking."

"When was that?"

"Around the same time that Perry came to talk with him. A few months ago I guess."

"So if I'm starting to get a clearer picture of Paul it is that his problems are women, booze and drugs in that order."

Lauren didn't say anything to that. She looked back at the rest of the orchestra, tuning and practicing.

"What was Paul's relationship with Sonia Varnier?"

"I don't know. He was very closed lipped about it. But I wouldn't be surprised if he used to have a relationship with her when he first started here. She is the reason he came here. I heard rumors she gave him a lot of money to stay and the apartment he has use of is probably worth at least a couple of million. Not something he could afford by himself. I'm afraid you'll have to ask her about their relationship, or him, if you ever find him. He never told me anything other than Sonia was very generous."

"I've heard she's one of the biggest patrons of the Philharmonic."

"Could be," said Lauren, "though I've never seen any of her largesse personally. Most of us haven't. Her generosity doesn't seem to filter down to the orchestra other than Paul. And what he gets from her I can't say."

I nodded at Lauren.

"Can you give me the address for your husband's work? I'd like to visit him tomorrow."

"Only if you promise to be discreet with what I've shared with you," she said.

"Scout's honor."

I was never a scout so I've never had scout's honor. But Lauren didn't have to know that. She gave me the address and I thanked her for her time. She had given up being flirty with me. It was just as well. I wasn't interested in married women.

# Four

I brought Rosanna Stewart down from the stage for my next interview. She was playing the piano when I called her. She wasn't wearing glasses and her skin seemed unblemished. She wore makeup to make her look paler than she was. My immediate impression of her was of a white geisha. She had brunette hair in curls that flowed past her shoulder. She was slim and attractive with a small mouth. She was taller than Lauren with brown eyes, and in my mind more attractive. But then I've always had a thing for brunettes over blondes.

She wore casual ripped jeans and a bulky blue t-shirt that had some sort of logo on that I didn't pay attention to. She was very polite. She offered me her hand and I shook it. She introduced herself and said how nice it was to meet me. Her mouth was full of lies, swarming with them like flies. But she meant well and I didn't take it personally.

"Do you really think something has happened to Paul?" she asked, trying to get a start on the conversation. Usually, that's a bad sign.

"I do," I said.

"What sort of thing?"

"That's hard to say. He could be lying in some back alley with broken kneecaps or maybe he's just in bed, hung over with some trollop next to him that isn't you or Lauren."

I smiled at her to see what she'd make of that. Her eyes fluttered but her composure didn't.

"That's not a very nice thing to say."

She held my gaze.

"I've found out that not very nice things have been going on with orchestra."

"Still, you don't have to be mean about it."

"I'm sorry," I said. "Perhaps I should have asked you why you're an adulterer."

I still had on my cheap, sticky smile. You can buy them by the dozen at any dollar store. Rosanna raised her eyebrows at me and shook her head slowly. Looked like she was shaking her head at her dog that just did his business on the kitchen floor. But I wasn't her dog and I was potty trained.

"That's such a crass word," she said.

"But it's accurate."

Rosanna offered me a fake smile. The kind they giveaway at fairs for free.

"Mr. Carrick. Your acerbic wit might work with most women, but I don't know you. I don't care to know you, and I certainly don't like you. But your words are the weapons of a small mind. I'll give you the courtesy of my time because Frank asked and because I care for Paul. But please, let's stop beating around the bush."

She had some sass. In fact, she had a lot of sass for a battered woman. I couldn't decide if that was what got her in trouble or if it was something new she was trying out on me first.

"I bet your husband loves it when you talk to him like that," I said.

"I thought you wanted to speak about Paul."

"I do, but it's so seldom I get a dressing down from a beautiful woman that I just want this moment to last."

She shook her head again, but didn't say anything.

"Why do you wear that hat anyway?" she asked, looking at my fedora on the seat next to me. "It makes you look like a dick."

She didn't say it with a lot of malice. I looked over at the fedora.

"That's because I am a dick, but my dick and me are private. See, that makes me a private dick. Like Sam Spade. Who also wore a fedora. It's an honored tradition."

She smiled pointedly at me.

"If it makes you feel like a big boy."

"Enough about me," I said, tiring of her loose mouth. "I'm beginning to understand why your husband slaps you around."

That turned her white cheeks red. The fires in her eyes flared.

"My husband does not hit me," she said.

"That's pretty much what every woman says whose husband beats her. What you don't know about me is that I had ten years on the job. I've heard it all before. But I'm here to talk about a missing man. The one you were sleeping with. Paul Klee. Let's get back on topic."

"Fine," she said, almost pouting.

"How long were you having a relationship with him?"

"A few years, I guess."

"And your husband found out, right? Kieran is his name?"

"Yes, he did find out a few months ago."

"And I understand he gave you a black eye over it. Did the same to Paul that very same week."

"Like I told everyone, I walked into a door."

"I know, I've heard it all before. Doors just seem to like smacking women in the face. Listen, I know he smacked you around. I'm not here about that. I'm here about Paul."

"How comforting. I'm sure you were a great cop."

"I did alright. Did Kieran tell you to break it off?"

Rosanna looked down at her lap and twisted her mouth off to one corner.

"He did."

"And did you?"

She shook her head slowly. Then she looked back up at me and her mouth wasn't twisted anymore.

"I was going to leave him for Paul. We were making plans."

"You're telling me that Paul was the settling down type."

She shook her head slowly.

"No, not originally. But over the last six months or so we started to get serious. He asked me to leave Kieran. Said he'd take care of me."

"And you were okay with that? You were going to leave a wife beater for a philanderer?"

This place was dripping with sickly sweet irony. The places I get myself into sometimes.

"No, it wasn't like that. I don't know what Lauren told you, but she likes to think things were more than they were with her and him. Her husband, Perry, had told her to call it off. She didn't want to, but Paul was going to. She got quite upset about it."

"How do you know?"

"Because he told me."

"And you believed him?"

Rosanna nodded her head.

"Yes I did. You wouldn't understand, but sometimes people can change. He had changed, his wicked ways were behind him. I don't know why. I never thought he would. When we first got together he wasn't like that. And I got tired of it. I guess he loved me, because he said he was going to leave his old ways and try and start fresh with me. He said he was getting older and he wanted to start fresh."

"What about his drug and alcohol problems?"

"He didn't really have drug and alcohol problems."

"That's not what everyone else tells me."

"Everyone else being Lauren. Like I said, she likes to live in a certain fantasyland. Yes, Paul drank a little and he took a little coke. But he said he would quit it once we were married and I believed him."

"When were you planning on getting married?"

"Next summer. But I still had to leave Kieran. I was planning on telling him this weekend. Paul told me he wanted me to tell him sooner but I was trying to build up my courage."

"So your husband doesn't know then?"

"I don't think so. I mean I don't have a black eye now, do I?"

She gave me her first honest, yet tragic smile.

"So you do admit that he hits you?"

"It's only happened a few times. Kieran's not been happy lately. He lost his job on Wall Street a couple of years ago and he hasn't found anything yet. He's a proud man and he wants to earn a living but nobody has hired him yet. He'll be better once he gets a job."

"You'll be better off without him," I said.

"I'm leaving him. I told you that."

"What will you do if Paul doesn't show up, or worse yet, he's found dead?"

Rosanna looked down at her lap. She shook her head sadly and slowly.

"I don't know. I hadn't thought of that."

"It's easy," I said. "You should still leave him."

"You might not know this, Mr. Carrick, but we don't make much money here at the orchestra."

"And Kieran's making a killing right now."

I smiled at her but she didn't say anything.

"He's like a dead weight holding you back. But that's none of my business. I'm just a dick like you said, trying to find out what happened to Paul."

Rosanna looked into her lap again, twiddling her fingers. She looked up at me with a sad face. A face lost and hopeless.

"I don't really know what I'll do if anything bad happens to Paul. He's my world."

"You'll carry on," I said.

"I don't know if I want to," she said, and I took her at her word.

"Had he changed over the last week or even the past few days? Did you notice anything different about him?"

"He seemed more nervous than usual. I mean, I shouldn't suggest that he was always nervous, but he seemed more nervous in the past few weeks. He wouldn't tell me why, but he thought he was being followed."

"Followed by whom?" I asked.

"I don't know. He wouldn't tell me. One occasion, about a week ago, we were walking back to his apartment together, and he seemed particularly concerned about these two men who were following us. At least he thought they were following us."

"Tell me about them."

"He said he'd seen them in the audience during that night's concert. He said that they were following us back home. I looked back and saw them. But when we turned the last corner and I looked back, I didn't see them anymore. To be honest with you, I didn't take them very seriously."

"Can you describe these two men who were following you?"

Rosanna shook her head.

"Not very well. Like I said, I didn't pay much attention because they weren't following use when we turned the last corner home. They also stayed back about twenty or thirty feet and it was dark. They looked big though, and they wore suits."

"How big?"

"Probably much bigger than you."

"Bigger or taller?"

"Both, at least the one was. The one man had a buzz cut like a marine, and he was big in the shoulder and chest and tall. Probably much taller than six feet. The other guy was just as tall but slimmer. He seemed to have longer hair. Not long exactly, maybe like yours but I think it was blonde."

"Did Paul ever submit a police report about it?"

"No, but he said that his apartment had been ransacked around the time that he started to notice these men first hanging around. He submitted a police report then."

"Have you seen these men before or since?"

Rosanna shook her head again.

"No."

"Did he mention if anything was taken when he was burglarized?"

"No, he said nothing had gone missing."

"Did he have any suspicion what they were after?"

"Not that he said to me."

"Did he have any valuables that you knew of?"

Rosanna kept shaking her head. I had to start asking different questions.

"Not particularly. He didn't spend his money on much. He didn't have a car, and the apartment was only his so long as he was with the Phil. Sonia Varnier owned it. He had lots of money. He told me that with his orchestral pay and Sonia's allowance he was making about a quarter of a million dollars a year."

"What did he do with all that money?"

"I'm not sure. He liked eating at fancy restaurants like Daniel's and places like that."

This meant nothing to me. The kind of places I like to eat at are working men's steak joints. Where the steak is large and the bill is small.

"So he had nothing of value then?"

"Well, no. He really took very good care of his violin. He had a few, but there was one he used for special concerts. It was a Stradivarius that his great grandfather had given him when he was eight or nine. When he started showing great interest and proficiency in the violin. And it's not a modern day Strad which is just a knock off really. This one was made by Antonio himself."

"You might as well be speaking in Italian," I said.

"I'll make it easier for you to understand then. This Strad that Paul had is called the Blount Strad. It was made in seventeen seventeen by Antonio Stradivarius himself, during what is called his golden period. His best violins were built between seventeen hundred and seventeen twenty-five or thereabouts. This Blount Strad, as it has become known, was bought by the English poet Alexander Pope. It was bought by him and given to his lover Martha Blount, thus becoming known as the Blount Strad. She was an amateur violinist who used to play for Alexander. Something which he apparently enjoyed. But that's not important. This Blount Strad is considered amongst the best examples of Antonio's violins. It has an exquisitely etched and carved tailpiece along with pegs and scroll. It is really one of a kind that way."

"I see," I said, trying to feign interest.

Rosanna shook her head vigorously.

"No, no you don't. You don't understand how beautiful this violin was. I've never seen anything like it. It was easily worth over ten million dollars. Paul in fact had it insured for that amount."

"I see, but who would have known how valuable this instrument was?"

"Well, quite a few of us on the orchestra, I'm sure. Especially other violinists, though Paul never made much mention of it actually. He usually downplayed how special this particular violin is."

"Anyone else?"

"I imagine there are those who understand violins and who study Stradivarius would likely know who owns the Blount Strad and its value. Other than that, it is quite a niche market. There are only a few hundred left remaining, and only a small handful that are considered his best work. This one being one of them."

"Where is this violin now?"

"I don't know. Paul usually kept in the basement here in the Lincoln Center. There's a safe in the basement where he would keep it. But over the last few weeks since he's become concerned about being followed, he's pretty much kept the violin on him. It's probably with him wherever he is."

So if we find the violin we might find Paul, or vice versa. I couldn't quite see how a violin was worth all this trouble, but we'd find out soon enough.

"Did Paul give any indication that someone was after his violin?"

Rosanna shook her head.

"No, not really. He wasn't sure what those two men who were following him were after. I don't think he ever spoke to them. But he became paranoid about the violin and started carrying it with him shortly after his apartment got broken into."

"That doesn't make a lot of sense," I said. "Surely the violin would have been safer in the safe."

"Well, I don't think Paul was that rational. He became a little paranoid. I told him the same thing. But he said that he couldn't trust anyone, not even Frank."

"Frank knew about the value of his violin then?"

"He must have, as he arranged for Paul to keep it in the safe under lock and key."

"And who has access to that safe?"

"I don't know. You'd have to ask Frank. I know he does for sure. I believe he gave Paul a key too, but other than that I don't know."

"If he was so worried about the violin, why not just keep it locked up and if it got stolen, then take the insurance money. I'm sure you could buy a few violins with that kind of money."

Rosanna shook her head and looked at me quaintly.

"It's not just the monetary value of the violin. It was the sentimental value of the violin too. His grandfather got it during the war in Nazi Germany."

"I see. From who?"

"I don't know exactly, but Paul said that he had verification of every owner of the violin from Alexander Pope, Martha Blount and through to him."

"But you don't know who that was?"

Rosanna shook her head.

"I don't. He never told me."

"Tell me about what happened to Paul the week you got your black eye from your husband."

Rosanna looked at her lap and knitted her fingers together. She might have been trying to make a scarf for all I knew.

"I don't know what you mean."

"Listen, Rosanna, I don't have time for this. You admitted that Kieran smacks you around. I want to know if he gave Paul the black eye too. If you really care for Paul, you'll be more forthcoming so we can get to the bottom of this."

She looked up at me, and then looked over at the orchestra. Nobody was paying us much attention. They were still a cacophony of screaming cats.

"Yes."

Her voice was barely a whisper.

"Yes what?" I asked.

"Yes, Kieran gave him a black eye. Paul said that Kieran had followed him home one night. Paul used to walk through the park to get home. Anyway, that one night when it was deserted, Kieran confronted him and they got into a fight. Paul said Kieran punched him in the face a couple of times and told him he better leave me alone. If he didn't, Kieran said he'd be really sorry."

"What do you think he meant by that?"

"I know exactly what he meant by it," she said. "Because I confronted him the next day, and he bragged about showing Paul that he wasn't going to allow him to get away with it. He told me that what had happened was just a warning. He told me that if Paul and I didn't call it off that he'd kill us both."

"Did you go to the police with this?"

Rosanna looked down and shook her head.

"So your husband beats you, then he beats up your lover, and then he threatens not only your life but your lover's life and you don't take it seriously. Do I have that right?"

Rosanna looked up at me, fighting hard to keep my gaze.

"I took him very seriously, Mr. Carrick, but I promised Kieran that it was over between the two of us.

"And yet you knew that was a lie. You told me earlier how you and Paul were going to get married next summer."

"I know."

Her voice was small and weak like a mouse's squeak.

"I'm sorry," she said. "I didn't really think Kieran would hurt Paul. I mean, we don't know that Paul's in trouble, do we?"

"We know enough for me to be concerned. Look, I'm gonna need to talk to your husband," I said. "Where can I find him?"

"If he's not at home he's at the bar."

"Which one?"

"The Pig and Bard," she said.

I nodded, making a mental note of it.

"But I don't think you should go and see him."

"Why is that?"

"Because he won't like it. He's got a quick temper, Mr. Carrick, especially if he's been drinking."

"Then I'll have to be quicker."

I looked at Rosanna steadily for a while. She glanced down at her lap.

"Look, you're an attractive woman. You can do better than a husband who beats you. Things aren't going to end well unless you leave him. That's my advice to you."

Rosanna nodded and offered me a small smile. A sample of what she might be capable of if she was a happier woman. I didn't know why I'd just given her advice. On less than one hand I could count the number of battered woman who took my advice when I was on the job. I eventually gave up offering it. It wasn't rocket science.

"Anything else?" she asked me.

I shook my head.

"I've got a lot of leads already. None of which suggest finding Paul unharmed. Is there anything else you'd like to offer?"

Rosanna shook her head, and stood up.

"I don't think so. And I really don't think Kieran would do anything bad to Paul."

"You mean other than punch him in the face like he had before? Listen, Rosanna, you don't seem to understand what's going on here. The best indication of future behavior is past behavior. Kieran has shown a lot of past behavior that doesn't make him a choir boy."

Rosanna looked at me for a while and then walked off towards the stage. I watched her go. She looked great from behind. This was the kind of woman who owned a gold mine and figured it for tin. From what I'd seen, neither Kieran nor Paul were any good for her. But that wasn't my concern.

I was trying to figure out why a concertmaster had gone missing. I figured his body would show up soon enough, and there were two suspects who might have something to do with it. And both of them had cheating spouses. If things continued heading in the right direction, I might just have this all buttoned up in the next day.

# Five

I called Patrick Francis down from the stage to speak with me. He was thin. Everything about him was thin. He had thin brown hair that was a dog's breakfast and salted with dandruff. His lips were thin and his beaked nose was thin. He looked sick and his pallor suggested the same. He was short. I wouldn't have put him past five eight. He looked like he might have been in his fifties, but I figured he was likely a decade or more younger than that.

He had on well worn jeans lashed around his waist with a black belt. He wore an old Rolling Stones t-shirt that had half sleeves. He was thin enough to have been a member of the band.

"Take a seat," I said to him.

"I'd sooner stand."

"This might take a while."

He folded his hands across his chest like a petulant teenager. I didn't need a fight so I indulged him.

"You told me earlier that you figured Paul was on another bender."

"That's right."

"Care to elaborate."

He just shrugged at me. Now he was beginning to get on my nerves.

"I get paid by the day," I said, "I bet you don't. I can sit here all day staring at you silently."

Patrick finally broke off his gaze and looked over at the orchestra. He didn't have his violin with him.

"It's not secret that Paul was a coke head," he said.

"And how do you know this?"

"Because I've seen him buy from Gary a ton of times."

"Buy what?"

"Coke, I just told you."

"Has he ever gone missing like this before?"

"No, but he's been late before. I think his problems are just getting worse."

"Which problems?"

"His drug and alcohol problems. Are you even listening to me?"

"Well, I see your mouth is moving but you're not saying very much. Were those Paul's only problems?"

"The biggest ones, and of course the women."

"What about the women?"

"He was a Casanova. Or at least he liked to think he was."

"With who?"

"The two women you just spoke with before me."

"Anyone else?"

"Yeah, there was this administrative assistant that rumor has it he knocked up. She's been gone some months now."

"What's her name?"

"Stephanie Perkins. Christina Tedder took her place."

"How long ago was that?"

"I don't know, a few months. Maybe half a year, I wasn't Paul's keeper."

"No, that's right. In fact, I heard you didn't like him much."

"He was a fucking asshole."

Patrick said it like it was a fact. There was no animosity in his voice.

"Tell me about that," I said.

"What's there to tell, he was an ass, plain and simple."

"Why did you think he was an ass?"

"Because he was uncouth and spoiled and a dilettante. Everyone was all over him like he was the best thing since Paganini, and he was nowhere near as good."

"Paganini who?"

Patrick rolled his eyes at me and shook his head.

"Paganini is only the greatest violinist to have ever lived. But you'd think it was Paul the way people fawned all over him. Paganini they say was at least gracious with his talent. The same could not be said of Paul."

"How so?"

"I think it must have started with his parents, but if Paul wasn't the center of attention then he would pout, miss rehearsals, or come late and generally act like a spoiled child. I remember one time, when he had just started here, he threw all the music stands over in a fit of anger because the conductor told him he had to practice his piece more. And that's just one example."

"I see."

"Lately, he had become even more contemptuous. He was using more drugs from what I can tell and his playing was the worse for it. He and Frank got into it one day after rehearsal about a week ago. It was a helluva shouting match. Frank told him he had to start smartening up and getting his shit together or he'd be demoted from concertmaster. Paul broke some of the chairs of the orchestra after that. In fact, if you go up on stage, you can probably see the marks on the wooden floor where he flung and thrashed the chairs all about."

"That's all quite fascinating," I said, "but I don't think those are the real reasons you didn't like him very much."

"Those are reasons enough," said Patrick, still standing with his arms crossed over his chest.

"Yes, maybe they are, but I figure your reasons run a little deeper. Your reasons are more personal."

Patrick looked at me but he didn't say anything. It looked like if I blew hard enough I could blow him over.

"A little birdie told me that you were really upset he got first violin and more upset that he got concertmaster."

"You wouldn't understand."

"Try me, that's what I'm here for."

"I graduated from Juilliard two years before Paul. I was promised a similar position in the first violin section just as he was, only it never happened. Before Frank, the musical director was a guy by the name of Doug Goodell. He was a much better director. He wasn't swayed by any of our rich benefactors. He ran the orchestra with an eye on what was good for the orchestra. Sometimes upsetting the benefactors, especially Sonia Varnier. Doug had promised me the first opening in the first violin section. He expected it to open up within three years. Almost three years to the day, after I got hired on by the Phil, Doug was let go. Sonia played a large role in it, and her lackey, Frank, is now the musical director. He was her first choice. Now, I have nothing against Frank except that he's an idiot, and doesn't know how to run an orchestra to save his life."

"So you don't like Frank or Sonia, because you didn't get your first violin position."

"That's part of it. Like I said, I don't dislike Frank. Sonia's another matter. I don't know if you know this or not, but the musical director is often the same person as the conductor."

"I didn't know that. So who was the conductor when Paul had his fit that you spoke about earlier?"

"That would have been Doug Goodell."

"Okay."

"Well, it's not okay. Doug was a superb musician, an outstanding conductor and a fine man. He had a real strong moral compass. I liked him a lot. And that's not just me. Ask anyone else around here and you'll get the same thing, just about everybody liked him."

"But not Frank."

"Well no, but you won't hear people complain about him unless they've got a couple of drinks under their belts. And not him. He's alright, it's the whole bit about him becoming the musical director and how Doug was fired that most of us aren't happy with."

"Why is that?"

"Like I'm trying to tell you, it's because Doug was excellent. There was no reason to get rid of him and he had no interest in retiring. It was all political so that Sonia could have her way. I mean come on, Frank's last post was as the first violin at the Chippewa Valley Symphony. That's in Eau Claire, Wisconsin for Christ's sake. And then bam, he's here as our musical director."

"That wouldn't necessarily disqualify him from the job," I said, having fun with Patrick's anger.

Patrick shook his head and rolled his eyes again.

"I'll forgive you because you obviously have no idea of what you're talking about. The New York Phil is a top five, some would say top three orchestra in the US. In the world, it's consistently ranked in the top twenty. You don't get to be the conductor at a world class orchestra without having conducted before, I don't care how good you are. And frankly, if you'll excuse the pun, Frank isn't particularly good."

It was fun seeing Patrick getting wound up about this issue. To me, I probably couldn't tell the difference between the New York Phil and the Chippewa Symphony. But he was passionate about music. That much was clear, and he earned my respect for that.

"Alright, I'll take you at your word. Frank's not the best conductor, or music director or whatever you want to call him. But you're upset because a first violin position went to Paul and not you."

"I'm upset because the esteem of the New York Phil is waning because of our incompetent conductor."

"But you just told me that this orchestra is consistently ranked in the top twenty around the world."

"Yes, but since Frank's tenure we've been steadily slipping down. We used to be in the top five, now we're number eighteen. The only reason we've stayed on that list as long as we have is because of our history and heritage."

"Okay then, tell me about what happened when Frank was made conductor."

"Within the first few months he fired one of the first violins and put Paul in his place. That's a position that should have gone to me. I'm just as good as Paul is."

"I'll take your word on that."

"You don't have to. The New York Times said the same thing twenty years ago when all this happened."

"That's a long time to hold a grudge. Why did you stick around?"

"I looked for other positions, but the top ten orchestras here didn't have any first violin positions open and I'd have to start from the beginning again as a second violin. I considered it back then, but only the LA Phil had a position and it paid less and they wouldn't cover my moving expenses. I stayed because I thought things would improve and in the early years Frank paid me lip service about getting a first violin position. When Paul made concertmaster it opened up a first violin position that was given to Milo Ellis. But by this time my mother was terribly sick and

I'm her only family in town, so I've resigned myself to stay here until she's gone, then I'll likely seek other opportunities."

"Or not," I said. "If anything unfortunate were to happen to Paul, you'd likely benefit, right?"

"Hard to say, I was supposed to get Milo's position. Who's to say who gets the next first violin opening. Besides which, Paul was on a self destruct mission. I didn't need to hurt him if that's what you meant."

"I was thinking you might actually have motive to kill him."

Patrick frowned his face and looked down his nose at me.

"That's pretty macabre," he said. "We don't know he's dead and saying such things is rather unpleasant. Look, as much as I disliked him, I didn't wish him dead."

"In my line of work I mostly deal with the dead. Paul missing now for over forty-eight hours isn't a good sign."

Patrick didn't say anything for a while.

"Why would anyone want to kill him?" he asked, genuinely puzzled.

"You tell me, but I can start. We have two pissed off husbands who wanted him out of the picture. We have you, and you feel like you should have been made first violin. Then maybe it's just a simple robbery gone bad. There's a whole bunch of people who might have liked his violin."

"So you're saying they stole it. Ha!"

Patrick tossed his head back.

"A violin as rare as his would be very difficult to resell. Everybody knows he owned it."

"Everybody in the violin world. But there is the underworld and there are private buyers for these sorts of things who wouldn't ask a lot of questions."

Patrick got a quizzical look on his face.

"Well, Paul isn't Jewish," he said as if that meant something to me.

It didn't.

"So what?"

"Well, Paul said he got his violin from his great grandfather, and his great grandfather got the violin during the Second World War."

"That's what I've been told."

"Yeah, well I looked into that a bit, and I found out that Paul's background is German. Paul's grandfather from what I learned was a guard at Mittelsteine. Mittelsteine was a German concentration camp for women. Paul's grandfather got the violin off of one of the first inmates there, a woman by the name of Anke Mueller. Anke died at the concentration camp, and just before the allies arrived, Paul's grandfather left for Switzerland under an assumed name."

"What was his name?"

"Ryszard Kucharski, or Richard as he became known. Though his real name I learnt was Swen Boehm."

"How do you know this?"

"Because of that first violinist who got fired that I told you about when Frank became the music director."

I nodded my head.

"His name was John Stampley and I kept in touch with him for several years after he was fired. He was really choked. He hit some hard times. Anyway, he spent a ton of money on a PI to look into Paul's background and this is what the guy came up with. He showed me some of the evidence the PI had uncovered. John said he was going to confront Paul with it, and if he didn't resign he was going to take the information to the authorities."

"And did he?"

"I don't know. I lost contact with him around that time."

"So you don't know if he ever told Paul that he knew all of this?"

"No, I don't."

"So how did Paul get the last name Klee?" I asked.

"The grandfather I'm talking about is his mother's father. His mother married his father and probably took his name."

I nodded.

"Do you know how I can get a hold of this John Stampley?"

Patrick shook his messy head of hair.

"No, I lost contact with him a while back. I can give you the last number I have if you'd like."

I nodded. Patrick fished a phone out of his front pant's pocket. He tapped away at it for a while and then gave me the number. I added it to the other notes I'd been making in my notebook.

Just as I finished up writing in my notebook, a uniform police officer came walking down the aisle and went straight up to Frank. Frank and he put their heads together, looking down. Frank nodded a lot but didn't say much. Most of the talking was done by the policeman.

The conversation didn't last long. I could see the cop mouth the word 'sorry', and Frank nodded, put on a brave smile and watched him leave. Frank looked up at us and waved us up to the stage.

## Six

Just as Patrick and I were exiting the row the cop came past us. Patrick started for the stage, I started for the cop.

"Just a second," I said.

The cop stopped and turned around. He was young, maybe not more than a few months out of the academy. He was clean shaven but still showed a five o'clock shadow. His name tag read 'Castiglione'.

"Anthony Carrick," I said, offering my hand, which he took instinctively and we shook. "I've been hired to look into the missing person's case of Paul Klee. Do you have any information?"

He looked me up and down. I smiled at him broadly like we were long last friends. He didn't return the gesture.

"All I can tell is what I told the musical director. This is no longer a missing person's case, it's now a homicide. The detectives will be here later to take statements."

Castiglione turned to leave.

"How, and where?"

"We found him in his apartment. He had been shot. I'm sorry, I can't tell you any more than that."

I nodded and thanked him for his help. I turned around to walk back up to the stage. I knew it. I knew this case was going to go south on me as soon as I'd arrived this morning and there'd still been no sign of Klee. Up ahead, on stage, a few of the women were crying. Rosanna and Lauren amongst them. Frank was trying to console them. He had his hand on Rosanna's shoulder.

If I didn't know any better, I would have thought Patrick was wearing the slightest hint of a smirk. I walked up to Frank.

"What did he say?" I asked.

Frank turned from Rosanna towards me. He looked even older and sadder than before.

"It appears you were right. Paul's been killed. They said he was shot, found in his apartment."

"I thought you sent somebody around to visit him?"

"I did, yesterday, but he didn't answer the door."

"Did the cop say how long he'd been dead?"

Frank shook his head.

"No, he didn't say much at all. He said the detectives would be around later this afternoon to take statements and to fill in some of the blanks for us."

"I know the timing isn't good, Frank, but I'd like to continue my investigations if you don't mind."

Frank nodded.

"Of course," he said. "We're not going anywhere, the police officer asked that we all remain here for the detectives, so please carry on. I don't think this changes our need for you."

I smiled and nodded.

"Thanks," I said. "I'd like to speak with Gary Johnson."

Frank called him over and I walked him off stage and back to the orchestra seating that had become my makeshift office.

## Seven

Gary Johnson was a tall, wiry guy. Wiry might have been generous. He was thin. He reminded me of Patrick's older and taller cousin, as I imagined an older cousin for Patrick. He was thin and looked old. His teeth were crooked and yellow. He had the same messy, mousy brown hair as Patrick, though his wasn't salted with dandruff. He wore gray pants, with a blue shirt and loose blue tie. He was the principal trombonist. His right index and middle finger were stained yellow. He was obviously a heavy smoker. Heavier than me.

He shook my hand politely and sat a seat away from me, leaving an empty one between us.

"I imagine you know why I'm here?"

Gary nodded, and smiled.

"You're here to find Paul. Unfortunately it now seems you might be here to find out who killed him."

I nodded.

"I understand that Paul wasn't well liked by everyone, though you and he were quite tight from what I've heard."

"We were friends, yes."

"I hear you were more than that. You were, in fact, his dealer."

Gary looked at me hard for a moment. His brown eyes like hard dried turds.

"I don't think I should be saying anything more without my lawyer," he said.

I laughed out loud. Gary looked at me with a furrowed brow deep enough to plant a hill of beans.

"You've mistaken me for a cop. You only need a lawyer if you're under arrest. And I'm not here to arrest you for drugs, Gary, I'm here to figure out what happened to your pal Paul. And if he was indeed your pal, you might want to help me out."

Gary thought about my proposal for a moment.

"Okay, I helped him get a few things he needed."

"Like what?"

Gary paused for a moment and looked around, and up towards the stage. I figured he wanted to make sure nobody could overhear us.

"You won't be taking this back to the cops will you?"

He looked at me steadily. I shook my head.

"Not unless I find out you killed him," I said.

"I didn't."

"Then we're golden."

"Paul was a coke head. In fact, it was getting out of hand."

"That's what I heard."

"Well, it was worse than anyone thought. I'd cut him off about a month ago. He was getting paranoid and I figured the coke wasn't helping him. He got pretty pissed at me for it. He threatened me, he begged me for more coke, but I wouldn't give him anything. That's a bit of a lie. I gave him one line, but he wasn't grateful. I tried to tell him that he needed to get off the stuff, that it was affecting him badly. He wouldn't listen to me, said he was being followed and he needed it to keep his edge up."

"Who did he say was following him?"

"I don't know. Two big men, that's all he said. Thing is, coke can make you paranoid if you start taking too much, and he was taking too much."

"So you cut him off. Did he start going through withdrawal?"

"No, because he didn't stop. He threatened to go directly to my guy."

"Your guy?"

"Yeah, the guy I get my drugs from that I used to sell to Paul. He said he was going to start going straight to him."

"And did he?"

Gary looked around the room again, and nodded.

"Yes, he did. I know this because Jamal told me. He said that Paul had come round looking for coke and said that I'd vouch for him. Only thing is, I hadn't vouched for him. I told Jamal that. I told him that Paul was unreliable with his payments at best."

"What did Jamal say?"

"You didn't hear this from me, but Jamal was pissed. He said he'd sold Paul a kilo of the stuff with only a twenty percent down payment."

"How much was that?"

"Ten grand."

"What did Paul want with all that coke?" I asked.

Gary shrugged.

"I don't know. I only found out about this a couple of weeks ago when I went to Jamal to get supplies. I think that Paul was probably looking to sell some on the side. He knew more high end clients than I did. Before all of this went sideways with him, he was always asking me for a gram here and a gram there to share with some of the higher class benefactors at events he attended. Not all of us get to attend all the charity and fundraising events."

"Did Jamal say what he was going to do if he found Paul?"

"No, Jamal's smart that way. He'll smile at you in the face while one of his men put a knife in your back. I tried to tell him that he'd get the money from Paul because Paul earned a lot of money. Jamal said he knew that Paul had a valuable violin that he promised to use a collateral if he didn't get the money to Jamal in a timely fashion."

I shook my head.

"Why would he do something like that for just fifty grand of coke?"

"Because he's an idiot," said Gary. "This was the kind of reckless behavior that Paul was into. He became paranoid about people following him which I didn't believe for a second. And he did crazy things. Addicts will do crazy things. And he was just about to lose his position here as concertmaster if he didn't smarten up."

"How do you know that?"

"Paul told me a few weeks ago, during one of his begging sessions for coke. He told me he'd had a harsh interview with Frank and Sonia. They'd given him a month to smarten up and get help or he was going to be fired."

"Was he going to do that?"

"No," said Gary. "He said he could sweet talk Sonia, just like he had done back in the day, and she'd make it all right for him."

"What did he mean by that?"

"Well, about twenty years ago when Paul first got on with the Phil, he managed it because he was charming and Sonia was a lonely and recent widow. Basically, he slept his way to the top. He had a relationship with her for years, until he started to get put off by her age. He still pretended to show interest in her, but secretly he was revolted by her."

"Charming," I said.

Gary shrugged.

"It's just the way he was. He was like that. Everything was about Paul. He wanted everything his way. I play trombone, I've made Principal Trombonist so I'm not in competition with him and I've got no further aspirations. He was fun to hang around if you weren't in competition with him and you knew what you were into."

"And you did?"

"Yes, I did. But when I cut him off, that was pretty much the end of our friendship. Like I said, he went straight to Jamal. And if he wasn't square with Jamal, then I wouldn't put it past Jamal to have him taken care of."

"Where can I find this Jamal?" I asked.

"I don't think you want to find him. He's not a fun guy especially if you're a cop."

"I'm not a cop."

"You might as well be as far as he's concerned. Listen, he'll sooner cut you up than talk to you about any of this."

"I'll take my chances," I said. "Just give me his address."

Gary gave me Jamal "JJ" Johnson's address which was someplace in Harlem.

"Let the cops deal with this. I can almost guarantee that Frank or Sonia or whoever's hired you is not paying you enough to get into the kind of trouble you'll get into with Jamal."

"I've been into all sorts of trouble. My shadow is like trouble, it just follows me around," I said.

Gary wasn't smiling.

"Well, I've given you fair warning, that's all I've got to say about that."

"And you've been a mensch about it," I said, smiling at him.

Gary frowned at me. I don't think he understood what I meant.

"Can you shed any light on his relationships with women?"

"You mean with Sonia?" Gary asked.

"Sonia, Lauren, Rosanna," I looked at my notes, "and Stephanie, the woman he got pregnant."

Gary looked up at the stage again. Everyone was huddled in small groups, commiserating or applauding, I'm sure there was a bit of both.

"Well, like I told you, I think Paul slept his way up to the top with Sonia. She took a real shine to him when he was at Juilliard. She's the biggest reason he's gotten as far as he has, but lately I think she's had enough. Like I said, they both told him he had to smarten up or he'd be shipped out. Paul's charm only gets him so far, though frankly, I'm surprised by how far he's been able to milk it. Just between you and me, I don't think Paul's the best violinist we have."

"Yeah, who would you say is the best?"

"No question in my mind, it's gotta be Patrick. Maybe on a good day when Paul was younger and he had his shit together he might have been as good as Patrick, but lately his playing has suffered. Patrick has a finesse, a deeper emotional understanding of the music than Paul ever had. But as you probably know by now, Patrick isn't very easy to get along with."

I nodded. He wasn't, but then again, he'd opened up to me easily enough. I wasn't one for beating around the bush, and Patrick was candid and forthright. I kind of liked it.

"Milo is also pretty good. But Milo is a shrinking violet. He's easy going, almost too easy. Anyway, I think Milo is just happy to be here."

"I heard he got the first violin position when Paul made concertmaster," I said.

Gary nodded, and then shook his head.

"Yeah, Patrick was pissed, and he had every right to be. Frank put Milo into that position because he and Patrick had a fight."

"Patrick and Frank?"

"Yeah. It easily should've gone to Patrick, but Frank might seem easy going but he can be a vindictive bastard if you cross him."

I was learning a helluva lot about this dysfunctional family. It seemed worse than mine.

"Was there anything specific?"

Gary shook his head.

"No, not really. The thing is, Patrick just doesn't know when to let things go. I can understand that to an extent, but music is like politics, you only get where you want if you curry favor with the right people. And currying favor was just not in Patrick's M.O."

"So he just kept pissing Frank off with his complaining and whining?"

"Basically," said Gary, "but it's not like Patrick didn't have cause. I mean he did, but he was fighting the wrong battle."

"Alright, so Paul pissed off Patrick most of all, would that be fair to say?"

Gary nodded and looked up at the stage again. Patrick was sitting in a small group. Perhaps the group that wasn't all that torn up about Paul's death.

"Do you think he could have killed him?"

Gary looked at me and then back at Patrick on stage. He shrugged and shook his head.

"Geez, I don't know. I wouldn't have thought so. I mean not before today. Now it seems anything is possible."

"Okay, let's get back on topic. You're saying Paul used Sonia to sleep his way to the top. But what about these other women?"

"Same deal."

"Can't be the same deal," I said, "because neither Lauren nor Rosanna have any power that Paul might have wanted access to."

Gary nodded his head up and down a few times.

"No, you're right. I didn't mean it like that. What I'm saying is that Paul just used them, the same way he did Sonia. But in their case he just wanted to sleep with them. It's that simple. Paul was incredibly spoiled. Probably ever since he was a child. Anything he wanted he figured he could get. And he was quite the lothario. He's probably tried to screw every woman in the orchestra, but he's only had success with the two of them."

"You're painting an ugly portrait of the man," I said.

One of the things I hated was gossip, and unkind gossip at that. Especially of the dead. But in my line of work that's pretty much the only kind I get.

"I'm not trying to, I'm just telling you what kind of a guy he was, that's all. Don't get me wrong, Lauren and Rosanna seemed happy to have his attention. He was very charismatic, very fun to be around, but if he tired of you then that was that. He was still charming about it though, and one kind thing I can say about him was that he didn't hold grudges."

"What do you mean?"

"Well, with the women he wasn't successful in bedding, he was still friendly with them."

"So if I take a poll of the orchestra, most of the musicians aren't going to be happy that Paul's kicked it?"

"That's right. Even Patrick. I bet if you had a heart to heart with him, you'd find that he's not really thrilled by Paul's death either. Even though they were enemies, like I said, Paul didn't hold grudges, he was still on friendly terms with Patrick, at least from his side. Not so much on Patrick's."

"Rosanna told me that Paul was going to settle down with her and marry her. She said the wedding was next summer."

Gary smiled at me. It looked like he couldn't help it.

"Is that funny?" I asked.

He nodded his head.

"Yeah, it is. I don't buy it for a second. Paul wasn't the settling down type. What he was thinking of doing though, was to cut off all ties with Lauren and Rosanna. One of the last conversations we had he told me that very thing."

"That he was going to call it quits?"

Gary nodded.

"Why?" I asked.

"He had been pretty shook up by his encounters with the women's husbands. Especially Kieran. He told me it was Kieran that had beat him up a few weeks ago. I don't think he told that to anyone else. Maybe Rosanna but he didn't want it to become a scene. He was scared of what they might be capable of. That and with those two men he thinks were following him, he figured he needed a fresh start."

"Why do you figure then, that Rosanna thinks they were going to get together?"

"Maybe because he didn't have the courage to tell her. I know he had indulged her that way before. He really seemed to like her. But like I said, he told me he was going to call it off. He'd had enough with the husbands."

"What about this other woman, Stephanie?" I asked.

"That was sad," said Gary, looking down and reminiscing.

"Tell me about it," I said, feeling like a psychotherapist.

"Plain and simple, he used her. She was the musical director's assistant, before Christina. He had a brief relationship with her and got her pregnant. When he did, she became very hopeful that this was going to lead to marriage and the white picket fence and all the rest. I don't want to sound mean, but she was really naïve. I think she was from the Midwest. Anyway, she became unbearable as far as Paul was concerned and he had her sacked, thanks to his pull with Sonia."

"That would have made her quite upset I'm sure."

"You have no idea. I heard that she went to pieces. After the abortion she tried to commit suicide. I believe she was hospitalized for a while after that."

I nodded. Seemed to me like Paul was a tornado, cutting a path of destruction and broken hearts in his wake.

"That's a lot of broken hearts he left behind," I said.

"That's just the way he was. Like I said, I happened to like him. He was fun to hang around, but it had to be on my terms. You had to know what you were getting into. Some people took him at his word and if you did that you'd get hurt."

"More than that, there's a lot of people out there who might have liked to see Paul get some of that hurt back on him."

Gary nodded and looked down thoughtfully.

"I suppose so."

I couldn't think of anything else to ask Gary. He'd filled in some gaps but also made it a lot more difficult to figure out where things were headed.

"Where do you think his violin is?" I asked.

"Probably wherever Paul is," he said. "He'd kept his violin with him lately. Everybody knew that. I think because he didn't want Jamal to get access to it too quickly."

I thanked Gary and asked him to bring Milo down to talk with me. I wasn't sure if there was anything new that anyone could offer me, but I needed to do my due diligence. You never knew what ripe fruit would fall from shaking the right tree.

# Eight

Milo walked down slowly towards me. Everything about him was average. He could be easily overlooked in just about any situation. I figured it would make him a great bank robber or assassin. He was forgettable and at the same time hard to describe.

He wore khakis that were a little too short. You could see his striped socks above his brown loafers. He wore a pale blue golf shirt with a little alligator over the left chest. He was soft. He looked like a marshmallow, a man who had an easy life, and who ate cookies and crumpets all day.

His eyes were watery and looked far away from behind round glasses. He had black neatly combed hair with a side parting. The only distinguishing feature about him that I could see was that he plucked his unibrow. His eyebrows were thick worms above each eye.

His face was white and he had very little stubble. He reminded me of an accountant or a nerdy scientist. He walked up to me and nodded, or rather tipped his head forwards and then backwards as if to nod more vigorously would send his hair tumbling to the floor. He offered a soft hand, which I shook thinking he'd performed a quick sleight of hand offering me instead his wet, warm handkerchief. Instinctively I wiped my hand against my trouser leg afterwards.

I offered him a seat and he took the one Gary had been in, leaving one between the two of us. He sat bolt upright, like a man who had a steel pole in place of a spine. He sat at forty five degrees towards me, his legs close together as if he were a modest woman, and his lady hands were in his lap, the right over top the left, looking like a shy turtle.

"Milo Ellis, right?" I asked.

He nodded. The same small nod that he had offered earlier. I got to thinking maybe he had a crick in his neck that stopped him from bending it any lower.

"Do you know why I'm here?"

I had a sense I had to start this engine nice and slow like it was my LeSabre I had left outside over night in a Fargo blizzard.

"I've heard you're here about Paul."

"That's right," I said, nodding at him more vigorously, showing him how it could be done. "How well did you know him?"

"I knew him well enough, but we weren't close," he said.

"Like him, you're a violinist."

More careful nodding of the head.

"And yet you weren't very close?"

"That's right."

"Why is that?"

"I'm here to practice and perform. I prefer not to mix work and pleasure."

"So you've never gone out with the group after a performance? You've never gone over to Paul's or anyone else's apartment?"

"That's correct."

I tried to keep my poker face, but it was hard to take this guy seriously. I mean who had never gone over to a colleague's place or had drinks after work? I couldn't think of one person. Yet with Milo sitting in front of me, I believed him.

"Alright then," I said. "From your observations, how would you describe Paul to someone like me?"

Milo looked over at the stage. Gary had joined the larger group that included Lauren and Rosanna. He was hugging Rosanna as Lauren looked on, none too pleased.

"Paul was enigmatic," said Milo.

"That's a mild way of putting it."

"As I said, I didn't really spend much time interacting with anyone here other than during rehearsals and performance. I like to eat my lunch alone and spend breaks practicing a piece or reading."

I wondered if he liked long walks on the beach and moonlight dinners by himself. I was pretty certain he probably lived with his mother.

"Did you know about his relationships with other musicians in the orchestra?"

"It would be hard not to know about that."

"Do you have any opinions about it?"

"No. I prefer not to put my nose in other people's business. If it's between two consenting adults then it really doesn't concern me."

Calling him a shrinking violet was putting it mildly. Milo was more like a ghostly eunuch or robot that was programmed to do nothing more than perform one task and that was all. I couldn't fathom a more boring person in my life. In fact, I figured staring at concrete was more inspirational.

"What about his relationship with Stephanie, the woman he got pregnant? Do you have any thoughts about any of that?"

"Not particularly. It was in character with how Paul was. But as I said, what two consenting adults choose to do is none of my concern."

"None of your concern, or you just don't give a shit?" I asked. My patience was wearing thin like the laddered stockings on a cheap whore.

The corners of Milo's mouth turned upwards. It could have been a smirk or maybe it was just a nervous twitch.

"I do, as you say, give a shit. But people's private lives aren't really something I care about. I feel sorry that Stephanie got herself into the situation she did. But she did it without pressure. I'm sorry that Paul got murdered, but it's not a real surprise."

"Now we're getting somewhere. What do you mean it's not a surprise."

The only thing that seemed to move on Milo's body was his head. It swiveled as if it were on a well oiled rod. He might have been sitting on a ventriloquist's lap. He reminded me of a puppet.

"You've likely heard all sorts of sordid details about Paul, most of which I'm sure are true. He was undisciplined and chaotic, if I can be unkind. It wouldn't take a seer to realize he was on a self destructive path."

"So you knew about his womanizing, his drugs, and his propensity for aberrant behavior and yet none of this bothers you, when it clearly bothers most of your colleagues?"

"It bothered me, don't get me wrong, Mr. Carrick. But it was not my place to change it. Frank and Sonia assured me they would take care of it."

"So you did speak to them about Paul's behavior?"

"I did. Only in so far as it was affecting the quality of the orchestra overall. Paul was a fine musician when he was sober. But that seemed to becoming a rarer and rarer event."

"Did you and he ever share any conversations? Do you have any insight into why he had become more erratic as some say he had in the last few weeks?"

"No, we didn't really talk much. Not outside of the music and performance subjects. I do agree though, that the last few weeks he did seem more odd."

"And you have no idea why?"

"I have an opinion."

"That's good," I said, "I'd love to hear it."

"I think that the chaos was catching up with him. He had recent altercations with Lauren's and then Rosanna's husbands. From what I heard he was also concerned about being followed. But whether that was part of his paranoia or real I can't say."

"So if I asked you who you think would have killed him, who would you finger?"

"That's an accusation I wouldn't like to make without very strong evidence. And I haven't seen any strong evidence yet."

"Indulge me, please," I said.

"Well, I can only think of those who might have been upset with him. That would include Lauren and her husband, Rosanna and her husband, Stephanie and one of the previous violinists, John Stampley."

"I thought Lauren and Rosanna were quite happy with him."

"I don't think so. They both seemed smitten with him, and neither one really likes the other. Now whether that's enough for murder I can't say. I'm just indulging you."

"How kind."

Milo smiled the fakest smile I'd seen the whole year. And I'd spent a lot of time around pimps, drug addicts and prostitutes.

"Are you, or were you, close to anyone here?"

"Not particularly."

"Do you have anything you might add to the discussion about Stephanie?"

I felt like a man dying of thirst trying to pump a dry well with a rusty handle. The effort was killing me.

"I know she was, how do I say this delicately, let go. But you probably already know that."

"What I know isn't as important as the flavor you might add to what I know. What do you know about that?"

"Rumors and speculations really. I don't make it my business to put my nose in other people's business, like I said before."

"Listen, Milo," I said, not unkindly, "in my business rumors and speculations are like treasure maps that get me to the crux of why bad things happen to people, whether they're good or bad. I don't care if you speak ill of the dead. I'm not here to judge your integrity. I'm just trying to find out why Paul was killed and who might have done it. Any morsel, any crumb, however irrelevant you might think, might get me closer to that goal."

"Fine," he said. "I heard that Paul got upset when he found out Stephanie was pregnant. The last thing he wanted was marriage, or worse than that, a child. Apparently he used up a lot of favor with Frank and Sonia in making sure they got rid of her. It was either her or him, is what I heard. So they got rid of her, paid for her abortion and gave her a large sum of money to be quiet."

"How large?"

"I heard it was half a million dollars. But like I said, this is all second hand information."

I wondered if it was a quarter mil or half a mil. Not that it made much of a difference, but when the details are not congruent oftentimes the big picture isn't.

"How did Stephanie take this?"

"Not well at all. I saw her leaving after meeting with Frank and Sonia late one afternoon and she was in tears. I asked her if she was okay."

Milo stopped and looked down at his turtled hands. His back stuffed full of iron pipe. Rigid. He made me feel uncomfortable just looking at him.

"What did she say?"

"She ran off. Told me she hated me and everyone to do with the orchestra. Thing is, I hardly knew her. I'd only said hello to her now and then in passing. This is why I prefer not to put my nose in people's business."

I nodded sympathetically.

"What happened to her after that do you know?"

"I don't. Some said she went back to the Midwest. I think she was from Muncie, Indiana if I remember correctly. Though I wouldn't put money on it. I also heard she was here, living in the Bronx someplace."

"So nobody knows what happened to her?"

"I wouldn't say nobody. I'm sure Frank or Sonia have probably still kept tabs on her whereabouts to make sure she doesn't misbehave."

"And Paul, did he have any remorse about what happened to her?"

Milo tossed his head back slightly and humphed.

"That's funny," he said. "I've never seen Paul show remorse or even admit to a mistake. No, he seemed in much better spirits after that."

"And when was this?"

"About a year ago."

"And these men that were apparently following him. What do you make of that?"

Milo looked at me with his watery eyes that seemed drowned in years and layers of disappointment. Though I might have been reading too much into them.

"Nobody ever saw these apparitions, and I certainly didn't. If you ask me, I'd say it was probably part of his paranoia or an attempt to create more focus on himself. There always had to be something going on with Paul. He always had to be the center of attention."

"I've also heard that his good graces were coming to an end with Frank and Sonia. Do you know anything about that?"

"Not as much as you. But I did hear that he was on his last legs as far as they were concerned. Especially Sonia. You see, Paul had used, how do I say this, his great charm and youthful vigor in the early years he was here. Sonia greatly admired that and I think it gave him a great advantage. But in the last decade or so, Paul had started to look the gift horse in the mouth if you know what I mean, and I don't think he liked what he saw. He had become on many occasions, and especially behind her back, quite insulting towards Sonia. The only thing surprising about this is how long he got away with his poor behavior."

"It sounds like you didn't care for him very much," I said.

Milo swiveled his head from left to right on the carefully oiled rod that was his spine and neck.

"No, not particularly. In fact, I didn't mind him at all. I had no qualms with him. You see, Paul was quite pleasant. Especially if he didn't feel threatened by you. But that doesn't mean I couldn't tell he was a wolf in sheep's clothing."

"What about John Stampley?"

"I arrived just at the changing of the guard. I believe Paul had been with the Philharmonic a year by then. I was hired on as a second violin as Paul was transferred into the first violin section. It all came as quite a shock to me. John was very upset. In fact, I remember him telling me that he hoped I was happy being an agent of his demise. Of course he was quite sarcastic about it. I didn't understand what he meant at first."

"But you soon found out?"

"Yes. Frank had fired John just so he could move Paul into the first violins. As you can imagine, I benefited by taking up Paul's then vacant seat as a second violin."

"So John was angry?"

"He was livid. The last I heard of him was when he made a scene during practice on his last day. He said he'd make sure that Frank and Paul paid for their deceit and disloyalty if it was the last thing he did."

"Could it not have been just sour grapes? Perhaps John wasn't performing up to snuff?"

Milo smiled at me, and shook his head slowly.

"No, everybody at the time said that John was one of the best violinists in the orchestra then. Under the previous conductor, I forget his name..."

"Douglas Goodell," I offered.

"Yes, that's right. Under Douglas, rumor had it that John was next up in line for the concertmaster position. He was in his early fifties at that point. That was about twenty years ago."

"What happened to him?"

Milo shrugged, as carefully as he did anything. Just the tops of his shoulders moved. Up and then down. I was beginning to believe he might not really be human.

"I'm not sure. I heard that he went on to offer violin lessons. But that was a long time ago. He could be retired by now."

"I heard something about Paul and his violin and John Stampley. There's a relationship there I think."

Milo looked at me and frowned.

"I don't think so," he said. "Paul had a Strad, a very valuable one that he used on special occasions. It sounded amazing. Such warm and thick tones. And the workmanship on it was astonishing. Really fine detail on the pegs, scroll and tailpiece. He bragged that he had it insured for ten million. Now I don't know if it was worth that much, though it could be because a seventeen twenty-one Strad called the Lady Blunt sold for almost ten million pounds not long ago."

I smiled.

"Never would I have suspected a piece of wood would sell for that much," I said.

"That's only because you don't have an appreciation for violins. There are only a few hundred Strads still around and far less in as good a shape as Paul's Blount Strad. Rare things generally become valuable."

"Yes, I suppose they do. How did he keep the violin safe?" I asked.

"He usually kept it under lock and key in the basement. There's a safe there that only a few people have access to. But lately he'd just been keeping it with him at all times."

"That doesn't seem particularly safe," I said.

"Well, yes and no. Just as you suggested earlier, not many people realize a piece of wood, as you said, could be worth that much. I mean a homeless guy playing fiddle down in SoHo could be using a million dollar Strad and who'd know? The only ones who'd know the value of Paul's violin were his fellow musicians like us, and collectors and connoisseurs. But you're right in a way, he should have kept it under lock and key, especially if he was so concerned about being followed."

"And yet he didn't."

"That's right. Though personally, I don't think his violin has anything to do with his death."

"You say that like it's a fact. And yet I've heard an interesting story that it was maybe stolen by his grandfather from a woman during the Second World War."

"I wouldn't know about that," said Milo, "but I wouldn't be surprised if that was greatly embellished. Adding a story like that to his violin, Paul probably thought it would make it more valuable."

"So you think that John Stampley looking into Paul's background and finding out that the violin was stolen and threatening to tell everyone if Paul didn't back down from his first violin position is not true?"

"I'm not saying that John wasn't looking for an angle to ruin Paul. I just think that Paul made up that story."

"Not according to Gary."

"And you're going to believe a coke head?"

"Why not?"

"Because he and Paul were thick as thieves. I think Gary's in on it."

I was just about finished with Milo when two detectives walked into Avery Fisher Hall. You could tell they were cops by the way they looked. The one guy was fat and his tie didn't reach his belt. He had a graying mustache and khaki pants. The other guy was slim with blue pants and blue shirt with a blue tie. He was clean shaven with brown hair.

The other thing that gave them away might have been their badges clipped to the front of their belts and their guns on their side. Neither of them wore a jacket.

# Nine

The two detectives walked right past us and up to the stage. I got up and told Milo we should go and have a listen. So we joined the group as they all jostled around the detectives. I stood next to Frank.

"I'm Detective Cooper," said the fat one, "and this is Detective Simms. You probably know why we're here. We'd appreciate your cooperation as we investigate your colleague's death."

Cooper had to take a pause to catch his breath. He fished out a handkerchief from his pocket and patted his brow which was blistering sweat. His underarm was stained wet. I could smell his cheap musky cologne over his stench, much like rotten meat.

His colleague seemed cooler and more collected. Simms had his hands in his pockets and he carefully studied everyone in the group as he looked around slowly.

"I'm Frank Moody," said Frank, offering his hand to Cooper who was nearest us, "I'm the musical director and I'll be happy to do whatever we can to help."

Cooper shook his hand and nodded.

"We'll need to interview everyone. Shouldn't take long. Hopefully we can get you home in time for dinner. Those of you who eat late."

"Can you tell us what happened?" I asked, throwing my line in the shallow waters.

"Who're you?" asked Cooper.

"I'm the hired investigator who was brought on to look into this," I said, smiling like we were old pals.

Cooper wasn't having any of it.

"I don't think so. This is an ongoing investigation. We don't need your help," said Cooper. "Though what you can do is hand over any notes you already have."

Cooper put a big, soft meaty paw out towards me.

"I don't think so," I said.

Cooper frowned his face and he looked like a hairless bulldog only less friendly.

"What did you say?"

"I said I ain't helping you out, copper, unless you help me out."

"That's not how it works, son." He said that like he meant it though we were probably of similar age, only he wore it like a crumpled suit, and me, well I wore it like a fine dinner tux. "The police investigate homicides and the public, which includes you, help us."

"You've mistaken me for someone who believes in the NYPD," I said.

"Just hand it over and stop pissing around with us."

I shook my head. I kept smiling at him. Out of the corner of my eye I could see Simms looking at me expressionless. His hands still thrust in his pockets. He was fondling the change in them. It didn't look good.

"We'll get it with a subpoena," said Cooper.

"If I'm still in town by the time you get it signed," I said.

"Let me talk to him," said Simms, looking at Cooper with a knowing nod. "Why don't you start on the interviews."

Cooper stared at his partner for a bit. Then he nodded and walked over to Frank and started asking him about the members of the orchestra.

"Could I have a moment of your time?" asked Simms, walking over to me.

He led me to a far corner of the stage. When we were alone he smiled at me and offered his hand.

"You look familiar," he said.

"I get that a lot."

"No really, you do. Were you on the job?"

"A while back yeah, in LA."

"What's your name?"

"Anthony Carrick."

Simms nodded and his smile broadened.

"I thought so," he said. "You boxed in the finals of the ninety-eight police games. You took the middleweight title from an NYPD narc named Steve Little."

I grinned at Simms. I remembered the bout well. One of the hardest I'd ever fought. And that was saying something. I could've gone pro but Racquel wouldn't stand for it at the time. She's now my ex.

"That's right. Hardest fight I ever fought."

"Steve still talks about it."

"You don't ring a bell though," I said.

"That's alright, I was in Little's corner, one of his seconds."

I nodded. I already liked Simms. I could tell he was a good cop. Better than his pal Cooper. Not just because he was stroking my ego. He knew how to find the inside track to someone. That was gold in my opinion.

"So you're no longer on the job then?"

I shook my head.

"Got out due to politics."

"Tell me about it. Listen," said Simms, "I'd like to help you. I really do, but Cooper over there is a stickler. I tell you what though. If you get Sonia Varnier to talk to the Police Commissioner we'll get you riding shotgun in no time."

"I appreciate the tip. I'll get on it," I said. "In the meantime, what can you tell me about the crime scene?"

Simms looked over at Cooper who was engrossed talking with Patrick. He huddled closer to me like we were deciding on a play.

"The missing persons was called in this morning," said Simms.

I nodded my head.

"So we sent some unis over just to do a knock and see. When they got there the neighbor met them, said the place had started smelling bad. The neighbor hadn't seen Klee since Thursday. Unis knocked on the door and got no response. They said it reeked. Smelled like shit and rotting garbage. They called it in to their sergeant. He figured that smelled like a dead body so he got a search warrant while they waited outside."

"I see where this is going," I said.

Simms nodded.

"Yeah, so the search warrant comes through. By this time there's a couple more unis at the place and the sergeant. They break down the door. First thing they see is Klee on the couch watching television. Loud, but not annoyingly loud for the neighbors. Just enough to distract you from a couple of suppressed gunshots. Klee's been tapped twice in the chest. Bam, bam."

Simms taps himself on the left chest, just above his heart.

"They were accurate."

"Was the place ransacked?" I asked.

Simms nodded.

"A total mess."

"Have you found prints?"

"A bunch, but we're not hopeful they're of the perp. It just looked really well done."

"I'd like to take a look."

Simms nodded.

"Speak with Sonia," he said. "She's got pull. She's your ticket inside."

I nodded slowly.

"So what do you make of it?"

"One of two things. Either this was a hit made to look like a robbery or it was a robbery, though it doesn't look like much, if anything at all was stolen."

"Did you find a violin?"

"We found a few actually."

"I mean an expensive violin. A Stradivarius?"

Simms shrugged.

"Dunno yet, we haven't catalogued everything yet. Why're you worried about a violin?"

"It might be nothing, but I've heard an interesting story about one of the vic's violins. He had a Strad, that was given to him by his grandfather."

"Doesn't mean much to me," said Simms.

"Didn't mean much to me either, until I heard it was insured for ten mil."

Simms turned his mouth down, raised his eyebrows and bobbed his head up and down.

"Yeah, I know," I said. "I never knew a piece of wood was worth that much. But it gets more interesting. This violin was apparently stolen from a woman by Klee's granpappy who was a guard at one of the concentration camps during the war."

"That's weird. Is this legit?"

"I don't know yet. I've heard it from a couple of the other musicians. I'm going to check it out. If it is, then it could be someone was after the violin."

Simms looked down at the floor and nodded thoughtfully.

"Could narrow down the suspects then. I bet not many know how valuable a violin like that is."

"That's what I figure. Though it could be a hit like you say. This Klee guy was a ladies man. Heard he was banging a couple of the married ladies in the orchestra. Had an altercation with both husbands just a few weeks ago."

Simms nodded his head for a bit, and looked at me.

"That's good intel," he said. "They might've known Klee had an expensive violin. Either of them could have set it up so as to look like a robbery."

"That's the thing," I said. "Just when you think it starts to look like you can narrow it down, there's a twist that opens it all up again."

"Ain't that the truth. Thanks for that," said Simms. "You're a good guy."

Cooper walked up to us.

"You ladies gonna stand around and talk theater or do you wanna help me with the interviews."

Cooper was looking at Simms. Simms patted me on the shoulder.

"Remember what I said," said Simms. "Better to stay out of this one. The NYPD doesn't like outsiders poking their noses into our business."

"I gotcha," I said.

Simms walked off with Cooper.

"I think he's good," said Simms. "We might even be able to use him."

He was talking to Cooper.

"He can give us his notes if he's got any. That's what he can do."

That was the last I heard of them. They split up and took different musicians to interview. Frank came up to me.

"I'm sorry about that," he said. "The police get quite territorial I guess."

"Looks like it," I said.

"But Sonia is close friends with the Commissioner. I'm sure she can have them soften their stance. She's really looking forward to meeting you. She's preparing dinner for you at her place tonight if you don't mind. She'll send the car round."

Frank looked at his watch.

"In fact, the car should be here for you any moment."

I looked at my watch. It was coming on five thirty. Frank stayed with me as we waited. And I decided to make a good time of it.

"This whole thing has turned as bad as I had feared," said Frank.

"It's a dog's breakfast," I said.

"Why do you think anyone would want to murder Paul. I just can't fathom that. I mean, I know he could be difficult at times, but that doesn't condone murder."

I turned to look at Frank.

"How did you manage to get your position?"

"I knew Sonia. We go back many years. In fact, she and I graduated high school together."

"Where was that?"

"Eau Claire in Wisconsin. Look, I know a lot of people aren't happy with me being here having taken over from Doug. But what's wrong with using the influence you have?"

"Nothing wrong with it," I said. "But having people fired so you can get it, seems a little unethical."

"What do you mean?"

"Doug was pushed out so you could come in as the musical director."

"That was Sonia's decision along with the board. I don't take responsibility for it."

"Do you take responsibility for firing John Stampley?"

I looked at Frank, he looked away. I followed his eyes as he watched the detectives interviewing his musicians.

"Yes, I take responsibility for that. You just don't understand, Mr. Carrick. Sonia is a powerful woman and she gets what she wants. She wanted Paul in the first violin section and so she got him in there. I was made the fall guy."

"And why was Paul chosen amongst all the others for that role?" I asked, looking at Frank as he looked at his musicians.

He didn't look at me right away. He crossed his arms across his chest and looked down at something on the floor. Maybe he was admiring the fine detail in the wood. I figured he was trying to come to terms with disagreeable thoughts. After some time, he looked at me.

"I think you know why. One of the musicians must have told you."

"I've heard a bunch of things," I said, "most of which I don't like. But I'd like to hear your take on it. If you hear something often enough it starts to feel like the truth, even if it isn't."

"Why would we lie?"

"That's an easy one. Because people don't want the truth to come out."

"Look, Anthony," said Frank, now at ease with my first name again, "I don't feel comfortable telling you about that."

"That's alright," I said, "maybe I don't feel comfortable working on this case anymore."

He looked up at me with a frown on his brow.

"What do you mean?"

"I mean, I might as well go back to LA and enjoy the last vestiges of summer before the cool wind comes in and I hibernate at my favorite watering hole. If the people who hired me to figure out this goddamn mess aren't going to be honest with me, I might as well stop before I've even started."

"Now, that's not necessary," said Frank, still frowning at me like I'd spilled milk on the floor.

"Your choice, Frank. You start being candid or I'm on the first plane back to LA this evening and you can explain it to Sonia."

Frank shuffled from foot to foot. He looked down and sighed. Then he looked back at me.

"Alright, Jesus," he said, "you can be an asshole." I grinned at that. "Sonia is a powerful woman like I said before. She tends to get what she wants. And she got Paul the position because he gave her what she wanted."

"And what did she want?"

"She wanted companionship after her husband died. Paul was very charismatic and charming and as you can probably tell from the photo of him you saw, he's also good looking. At least to a lot of woman from what I can tell."

"I'm not buying the companionship," I said.

"You know what I mean when I say companionship. I'm sure intimacy was involved too, though I don't know for sure and I don't care to know. But it certainly seemed like that was part of the deal. Listen, this wasn't just Sonia getting her way, I think Paul was quite into it too. Sonia was a good looking woman, still is, but fifty years ago she was still clinging to the ends of youthful vigor."

"I get that," I said. "Paul's sleeping his way to the top, and Sonia's getting whatever it is she wants out of the deal, and you've been put in place as the rainmaker to make it happen. But things had soured lately right?"

"Well, they started souring about ten years ago. Sonia kept getting older and Paul started getting put off by it. Not that he told me, but I overheard him expressing his revulsion with Sonia as she got older. He managed to hide it well until about three years ago, just after he got the concertmaster position. Since then he's been less inclined to play ball."

"With Sonia?"

"With everything. His flamboyant lifestyle, if I can call it that, started overtaking his professional life. He started taking more drugs and coming in late to rehearsals, finishing them early and becoming a pain in the ass generally."

"Right, so you and Sonia had words with him," I said.

Terry entered the hall and started walking down the aisle towards us.

"Your ride's here," said Frank, nodding his face towards Terry.

We waited until Terry came up stage and joined us.

"Are you ready, Mr. Carrick?" he asked.

"No," I said. "If you don't mind giving me a few minutes."

"Certainly."

Terry bowed himself away and went and sat in the audience seats, about half a dozen rows out from us. Frank looked back at me.

"Yes, Sonia and I had words with Paul about a month ago."

"What kind of words?"

"Frankly, Paul was given notice. He was told if he didn't get his act together by the end of the season, which is in six months time, then that would be the last season he'd play with us."

"And how did he take that?"

"Not well. He had a tantrum and told us that he was the sole reason that the Phil was so successful and that without him we'd be nothing. After he calmed down a bit, we told him we were serious. Then he stormed out. Later that day, Sonia had a private conversation with him and told me that he had promised her he was going to change. Sonia believed him, though to be honest with you, I didn't."

"Why not?"

"Because he had become irrational and unreliable. He'd always been spoiled with a big ego, and most of us knew how to cater to that, but lately, nothing seemed to reign him in."

"What do you think was going on with that?"

Frank shrugged his thin shoulders.

"He had all sorts of excuses. One day it would be the husbands of the women he was screwing, the next day it would be the drugs and then it would be his paranoia."

"The men who he alleged were following him?"

Frank nodded.

"When I came to see you, you told me Paul had never missed a rehearsal. Is that true?"

"No, what I meant to say is that we'd always been able to get a hold of him. This time was different, because we couldn't get him on the horn."

"Tell me about Paul's Strad," I said.

"What about it?"

"Was it as valuable as everyone is making it out to be?"

"Most certainly. He had it insured for ten million, and I'm sure it could have sold easily for that much if not more. It was very rare, with a storied pedigree."

"You mean his grandfather stealing it from a concentration camp woman?"

Frank looked at me steadily and the corners of his mouth smiled at me.

"You don't mess about, Mr. Carrick, do you? I can see you're proving to be well worth your money. I've heard rumors of that story. Frankly, I don't buy it."

"Why not?"

"Because most of the art, and you could call this Blount Strad art, that was stolen by the Germans was returned to its rightful owners. There are very few items still missing. In any event, Paul assured me this wasn't the case. His grandfather wasn't a guard at any concentration camps and he said he had the papers to prove who had owned the violin since Pope bought it for Martha Blount."

"And you saw these papers?"

"No, I didn't feel it was necessary. The authorities would surely have caught up with the violin by now if it had been improperly obtained."

"Where did Paul keep the violin?"

"Ah, that's the strange thing. We had offered him full use of our basement safe, which he had used since we first became aware of the value of his violin after he joined us. But lately, about three weeks to a month ago, he had taken it from the safe and kept it with him at all times. I thought it was quite odd and tried to encourage him to put it back where it would be safer. He wouldn't hear of it, said he didn't trust anyone and he was being followed. I said that was even a bigger reason to keep it under lock and key. He said that's exactly what they'd expect and then they'd break into the safe and take it. He said this way, they'd have to kill him if they wanted to get it. I just thought he was paranoid. Maybe he wasn't that paranoid after all."

"We don't know that yet," I said. "The police are still cataloging what they found at the crime scene. Who had keys to this safe?"

"Only me, the caretaker and Paul. Though it's hardly relevant now I think."

"How long has the caretaker been with the Philharmonic?"

"Funny you should ask," said Frank, ironing out his frown. "This caretaker is new, only been here about three months I think. The previous one just stopped showing up, so we had to hire someone new. Worked out really nicely. This guy just happened to show up at the right time when we needed him. German fella, but speaks good English. They're detailed you know, he does a good job. Not me you understand, I didn't hire him, the management group of Lincoln Center."

I nodded my head slowly. Things were starting to fall into place, but I couldn't be sure of the reason that Paul was murdered. A violin seemed unlikely. What seemed more appropriate was jealousy and infidelity. That's the direction I was gonna head in first.

"How did this guy say he knew about the job?" I asked.

Frank shrugged.

"Said he heard some guys talking about the caretaker not showing up, so he thought he'd come in and see if we needed help. Perfect timing."

"What was this caretaker's name?"

"The new one?" Frank asked.

I nodded my head.

"Martin. Martin Maurer I think. Why do you ask?"

"It's what you hired me for. To ask questions of people, and I want to ask Martin a few questions. Who was the guy before him?"

"Wit Walczak."

I smiled at Frank.

"Really, you only hire caretakers that have the same initial in their first and last names?"

Frank didn't find that particularly amusing. He shrugged his shoulders in his big jacket.

"I hadn't thought of it like that. Besides, I don't do their hiring."

"Speaking of which, is Martin still around?"

"You're suggesting that he's involved?"

"I'm just asking a question," I said.

"I don't see how. I think it's just coincidental. Anyway, like I told you, Paul took his violin out of this safe a few weeks back. Why would Martin stick around if that's all he was interested in?"

"To make it not look obvious," I offered. "But instead of arguing with you I'd prefer if you just answered my question."

"Yes, Martin's still around. I saw him yesterday. Though you won't find him today or tomorrow, he doesn't work the weekends."

I nodded.

"We'll see if he shows up on Monday."

"I don't see why he wouldn't."

"One last thing. Who benefits the most from Paul's death, here in the orchestra?"

"Probably Milo Ellis," said Frank, looking over at the orchestral musicians. Milo was being interviewed by Simms. "You don't think he'd have something to do with it?"

Frank looked at me with a genuinely questioning face.

"It's too early to say."

Personally, I didn't like Milo for it. There was something insipid and uninspiring about him. But I liked to keep my options open, and when gathering intel on a case it's best to let others keep their minds open too.

"I think that'll be all, Frank. How can I get a hold of you tomorrow if I need to?"

"I'll be here. We all will. There's a matinee and an evening performance."

I nodded, and walked off the stage towards Terry. He got up and met me in the aisle. Terry wore his black chauffeur's suit better than Frank did. Though to me he looked more like an undertaker, and that was appropriate.

SECOND FIDDLE (AN ANTHONY CARRICK MYSTERY)

# Ten

Terry drove very sedately away from Lincoln Center. Terry got onto W 58th and headed south. I knew that from the street signs. I was making note of my whereabouts. We passed behind the Ritz where I was staying and then onto Madison Avenue where he headed north to E 61st. New York, it seemed to me, had more one way streets than the path to hell.

I was starting to get dizzy by the time Terry turned left again onto Fifth. He dropped me off across from the park and right outside the main doors of what looked like a hotel. I saw the name on the awning. It said "The Royce", and it looked like the Rolls Royce of hotels.

"Just let the concierge know you're here for Mrs. Varnier and he'll escort you up."

I thanked Terry and got out of the car carrying my hat. I walked into the opulence that is The Royce. The foyer was outrageous. It consisted of marble flooring that sparkled as if it were winking at me a shared joke. The ceilings were huge and a large waterfall splashed in the middle. An abstract Zen suggestion of a water fall. It must have been twenty feet high. The ceiling was painted like the Sistine Chapel, but it didn't look religious in motif. I found the concierge desk and walked up to the older man who wore a dark blue suit with matching blue gloves that you might have mistaken for skin except his face was the polished brown of walnut.

He smiled at me as if I was an old friend. His teeth were large and white and his nostrils flared out like a race horse. His hair was short and reminded me of salt dusted peppercorns. He was a couple of inches taller than me and thicker around the chest and waist.

"Good evening, sir," he said.

He had a relaxed almost grandfatherly warmth to him.

"Hello," I said. "I'm here for Sonia Varnier."

"Of course, can I get your name please, sir?"

He was polite and warm. His smile seemed almost permanently carved into his face. I told him my name and he asked for ID. He was very gracious about it, explained how they'd had some ne'er-do-wells recently. And well, you know, precautions being how they are. I nodded all the while, sizing this fellow up. When he was satisfied he handed me back my driver's license and asked me to follow him. I did, and I watched him walk towards one of the far elevators. His blue gloved hands hung like swinging hammers. He moved softly and quickly on his feet without much effort. I'd put money on him having been a boxer. He had the graceful movement of one.

We got into the elevator together. He pulled out a key from his pocket and put it into the control panel. Then he pushed the button that had V on it. There were only three buttons on this elevator. M, 1 and V. I figured this was Sonia's private elevator. Jeremiah, as he had introduced himself to me, and as his name tag indicated, didn't say a word to me. He stood the whole journey with his hands clasped loosely in front of him and facing forward, though I could feel him watching me the whole time.

When we got to floor V, which I figured was somewhere really high up, he insisted that I get out first. I did. His insistence was patient but forceful. I had the suspicion we'd head back down if I didn't do as he asked.

There was only one way to go and that was straight down a short hallway to two large solid wood, intricately carved doors along a soft but intricately woven carpet. I stopped at the doors and Jeremiah came up to my right. He pushed the button and I heard a song hummed inside somewhere far away.

A short while later I heard high heels clicking towards the door. A short, slim woman opened the door. I put her in her seventies. She wore it well. Her hair was short and curly and brown. Not her natural color. She wore a navy suit with a white blouse underneath. Her bosoms were ample and surprisingly firm. She wasn't stunning, rather quite plain, and she didn't wear much makeup, but she still had a charm. I figured in her youth she would have been a lot of fun.

She smiled at Jeremiah, and then at me. She held out her hand and I shook it delicately like I was holding a baby kitten.

"You must be Mr. Carrick?" she said, "I'm Sonia Varnier."

"Please call me Anthony, Sonia," I replied.

Sonia looked over at Jeremiah and nodded at him.

"Thank you, Jeremiah."

He nodded at her and walked back down the hall towards the lift. Sonia opened the door wider and invited me in. I stepped into a foyer that seemed as large and as opulent as the main foyer many floors down.

"Nice place you have," I said, trying to start the conversation with the kindling of small talk.

"Thank you, Anthony," she said. "My husband bought this place only a few years after we were married."

"It's a nice apartment."

"It is, though I meant to say he bought the building at the time. The apartment was convenient for us to move into."

"I take it that's how you made your money?"

Sonia smiled at me and invited me further into her home towards a bank of couches and chairs. I figured it was the living room but it went on for years so I couldn't be sure.

"That's how my late husband made our money. I don't have much involvement in the business anymore. My son, Garrett, runs the company now, I just have an honorary chair on the board."

I nodded at her and followed her as she walked over to the first couch and chair. She took a well padded lounge chair and offered me the couch in front of her. I sat down in it and felt lost in its expanse and softness. It was more comfortable than my bed. In front of us was a wooden table with small sculptures on it of the female form. They were as realistic as Barbie dolls, but nevertheless tempting to look at.

A butler walked up to me, dressed in a tuxedo and white gloves. He was in his fifties with black hair and roundness around his midsection that suggested he was paid well to wait on guests.

"Can I offer you a drink, sir?" he asked, leaning forward towards me.

"I'll have a Scotch if you've got it."

"Blended or single?"

"Single."

The butler bowed himself away towards the far end of the room where he got my drink ready.

"Alfred has been with me for twenty-five years now," she said, looking at him as he prepared my drink.

He hadn't offered her one, and I could see why. She was sipping on a glass of red wine.

"My late husband hired Alfred just before he passed."

"I'm sorry to hear that," I said.

Sonia smiled kindly at me.

"Not at all, that's been almost twenty-five years ago now."

"He must have been a young man," I said.

Sonia nodded and took a sip of her wine.

"Yes, he was only fifty-five. It was a sudden heart attack. Took me by surprise, he was very fit."

I nodded. There wasn't much more I could say. I was talking to a stranger about her late husband who meant nothing to me, and she likely had more money than she knew what to do with, and most likely didn't need my fake sympathy. Not that I wasn't sympathetic in a small way. I was, but better people are cut down in the prime of their lives all the time.

Alfred came back carrying a silver tray, that from the dull shine of it was probably made from real silver. It had an intricately formed lip. On it was a bottle of Scotch and a tumbler and another glass full of ice. The bottle of Scotch was Macallan 1949. It was two thirds full of its golden liquor.

"Will this do, sir?" asked Alfred, leaning down towards me.

"Looks fine," I said, "thanks. No ice."

Alfred poured me a generous three fingers and placed the glass down on a coaster in front of me. He looked at Sonia and she nodded at him. He bowed himself away and moved just out of earshot but still attentive.

"My husband was a Scotch drinker too," said Sonia. "He loved his single malt. It's not often I've been able to offer some of his single malts to guests. Seems that Scotch is an acquired taste that not many young men seem to take to anymore. That's a shame."

"A crying one," I said.

I put my hand out for the Scotch and took a sip. It was smooth and warm and I tasted hints of burnt mango smoked over oak. That wasn't really so. I wasn't a snob about my whisky. It just tasted like more so I had another sip. Yeah, it was good. I'm sure it cost a few bucks.

"Do you like it?" asked Sonia.

"Very smooth," I said.

"A bottle like that sells for almost twenty thousand dollars nowadays," she said.

"I'll try not to spill any then."

I smiled at her.

"You're not very impressed by wealth, are you, Anthony?"

"Not particularly," I said.

"What does impress you?" she asked.

"Sleeping babies, honest, hard-working men with leathery faces and scuffed hands. Women with short skirts and ample breasts. The curve at the bottom of her calf like a knowing smile when she wears high heeled shoes."

Sonia smiled at me.

"Are you always this facetious?"

"You asked what impressed me, those are some of the things that impress me. I'll tell you another thing that impresses. Men who can live good lives when all around them temptation comes calling. The same goes for women."

"I have the feeling that's a pointed remark in my direction," said Sonia.

"You never remarried?"

"No, I never found the right man."

"Or were you grabbing at the fragile, fraying edges of youth."

"You're a quick study," said Sonia. "I admit to having had a weakness for youthful vigor, though I gave up on that a few years ago."

"You gave up on it, or he did?"

"Does it matter?"

"I suppose not."

I leaned back into the couch and swirled the Scotch in my glass. The light in the room was soft and warm, and my belly was feeling light and happy. I was hungry, and Sonia wasn't in the kitchen cooking. Not that I expected she would have been. I figured that Frank telling me she was making me dinner was a figure of speech not a literal telling of what was happening. Seeing the butler, I wouldn't have been surprised if she had an Iron Chef in her kitchen right now.

"Do you have any dietary restrictions?" asked Sonia, sipping her wine.

"I'm not fussy."

"Then I hope you'll enjoy what my chef has prepared."

"I'm sure I will, so long as it isn't poisoned."

I smiled at her and took a sip of Scotch. I was thinking I could get used to a place like this. I could huddle deep within these walls, drinking Scotch, eating steak and getting soft, and being as depressed as the best of them.

A Hispanic woman in a black French maid's uniform came up and spoke to Sonia. She told her that dinner was ready anytime we were.

"Are you hungry?" asked Sonia.

"I could eat."

"Then why don't we go to the dining room."

Sonia got up and led the way to a dining room that was bigger than my apartment. At least that's what it looked like. There was a dark brown table spread out along its length. Around it were the same dark brown wooden chairs with soft cushions on the seat and backrests with arm rests that weren't covered with cushions. I counted ten of them. At the head of the table was a setting and to the right was another setting.

Alfred pulled out the chair at the head of the table for Sonia and tucked her in when she sat down. I now knew which seat was mine. I went to sit down and Alfred tucked me in too. I didn't like that, but I didn't complain.

We were served weeds that looked like they had been plucked from the cracks in New York city's sidewalks. It was a small bowl and got me wondering how vegetarians survive. It wasn't bad. I tasted a mustardy flavor to the dressing. Next up was a serving that looked like some sort of fungus you might find in a wood. I was certain it wasn't edible but Sonia assured me it was. It must have been the look on my face. She told me it was black winter truffle with scallions and tamari. It tasted good if I were to be honest.

The next dish to be served was the one I thought was going to be dinner. The places I go to are usually a one plate meal. I like the simple things in life. Having eaten two meals already I was wondering how long this meal was going to last.

The chef served us this course, which I figured was the main course. He served Sonia first, and explained how it was a duck confit with fork crushed fingerling potatoes, pickled pearl onions, fines herbes and au jus. I had no idea what it meant, but Sonia nodded with twinkling eyes and a big smile. I guess it was to her satisfaction.

Next he placed a filet mignon in front of me on a plain white plate. It had a hash brown potato patty next to it, which the chef called a hashed brown potato cake. My filet mignon was also wrapped in bacon which I figured was overkill. I usually like to eat just one kind of meat at a time. This the chef informed me was applewood smoked bacon. The whole thing had a brown gravy drizzled over the top of it. Only it wasn't gravy. The chef smiled at my description. He called it a Bordelaise sauce which he explained is made with butter, red wine, shallots, sauce demi-glace and bone marrow. The last bit had me losing my appetite. I nodded at him and tried to smile. I couldn't figure out what was wrong with just a plain old steak with a nice and classic mushroom or Béarnaise sauce.

The chef offered me red wine. I didn't pay attention to what kind it was, but he said it would go better with the meal than my Scotch. Who was I to argue with him. He topped up Sonia's glass as well. When he replaced the bottle I saw it was a Cabernet.

110

I peeled off my bacon and put it to one side, and started in on the filet mignon. It was damn good. Probably the best filet mignon I'd ever had in my life.

"Everything okay, Anthony?" asked Sonia, popping a piece of duck into her mouth.

"Very good, actually," I said, and I didn't even have to lie.

The chef grinned and removed himself from the dining room. We sat in silence for a little while, working our way through the meal and sipping red wine.

"Why did you want someone from LA instead of New York?" I asked Sonia, looking at her as she speared an onion with her fork. "There must be some good PIs here."

"I didn't just want anyone from LA, I specifically wanted you."

"That's very flattering," I said, "but why?"

Sonia took her time eating the onion and looking down the far end of the table at ghosts. Maybe she envisioned her husband down there. After she had finished chewing she looked at me and smiled.

"I have friends in Hollywood," she said. "They spoke highly of you. Not only of your abilities but of your discretion as well."

"The Max Ernst case," I said.

Sonia nodded.

"I also followed up by talking with Chief Burton."

"That surprises me," I said.

"Why?"

"That you'd still want to hire me after speaking with him."

I put more filet mignon in my mouth and chewed on it, watching Sonia.

"He acknowledged the two of you hadn't seen eye to eye, but he told me that you were the best homicide detective he'd ever known."

I guess water could wash away under a bridge. I smiled at Sonia and she smiled back.

"Besides, you're cheap."

"Is that so?"

Sonia nodded.

"I always thought I might be easy, but never cheap," I said, grinning at her.

"Half the price of most of the better PIs I inquired about here in New York," said Sonia.

"I see, perhaps next time I'll negotiate higher rates."

We ate in silence and I sipped my wine. I looked around at this massive room and the even bigger apartment which was at least two floors high if not three, and I got to thinking that this woman must be lonely in here all by herself. No wonder she took a shine to Paul.

"I'm sure by now you realize this case has turned into a homicide investigation," I said.

Sonia nodded, but she didn't look at me. She put a piece of potato in her mouth and chewed it slowly.

"Does that change your rates?" she asked.

"No."

Sonia looked at me and offered a weak smile. I'd seen more teeth from the local toothless bums in the park earlier. Sonia picked up her napkin and dabbed at her eyes. They filled with water but she held the flood back. She dabbed at them again.

"Sorry," she said. "I just heard a couple of hours ago. I'm still trying to understand it."

I looked at Sonia. She was as fragile as the last autumn leaf on a maple tree in winter's gusts. Money couldn't assuage the pain of loss, and as much as I had my opinions on her and Paul, it was apparent that she cared for him. Deeply.

"You were close to Paul, I understand?"

Sonia looked at me, blinked her eyes and nodded. Her face had turned soft and vulnerable like that of a puppy. She scrunched up the napkin in her lap and a tear rolled down her

112

cheek. She dabbed at it. I felt like a Presbyterian minister at the Pope's funeral. So I tucked into my food and looked across at the empty chair.

"He was really quite special," said Sonia, after some time.

I looked over at her. She was looking down the length of the table at the far empty chair across from her.

"I've heard that," I said, trying to offer some comfort.

She turned and looked at me and smiled the fragile smile of babies and old people.

"I don't know if I'm mourning the loss of a son or a lover."

She looked away quickly then, and picked up her fork and had more duck.

"Perhaps it is both," I offered.

She nodded at her plate, and chewed her food. I was cutting big chunks off my filet mignon. I'd soon have it tamed.

"I imagine the main reason you invited me here tonight is to discuss this case. It is why you've hired me," I said.

Sonia looked at me and nodded.

"It's more important to me now that you find whoever did this and bring them to justice."

"That's what you've hired me for."

"There'll be a large bonus in it for you," she said.

"That's not necessary," I replied, eating the last bit of my filet mignon.

"I just want to be sure you're motivated."

"I'm always motivated," I said. "If you spoke to Frank, not Moody, but Burton, then you know I've never lost a case."

"He said that, yes."

"But what that means," I said, taking a break from my food and putting my cutlery down and looking at Sonia intently, "is that I ask questions that people don't like to answer, and I don't make friends. And that might include you."

Sonia held my gaze for a while and then nodded curtly.

"Very well, you can ask me any questions you'd like. Though I trust that your discretion is as discreet as I've been told."

"It is," I said. "Unless I find out you killed him. In that case I'll go to the cops with whatever you've told me. If you had nothing to do with it, then I'll go to my grave with what you tell me."

Sonia liked that. She smiled and nodded.

"I'm sure you've heard no end to the rumors about Paul and I."

"I've heard some things. What I'd like is the truth from the horse's mouth."

"Paul and I did have a relationship if that's what you're wondering."

"It's more than that," I said. "It appears that you've used your quite considerable influence to mold the Philharmonic in your own image, if I can put it that way. And that's upset a lot of people."

Sonia looked at her plate and ate some more food. I did the same. I was working on the bacon now. Mighty fine tasting bacon too.

"Perhaps I did overreach," she said.

"I'd like to start at the beginning. When did you and Paul first meet?"

"I met Paul at a Juilliard recital when he was in his third year. I've been a benefactor of both Juilliard and the Philharmonic for as long as I can remember. Forty years perhaps. It was something Philip and I got into not very long after we were married. I've continued with it since Philip died. I like feeling that I can contribute to the development of music and it gets me out and about."

I nodded and finished putting the last bit of bacon in my mouth. I topped up Sonia's wine and did the same for myself. I didn't think I needed to loosen her tongue with Bacchus' grapes, but it wouldn't hurt.

"Paul was always so very charming. You might find this odd, but there was a chemistry between us from the beginning. Though it was a few years before we got intimate. It was his twenty-fifth birthday if I remember correctly. I had hosted a party for him here and he stayed overnight after the last guests had left."

"That was after he had been given a first violin position?" I asked.

"Yes, Paul was given a first violin position after a year, I think, that he was with the orchestra. That would have been two years before."

"Some I've spoken to believe that Paul, if I can put it crudely, slept his way to the concertmaster position."

Sonia looked at me and smiled somewhat embarrassedly.

"I suppose that wouldn't be wholly inaccurate. Though I made sure he got the first violin position before we became intimate. But regardless, Paul made me feel young. He was attentive and kind and flattering. He had such charm. Even if we had never been intimate, the way he made me feel I would have made his dreams come true. So I'd say no, it wasn't just about the sex. There was so much more to Paul."

"You paint a very different picture of the man I have in mind."

"What have you been told?" Sonia asked.

"I've come to see him as a petulant and spoiled child in many ways."

Sonia smiled off at the far end of the table.

"I suppose that wouldn't be terribly inaccurate either. He was spoiled and he was petulant, but all great artists are. But with me, up until recently, he was very different. Though I had seen those sides of him."

"If I can be honest with you, Sonia. I'm seeing a portrait drawn before me of a man who was a borderline sociopath, a user and a narcissist."

Sonia looked at me and smiled again.

"I sometimes wondered about that," she said, "especially recently. But even if it's true, I would do it all again. Perhaps you can't understand. The good times were so good that they more than made up for the bad. And I loved him. If I'm to be honest with you, Anthony, I loved him. Almost as much as I loved my dear Philip."

Sonia's eyes misted up again. She took her napkin and dabbed at them. I placed my hand on her forearm.

"Love ain't easy," I said, knowing all about that.

She looked over and nodded. I took my hand away.

"You said things seemed to have changed between the two of you recently. Can you tell me about that?"

"He became less attentive. He became less interested in me. I think he was becoming put off by my age if I'm to be honest. It started shortly after I helped him get the concertmaster position. It wasn't obvious, but all our intimacy stopped and he seemed to have very little time for me. And when we were together, he was short with me, distant and constantly distracted."

"So this has been going for three years then?"

Sonia nodded and pinched her lips together.

"You could have still had him removed from that orchestra if you wanted."

"Yes, I suppose so, Anthony, but it's not that easy. He hadn't been cruel or mean, though I'd heard rumors that he was saying nasty things about me behind my back. In any event, love can still survive as a fire in one heart, it doesn't need both flames to be burning."

I knew all about that too.

"And I still loved him. We've been together almost as long as I was with my late husband."

"I understand that. And yet you must have known that Paul had a roving eye. You paid off one woman who he got pregnant, and that's probably just the tip of the iceberg."

"You are thorough," she said, "you've already done your homework."

"That's what you're paying me for."

"You're right. I regret that. I still feel bad for what I put that poor woman through. She was very upset."

"How much did it cost you to keep her quiet?"

"I paid her half a million dollars," said Sonia, "and I got her the best doctors to take care of her pregnancy."

"You mean for the abortion?"

Sonia shot a sharp look at me.

"Yes, if you must say it like that."

It wasn't my place to question a woman's reproductive rights. But what I didn't like was blackmailing someone into a position they might not have taken otherwise. Sonia sensed my dissatisfaction with what she'd done.

"I regret that, Anthony. I really do. That was some years ago when I was still quite smitten with Paul. That veneer has since tarnished, but I did what I did. If it makes you feel any better, I still keep in touch with Stephanie and make sure that she's taken care of. She's married now and has two small children, a boy and a girl."

"So everything's great then," I said sarcastically.

Sonia didn't take the bait. Just as well, I would've felt differently about her if she had.

"I'd like to see her. Do you have an address and telephone number for me?" I asked.

"I'll get it for you before you leave."

Alfred came back in and took our plates away. We'd finished. The bottle of wine was finished and my glass was almost empty. Sonia was taking her time about it. Alfred came back in with our last course which was consisted of dulce de leche, candied almonds all atop of a milk gelato. I finished the last of my wine and took a sip to water to cleanse my palate.

"Surely you don't eat like this every night?" I asked.

Sonia looked over at me and smiled.

"Good heavens no," she said. "Only when I have guests."

"I wouldn't know how you kept yourself so trim otherwise."

"Decadence is to be shared, Anthony, simplicity can be enjoyed alone."

I took a mouthful of dessert. It was like eating soft, cold, wet pillows of heaven. Just as sweet but perhaps more decadent.

"What is your next step?" asked Sonia.

"I'll know that once we've finished discussing all that you know."

Sonia looked over at me and nodded. Then she took a taste of her dessert.

"You knew about Stephanie. Tell me what you knew about Lauren and Rosanna."

"I know they're both married and that Paul was behaving badly with them."

"What do you mean by that?"

"Well, as you said before, he had a roving eye. I always knew it, but for the first ten or more years while we were intimate he either wasn't seeing anyone else behind my back or he was doing it very carefully behind my back that I didn't know about it."

"Which would you put money on?" I asked.

Sonia looked across the table but where her mind was, was very far away.

"I'd rather not speculate," she said.

In other words she was worried that he had been banging other woman all this time. A leopard doesn't easily change its spots. But I wasn't here to pop her balloon. The woman had seen enough pain and perhaps embarrassment. She also hadn't done much wrong other than behave badly. But certainly no worse than others, and in many ways better. Paul, on the other hand, had met his match so it seemed.

"And lately, with these women?" I asked.

Sonia looked over at me and then back at her bowl of ice cream. She took another taste.

"He was sleeping with them if that's what you mean. I told him it wasn't a good idea, but he was long past listening to me by then. I suppose now, looking back, that we'd coddled him for too long. He just thought he could get away with anything really."

"But it would appear that he hasn't."

Sonia nodded.

"I suppose not. If he'd only listened to me. I knew he was courting danger I just wish he hadn't found it."

"How was his relationship with these other women? Can you speak to that?"

"Not very well," she said. "That was a part of his life that he kept from me for good reason. Though I confronted him with it when he got his black eye, from Rosanna's husband I think it was."

"And what did he say?"

"Well, he denied it of course. At first. But I told him I knew about it. He eventually confessed but told me he was having a hard time ending it. He said they just wouldn't take no for an answer."

"Both of them?"

Sonia nodded.

"That's what it sounded like. He didn't go into much detail with me about it, but he did swear that it was over, that he was going to start over."

"Did you believe him?"

Sonia looked at me steadily.

"I wanted to. I really did, but I think there's a part of me that didn't believe him."

"Because at this stage you'd already given him the gypsy's warning," I said.

"Yes, about a month ago, Frank and I had a meeting with Paul about his performance in the orchestra."

"So it wasn't specifically about his relationships with these other women?"

"Not particularly. It was more to do with his lack of respect for the other musicians. Missing practices and not performing to the highest standings for someone in his position."

"Maybe he wasn't up to the task? I've heard that other musicians seemed as capable."

"You're referring to Patrick. That's who Doug would have had in the first violin section rather than Paul. He likely would have made him concertmaster in time too."

"You don't think Patrick's as good?"

"I do, Patrick was just more difficult to get along with. At least he was with me, but that could have had something to do with the relationship between Paul and I."

"Might have had everything to do with it."

Sonia sighed.

"It's all moot now," she said. "Everybody wins now that Paul's dead. Everyone except for me."

"You mean Patrick, because he'll get a first violin position?"

"Yes, and Milo, he'll likely be up for concertmaster. And the two women. In a roundabout way I suppose, their marital lives can perhaps go back to normal."

"So you're suggesting that any one of them could have killed him."

Sonia looked at me and she furrowed her brow.

"No, good heavens no. That's not what I'm suggesting at all. I don't think any of them would have done it. Perhaps one of the disgruntled husbands but surely not Rosanna, Lauren, Milo or even Patrick. I just can't see it."

"What about Doug then, or John?" I asked.

Sonia shook her head and put more ice cream in her mouth. I did the same. I was quickly nearing the end of it.

"No, not Doug. If anything, he was most upset with me. Had quite a few strong words with me when he was let go, and Frank too."

"What happened to Doug?"

"Last I heard, and this was many years ago, he was teaching high school music."

"What about John?"

I scraped the bottom of my bowl, and managed to come up with almost a spoonful's worth of ice cream. Sonia still had a few bites left. She studied her spoon in the bowl for a moment before she spoke.

"Maybe," she said, "but that's an awfully long time to keep a grudge. Why wait so long?"

"I have my theories."

"Perhaps you're right. I didn't know him very well, but I do remember Frank telling me how absolutely blindly mad he became when he was let go upon hearing that Paul was taking a first violin position."

"Had Paul mentioned anything about being followed lately?"

"He had, he seemed quite upset about it. I even offered to hire a bodyguard for him. He was that upset, though I don't know of its veracity. You see, Paul could be quite paranoid. I think it was the drugs he was on."

"Is that why you had the talk with him? You and Frank?"

"Yes, Paul was getting quite out of control."

"Do you know what drugs he was on?"

"I heard he was on cocaine, but I never saw him take any, obviously, I wouldn't allow that here."

I nodded and pushed my bowl out in front of me. I took a sip of water to clean my palate. Then I grabbed my tumbler and had a drink of Scotch.

"Let's retire back to the living room," said Sonia.

She took a last spoonful of her dessert and got up. I stood up with her and followed her into the living room where we had sat when I first arrived. There were windows just off to my left that I could see out of all across Central Park. It was a view worth a few bucks.

"So you didn't believe him about being followed?" I asked, taking a sip of Scotch.

Sonia was holding her wine glass which still seemed half empty. Perhaps much like her life had now become.

"I wanted to believe him. And a small part of me did believe him, but I never saw any evidence of anyone following him."

"Yet you still offered to hire a bodyguard."

"I did. He seemed very agitated about it."

"What happened about that then?"

"He said it wasn't necessary. I pushed a couple of times but he didn't take me up on the offer."

"Perhaps he didn't want to be followed."

"I don't know what you mean," said Sonia.

"Well, from what I've heard he wasn't on the up and up even as recently as a few week ago."

"So he hadn't ended his relationships with those other women?"

"Doesn't sound like it, but that's not my biggest concern."

I looked out across the park. I wondered how many little ant people were crawling across its belly right now, eye deep in their own excrement.

"What is your biggest concern?"

"I have a few. Though one that comes to mind right now is his drug use."

Sonia shook her head and sipped some wine.

"I had offered to pay for the best rehabilitation clinic for him. He said he'd go, he just needed to tie up a few loose ends."

"I heard he recently bought a kilo of coke from a dealer here in town."

Sonia frowned.

"That's worth around fifty grand."

"Good heavens," said Sonia.

"That's not the worst of it. He only put a down payment on it."

"How much?"

"Twenty percent. Though I'm wondering why he didn't just pay for the whole thing with cash."

I looked at Sonia like she had the answer to my question.

"Weren't you paying him a substantial income as enticement to be with the orchestra?"

Sonia looked at me.

"I suppose that's what everyone thinks. I imagine Paul would let them believe it. He always liked to exaggerate how well he was doing. But to answer your question, Anthony, no, I didn't pay Paul a substantial income. The enticement was an apartment in lower Manhattan and income as needed to cover incidental expenses. I've never given him more than fifty thousand dollars in a year. The rent on the apartment, however, is worth one hundred and eight thousand dollars a year."

"Must be a nice apartment," I said.

"Paul liked it."

"Where is it? I'll need to take a look at the crime scene later."

Sonia gave me the address. It wasn't far from where I was staying at the Ritz. It looked across the park. Sonia said Paul insisted on that, and he wanted to be close to work.

"How much did he earn as the concertmaster?" I asked.

"I think he was getting one hundred and twenty thousand per year, with a share of proceeds, though the last couple of years that wasn't much."

"What do you mean a share of proceeds?"

"It means that if the audience numbers and revenues met a certain threshold then Paul would get a share of any revenue above that threshold. But with the economy not doing very well, I don't think he received much of that for the last few years."

I took a sip of Scotch, thinking about how I was in the wrong line of work. Nevertheless, I didn't know how to play the triangle let alone the violin.

"He had a very expensive violin, I heard."

"Yes, he did. It was an original Stradivarius. I made sure he insured it for ten million. I paid for that."

Sonia looked at me for a while. Looking for something.

"Do you know where the violin is?"

I shook my head.

"Not at the moment, but the police are still doing inventory of what they found at the scene. There were a few violins."

"Should be five violins," said Sonia, "including the Stradivarius."

"I heard he had been keeping the Strad on him for the last little while."

Sonia nodded.

"I told him I thought it was a very bad idea. I said it would be safer in the safe at Avery Fisher Hall. But he was paranoid that it would get stolen. He seemed especially wary of the new caretaker, but we run background checks on everyone we hire. He told me that if they wanted to get the violin, they'd have to pry it out of his cold, dead hands."

"Yes, I heard that too," I said. "And yet I'm puzzled. He was so adamant about protecting the violin with his life that he carried it around everywhere. But then he uses it as collateral for coke buy."

Sonia brought her hand up to her mouth, and frowned again. She'd been doing a lot of frowning during my conversation with her.

"I can't believe it," she said. "Why on earth would he do something like that?"

"Drug addicts are unreliable," I said, "even when they're not high. But I'm planning on visiting this dealer and having a talk with him to figure it out."

"God, you don't think some criminal has a violin like that?"

"Hard to say, though I'm thinking if they have the violin then why kill him. But you never know in these situations. That part of society has different and sometimes changing codes."

"God, I hope not. I'd hate to think that Paul was killed by a drug dealer over a violin."

"Would it better if he was killed by a disgruntled husband over infidelity?"

I looked at her steadily over the rim of my Scotch glass as I put it to my lips. That was the end of the warm liquor. Alfred came up dutifully and offered me a refill. I took him up on the offer.

"I suppose when you put it that way it doesn't really matter, does it?"

"Not in my experience," I said. "Murder is foul however it's delivered. Now accidental death, that's a tragedy."

"Tell me about how Paul obtained such a valuable violin."

"He got it from his grandfather. It was originally brought by Alexander Pope for his lover Martha Blount. Hence it's become known as the Blount Stradivarius."

I nodded and sipped on fresh, expensive Scotch. It tasted as good as the twenty dollar bottle in my apartment.

"I heard all of that," I said. "How did his grandfather obtain such a valuable violin?"

"Paul told me that his grandfather helped Jews escape through Poland and into Russia during the war. He was given the violin as a gift of thanks from one of these families."

I smiled at Sonia. A big, wide, knowing smile that felt happy with itself.

"You don't believe me?" she asked.

"I believe that you believe the story, and it could be true. I've just heard a different story."

"What story's that?"

"I heard that Paul's dear old granpappy was a guard at Mittelsteine, a concentration camp for women. He stole the violin from a woman there. A woman whose name was," I fished out my notebook and leafed through a few pages, "Anke Mueller."

Sonia frowned at me some more. She'd be spending a lot of money on Botox at this rate. Though to be fair, it didn't look like she did much self-mutilation like that.

"You can't be serious," she said. "That sounds totally outrageous."

"Paul's grandfather's real name was Swen Boehm, which he changed to Ryszard Kucharski, or Richard when he came across the pond."

Sonia shook her head.

"I can't believe it," she said.

"Perhaps Paul didn't know about it either," I offered. "Fact of the matter is that this is what I've heard. John Stampley hired a private investigator to dig up some dirt on Paul and this is what he found out. I'm going to speak to John about it to find out what he did with this information. The idea was, he was going to confront Paul about it and get him to give up the first violin position or John was going to tell everyone about what he found out."

Sonia looked down at the coffee table between us and twirled her glass with the wine very nearly escaping. She shook her head slowly.

"I can't believe it. This sounds awful, and that was so long ago. Paul never said anything about it."

"It's shameful knowledge to have. And it also would have meant, if it was true, that he would have to return the violin to its rightful owners. The heirs of Anke Mueller. Do you think that was something he might have been willing to do?"

Sonia was mesmerized by her swirling wine. It seemed like some big black hole that was going to suck her into its enigmatic charm.

"I can't imagine him giving up that violin for any reason," she said. "He loved it more than he loved women."

She looked up and smiled at me sadly. Across the plain of a dawning realization that perhaps her life to this point had been a barren burnt field that the sun was just now burning the fog off.

"Perhaps there is something to it then," I offered.

I drank more Scotch and started to feel soft and warm all over, like someone had covered me with thick honey.

"Was Paul Jewish?" I asked.

Sonia shook her head sadly and slowly.

"No."

She paused for a long while. Looking out across the expanse of room she had in her large home. It was filled to the brim with expensive decorations and furnishings, yet she was as empty as a cracked egg.

"I don't know, Anthony. I don't know about much anymore it seems. He was so careful with that violin and yet he put it up as collateral for a drug deal. I can't understand why he'd do that. I mean, what was he going to do with all that cocaine anyway?"

"What most drug dealers do that with that amount of cocaine. Sell it," I said.

Sonia looked up and behind me. She was lost in thought, and she looked like an old woman full of regrets and loss.

"It seems that Paul wasn't everything I had thought he was," she said. "Perhaps my feelings for him blinded me to the obvious truths."

She paused and took a sip of wine and then looked at me with a sad smile that had earned its keep over the years.

"But he was such a talent. He really was. I wish you could have heard him play. When he was up there in the orchestra, it was as if he were an angel. He never looked so beautiful and fragile and pure."

Her gaze drifted down to her wine glass and she swirled it again.

"People remain to us how we choose to remember them," I said.

She nodded, looking down at her wine.

"That's kind of you to say. I should hope to remember him in the best light then."

We sat and I drank for a while. I watched the green of the park shimmer as the sun started to fall towards earth in the west. As it died a blood red each evening, so did the chapters of many lives. It was a morbid thought, but I was dealing with a morbid matter and it felt appropriate.

"You will solve this murder, won't you?" asked Sonia. "I'd really like to see justice served."

I looked at Sonia and smiled.

"I'll solve it, though justice doesn't always dine at the table of our desires."

Sonia looked at me and smiled.

"You're quite poetic for a private investigator," she said.

"Sometimes it's only poetry and philosophy that make sense of man's madness."

We sat in silence again. I didn't have much else to ask her. But her couch was comfortable and my Scotch not quite done, so I bided my time. I was going to have a heart to heart with Kieran tomorrow morning, see if he did it. After that, I'd let life jostle me towards other shores.

"I like to get in and see the crime scene," I said.

"You know where Paul lived, don't you?"

I nodded my head.

"I do, but the local constabulary is not being particularly helpful. I was told you're a close friend of the Commissioner."

Sonia nodded.

"I'll speak to him tonight. You'll have their full cooperation by tomorrow, I'm sure of it."

"That would be very helpful."

I took the last drink from my Scotch and sat the tumbler down. Alfred started towards me again. I figured it was best to stop while I was ahead. And it wasn't often I was ahead. So I waved him off. I stood up and put on my hat. Sonia stood up too.

"I'll call my driver," she said.

"That won't be necessary. I'd prefer to walk and let things settle in."

Sonia nodded.

"I'll walk you out then."

I followed her to the front door and then out the hall to the elevator. I pushed its white button which lit up a dull yellow. We stood and waited.

"You've been helpful, Sonia," I said. "I'll keep you up to date as I find out more."

Sonia nodded and thanked me.

"I appreciate you not being judgmental," she said.

She offered me her hand and I shook it tenderly. It still felt to me like a fragile bird or a kitten's paw. Perhaps I was reading too much into it, or perhaps life had recently whittled her away. Whatever it was, I was in a big city, a big apple, whose core seemed somewhat rotten though the skin shone brilliantly.

The elevator opened up and I stepped into its gaping maw. The last I saw of Sonia was her smiling face and her hands clasped in front of her in a gesture of hope. I rode the elevator down to the main floor with the numbing music of its namesake. I strode through the opulent foyer like a man walking on hot coals.

Jeremiah smiled warmly at me and wished me a good night. I wished for a good night too, but it wasn't always like that. I got out of The Royce and stepped onto the sidewalk of 5th Avenue. I lit up a cigarette and looked out over the park and into the dusky evening. Through the cacophony of sound, somewhere a baby was crying, and someplace else a man was dying.

# Eleven

From the Kings and Queens you head east into Nassau and Suffolk counties on Long Island. I understand they're most commonly just called Long Island and that was where I was headed. I was in a yellow cab and the meter was a blur of red numbers doing what looked to me like logarithmic math.

I started thinking that I should have taken Terry's taxi. Sonia had offered his services to me as needed. But I hadn't thought of that heading out this morning and I ducked into the nearest cab, now well aware of my mistake. Not that I cared particularly, my fee is five hundred plus expenses. A taxi fare was expenses.

I was heading out to see Kieran. I'd learnt yesterday that Kieran was working now. Just odds and ends, doing some woodworking for Perry. Funny how misery likes company. Perry had hired Kieran for a recent job. Maybe they'd been in on this murder together. Or maybe they were just two sad sacks trying to help each other out.

By the time we got to Brentwood which was a nice middle class suburb where there are not white fences but the lawns are green and the trees in bloom, the meter was over a hundred bucks. The cabbie pulled over by the side of a house that looked like it had been in a hurricane. It wasn't far from the golf course and there were two guys in overalls fixing the siding. I paid my fare and got out of the cab. I walked up the driveway towards the two men. One guy was much bigger than the other. He was muscled too. I could tell because he wasn't wearing a shirt under his overalls. When you're in a tight spot, it's always best to start with the big guy.

"Can I help you?" he said, trying to sound tough.

The smaller guy was thumping a hammer against his thigh and giving me the eyeball.

"I'm looking for Kieran Stewart. Is he here?"

"What's it to you?" he asked.

I looked at the big guy in front of me. He had a large Adam's apple that would cause a whole world of hurt if I hit it just right. The problem with big guys, and this guy was an easy six three, is that they're slow, and most times they're not used to getting assaulted.

"What does that even mean?" I asked him. "What's it to me. Jesus, none of your business."

I was getting a bit testy with him. I admit that. But it was just after nine a.m. and I was nursing a slight hangover.

"I'm afraid you've got the wrong place," he said.

He was a bad liar. I nodded at him and sidestepped him to head into the house. He moved to block me. His buddy came along too as if they were attached by an invisible string.

"I'm the termite inspector," I said, dead serious.

"Sure you are," said the big guy with a shit eater's grin on his face.

I jabbed him real hard into the larynx. His eyes went wide and he grabbed at his throat gasping for air. This was helpful to me. It meant his stomach was soft and exposed. So I hit him hard, right in the solar plexus. He buckled over and that let me rest his nose on my knee, hard. He fell to the ground then, blood streaming from his nose, gasping for air.

Buddy came at me with the hammer. He was an inch or two shorter than me which meant I had greater reach. Except for that damn hammer. He swung it wildly and I danced back and round for a while as I took off my windbreaker.

"Take it easy, son," I said to him, "you'll hurt yourself with that thing."

I wrapped my jacket around my arm for a little protection, and as he swung at me I hesitated for just a moment before rushing him on his down swing. The hammer was heavy and he wasn't fast enough to bring it up again. By the time he decided that's what he needed to do I was hugging. Because we were being so intimate I decided to give him a kiss too, a Glasgow kiss.

He staggered away from me, dropping the hammer. I jabbed at him, feeling the distance before knocking him on his ass with a right. He had a glass jaw.

I unraveled my windbreaker, put it back on and walked into the house like I was the owner. In the kitchen a guy about six feet had his back to me. He was in similar overalls with black, wavy hair and medium build. He wasn't fat, and he didn't hear me coming in. Maybe he was deaf.

"Kieran Stewart," I said, standing across the kitchen island from him.

His head cocked up and steadied for a moment before he turned around. He had a carpenter's pencil in one hand. A hand that was big and rough for his size.

"Who wants to know?" he asked, crossing his arms in front of me.

"Me."

"I'm not gonna play games. This is a private residence and you're not supposed to be here. So why don't you just fuck off before I call the police."

"I don't see a phone anywhere near you."

This took him off guard. His eyes moved looking around for a moment. He was thinking about what to do. I was hoping he'd take a go. He didn't. I guess he was smarter than I'd figured.

"Alright, what do you want?"

He kept leaning against the far counter with his arms crossed over his chest, the pencil still in his right hand. I took a look at his tool belt. There wasn't much there I needed to be worried about.

"I want to talk to you about Paul Klee."

"The violinist?"

"The very same."

"What about him."

"He's dead."

"You're not the cops."

He looked me up and down. I didn't look like a cop. Cops nowadays don't usually wear fedoras much.

"I didn't say I was."

"Then who are you?"

"A gumshoe."

I smiled at him and he frowned at me.

"What?"

"A private investigator."

He nodded like that didn't impress him.

"I don't know anything about that," he said.

"Probably because you aren't one."

He shook his head.

"I meant I don't know anything about Paul's death, smart ass."

I still smiled at him.

"Great, so I wasted an hour in a cab and a hundred bucks for nothing."

"Seems so."

"Alright, I guess I'll be on my way," I said.

I was still smiling at him but I didn't move.

"I'm waiting," he said.

"On second thought, let's talk about wife beating."

He didn't like that one much. He took a couple steps towards me. I moved around from the kitchen island so he could reach me easier. He thrust his chin out at me.

"That ain't none of your business."

"I'm making it my business."

I was still smiling like we were old chums sharing an inside joke. I was beginning to feel a lot better. The hangover was almost gone. I figured another round with this clown and I'd be right as rain. Kieran started jabbing at me with the pencil in his one hand.

"I reckon its time for you to leave, asshole. Before I put a world of hurt on you."

And with that last word he jabbed the pencil into my chest for emphasis. Not hard, it didn't break the skin, but it was his mistake. I grabbed his wrist with both my hands and swung around him like we were dancing. There was room enough in this kitchen that he followed my lead. And when I came to a stop he had dropped the pencil and his face came to a stop against some very fine cabinetry.

I let him go. He was dazed for a few moments and brought his hands up to his face. His nose wasn't broken, nor was it bleeding. But I bet it felt like a thousand bees had stung it. His eyes went crazy and he came at me with a big, wild swing that telegraphed all the way from LA. It was easy to miss and as it kept going it opened up the soft of his right side. I planted a hard upper left into his lower ribs and kidneys. As hard as I could. Probably harder than I needed. I figure I likely broke something. He dropped like a shit bag to his knees, gasping for breath.

He leaned back against the kitchen cabinets just below the sink, wheezing like an octogenarian on his second pack of cigarettes. I waited and gave him a moment to catch his breath.

"What the fuck do you want?"

He used foul language but there was no mustard in the tone. I looked down at him. I wasn't smiling any more.

"Don't feel so good on the receiving end, does it?"

He looked away from me.

"You touch your wife again and you and me are gonna keep having heart to hearts," I said.

He didn't look at me.

"You understand?"

I squatted down close to him so he could see my five o'clock shadow and smell my cheap cologne. He looked at me and nodded his quickly. He massaged his throat.

"Now tell me why you didn't kill Paul Klee."

I stood up again, my knees don't take kindly to squatting for any length of time. Kieran wheezed and coughed and tried to clear his throat.

"Because I didn't, that's why," he said.

"That doesn't tell me anything. Let me give you a hand. Your wife was banging him. You were upset about it, so you went and paid him a visit. Now he's ended up dead and you look good for it."

Kieran shook his head.

"No, I didn't kill him. Hell, I don't even know where he lives."

"Then tell me what happened."

Kieran nodded his head.

"Okay. I found out that asshole was banging my wife, so I went to speak to him about it. I was gonna tell him to back the fuck off. So I followed him through the park one night and I confronted him about it. He told me he was finished with that skanky whore anyway. And what's more, he said, shouldn't I be dealing with my wife and not him. After all, she's the one stepping out. So I lost it on him and smacked him around a bit. I told him to lay off."

"Or?"

Kieran looked up at me and then back down at the floor. His wrists were dangling limply off his knees.

"Okay, I threatened him. I told him he better lay off or I was gonna come back and do worse. But I didn't kill him."

Kieran looked up at when he said the last bit. He didn't strike me as a man who was capable of murder.

"Do you have any handguns?" I asked.

He shook his head.

"Did Paul say anything else before you clocked him?"

Kieran looked up at the ceiling for a moment.

"Actually he did. When I first caught up with him and tried to get him to stop so I could talk he told me he didn't have time, that he was being followed."

"And did you see anyone following him?"

"No, I was more interested in giving him a piece of my mind. But after we'd finished our chat, he took off like a rabbit. That's when I did notice a couple of men in gray suits follow after. They were walking hard in his direction but they weren't running."

"What did they look like?"

Kieran shook his head and hung it low for a while before looking back up at me.

"Man, I dunno. I was more concerned about delivering my message than anything else."

"Give me something to go on."

"They were well dressed. The suits fit them well. They were both tall, taller than me by a few inches or so. The one guy was thin, the other guy was thick."

"What about their hair color or styles?" I asked.

"The thick guy had a buzz cut. They both had dirty blonde hair. The taller one's hair was normal length. That's all I got."

"Do you think you could recognize them if you saw them again?"

"I don't think so. I mean I didn't get a good look at them. Maybe if they were dressed the same, they were big. But I couldn't ID them in a lineup."

I walked out to the end of the kitchen. It was an open floor plan. Where the kitchen stopped a creamy colored sea of carpet with frothy peaks spread out into the living room. At the end of the living room was a fireplace and on top of the mantel were photo frames with a photograph of what looked like a nice African American family. It was too far away to make it out very well. I turned around and looked back at Kieran.

"Did your wife tell you she and Paul were going to get married next summer?"

I smiled at him. I do that sometimes just for fun. He looked at me, searching for the sincerity of what I'd just said.

"I guess that's gonna be called off then," he said.

It was funny as hell, but I didn't get the impression he'd said it with that intention.

"I'll give you a tip for your pain and suffering. It's better to leave a cheating wife than stay and end up the chump."

He looked at me.

"We've been together since high school," he said.

"Seems to me then that it's time to graduate."

Kieran was heading down a one way street called misery. And if he kept going he'd end up a wreck at the T junction. He looked down and shook his head. Then he combed his hands through his hair.

"I've been down that road, friend. Better to let her have half now than take it all from you at the bitter end."

He looked up at me and nodded slowly.

"Yeah, I guess you're right."

I nodded at him and looked around the kitchen.

"You've done some good work here," I said, and I turned and walked out the house.

In the yard, the two yahoos were dabbing at their upper lips to try and clean themselves of the residual blood. The middle of their noses were thick and swollen. They looked at me with hard stares that had no stones behind it. I smiled at them and tipped my hat.

"Stay out of trouble, son," I said to them, and I walked on down the road.

I figured I'd make a stop at the golf course. A little hair of the dog might not be a bad idea. A golden, liquid brunch with a sandwich on the side might just do the trick. I fished out my phone and dialed a number.

"Terry," I said, when the voice on the other line answered, "would you mind picking me up at the Brentwood Country Club in about an hour?"

# Twelve

Terry picked me up. It was more comfortable and cheaper driving in the Maybach than it was in the yellow cab. I was grateful for that. We were on our way to the Bronx Zoo. I don't regularly go to zoos. They remind me of prisons, and I'd sooner not visit prisons either.

So your question might be, why am I heading to the zoo? And that's a good question. I was hoping to interview a monkey. I'd seen one earlier in the day out on Long Island, and I figured while I was dealing with one chump, might as well deal with others.

Perry Alcantara's construction firm had won the bid to renovate the Bronx Zoo's cafeteria. Not a huge job, but in this economy beggars couldn't be choosers.

Terry dropped me off at the parking lot just off Southern Boulevard. He was gonna wait for me, Sonia didn't need him and I didn't think I'd be longer than an hour. The admission price was over twenty bucks by the time the man had taken his share. Tax was the biggest legalized racket I'd ever encountered. At some places in LA I can get a steak dinner for the same amount. And it'd be more satisfying.

Didn't matter in the long run anyway. Like I've said before, these are expenses. Something Sonia or the Philharmonic were going to pick up. And I didn't think Sonia would be all that concerned about a Jackson for some monkeys.

I grabbed a map and found that the cafeteria wasn't far from the parking lot. I made my way there. Half of the cafe was closed for renos, that was the half I was looking for. I called over one of the laborers and asked him to fetch Perry for me. He did. He was just one of those guys who didn't ask too many questions. I liked that.

After a short while an average looking guy walked out from behind the construction sheets. The laborer pointed at me and this guy walked up to me and introduced himself. He was about my height, but about nine months pregnant. His stomach was hard and round though the rest of him didn't seem all that fat. His face was a bit puffy though and he shaved his head because the top of it was getting sparse. He was clean shaven and he had a pleasant demeanor. I didn't think I'd have to be strong arming Perry like I had with Kieran.

"Anthony Carrick," I said, after he'd introduced himself. "I'm looking into the Paul Klee situation."

Perry nodded and smiled at me. He pointed his hand out.

"Right, you're the private investigator that the orchestra hired."

I nodded.

"Do you mind if I take a few minutes of your time?"

"Not at all," he said, then he turned around and shouted. "Alvarez, you're in charge until I get back. I'm taking a break."

A guy kneeling down over some blueprints with short, black, curly hair and a heavy five o'clock shadow looked up and nodded at him.

"Have you taken a look around the zoo?" asked Perry. I shook my head. "It's quite something. How about a walk?"

A walk suited me just fine. The weather was warm and the vegetation was lush, and if this got Perry chatting then I was all for it. We exited the cafeteria and headed towards the Butterfly Garden. The zoo was busy. We walked slowly, casually, as if we were two old friends with nothing new to say to each other. So I decided to start.

"You've probably heard about Paul's death."

I looked over at Perry as he walked hands in pockets. He nodded but kept his gaze on the ground in front of him.

"Yes, I did. My wife told me. Quite unfortunate."

Quite unfortunate was one way of putting it if you didn't particularly care for the man. And I figured Perry didn't care for him. From what I'd heard, Paul probably wouldn't have buoyed my boat.

"You don't seem all that upset," I said.

Perry looked over at me.

"I'm not." Then he stopped for a moment and faced me. "Listen, you've spoken to my wife already, you know I was no fan. But just to get it out into the open, I didn't kill him."

"I've been hearing that a lot the past couple of days," I said as we started walking again.

"What? That I wasn't a fan or that I didn't kill him?"

"Both. Seems he wasn't likable if you had something he wanted. Though the ladies seemed to like him."

Perry didn't say anything to that. We walked on, passing a family with two kids. Both kids, a boy and a girl, engrossed in their ice cream cones.

"How well did you know him?" I asked.

"Not that well. I'd only met him a handful of times over the years. He seemed nice enough on the surface, though I got the sense he was a bit arrogant. Everyone was always fawning over him like he was the best violinist the world had ever seen."

I nodded as we walked on. We veered right before the Butterfly Garden, heading towards the Mouse House. It was peaceful to be in nature, as fake as it might be. The people were the problem. Too many of them.

"You had a heart to heart with him a while back."

Perry nodded.

"Yeah, I went to speak to him about screwing around with my wife. It got pretty ugly."

"What do you mean by that?"

"Well, I just wanted to tell him to stay clear. He thought it was funny. He made fun of what I looked like, saying it was no wonder that Lauren was stepping out on me, a fat blue collar worker. That got me going, so we got into a shoving match. The musical director stepped in before it got worse. I swear to God I wanted to smack that grin off his face."

We passed on by the Mouse House on the right side. I got to thinking about that. Mouses in houses, if you'll indulge me, didn't seem to be an attraction. Most folks I know are trying to get rid of the mouses in their houses. On a side note, doesn't that sound better anyway, rhyming it like that?

"I heard something similar from Kieran," I said.

Perry nodded.

"Yeah, I think Kieran came by to talk with Paul a couple of days after I did. From what he tells me though, he let his fists do most of the talking."

"And that's how you and Kieran got to know one another?"

Perry shook his head. We stopped to look at the giraffes and ostriches. They generally ignored us.

"I knew Kieran from some time before. Occasionally, the Philharmonic had family days where the families of the musicians got together for BBQs and picnics and things like that. It's happened here at the zoo more than once. Anyway, I knew Kieran that way. But after I heard what he'd done to Paul I had

144

renewed respect for the man. So I reached out and contacted him."

"So it didn't bother you that he was beating his wife."

Perry leaned on the railing and looked over at me.

"I don't think you're getting the full picture of the man. He lost a really good Wall Street job a couple of years back. That was around the time that we both started finding out that our wives were sleeping with dick face. I'm not condoning what he's done, but Rosanna and him had a good marriage before that. I think the stress just got to him."

I nodded and took off my hat. It was making my head hot. I looked out across the African plains, that didn't look like any African plains I'd ever seen.

"And you gave him a job?"

"I offered to give him a few gigs if he wanted. I'd learned that he had always enjoyed woodworking. And he does good work."

I nodded.

"He does indeed."

"You've been to see him then?" asked Perry.

"Yeah, had a heart to heart with him out in Long Island this morning."

"And the work's good right?"

"Yes, it is."

Perry looked out at the giraffes, and then straightened up and we started off walking again around the Zoo Loop.

"So you two became friends?" I asked.

"Yes, in a way. I really like him. Perhaps it's a shared pain. Whatever, he's a good guy really. I'm happy to have him work with me until he can find something he likes better. Though he might stick around for a bit. I think he likes the work."

"Your business wasn't hurt during the recession?"

Perry turned to look at me and smiled.

"No, I was hit just as bad as everyone. I don't have a big business, and maybe that was a bit of a lucky break. I don't do big projects, but building houses almost came to a standstill and renos dropped by more than half. It's just been in the last couple of years that I've been able to get back to where I was before and rehire all the guys I had to let go. I didn't hire Kieran for charity, I needed the help. It's been mutually beneficial."

"You know what a cynic might suggest listening to this?"

"No I don't," said Perry.

"He might think it's strange that the two of you get to working together just weeks before Paul ends up dead. I can't think of any two men who had as much of a vested interest in Paul's death than you and Kieran."

We were heading towards Somba Village. Perry stopped again for a moment and looked at me.

"Listen," he said. "Like I said before. I didn't like Paul. He was fucking my wife. I get that, but that's no reason to kill a man. If anything, I was going to leave Lauren, but to suggest that because I help a man get back onto his feet means that I killed Paul is a reach. I'm only talking to you out of courtesy. It'd be much easier for me to wait for the police when they finally get around to interviewing me."

I smiled at him. He was an agreeable sort, but I got the feeling that I was starting to needle him a bit too much.

"I'm not thinking that you helping Kieran is why you killed Paul. I'm just saying, that the two of you have a shared anger and that anger was towards Paul. I'm not saying it was unjustified, I'm just saying it gives you motive."

Perry started walking again and I kept to his side. Our steps were in unison as they often are when walking with someone of similar stature.

"I can see how it gives us motive. I'm just saying I didn't do it, and I don't see Kieran doing something like that either. What it really is, is coincidence. Nothing more. I mean, we had a shared anger towards our wives too. And they're not dead."

He had a point. I'd become more pissed off at Racquel when she stepped out than the douche bag she's since married.

"Still," I said. "The cops are gonna ask for your whereabouts on Friday."

"What time are we talking about?" he asked me.

"Dunno yet, they haven't determined TOD."

"TOD?"

"Time of death."

Perry nodded as we strode past Somba village through the thick forests, keeping to the nicely paved pathway, weaving between thick clots of families and toppling old ladies.

"Well," continued Perry, "I was working here most of the day. I got in at eight in the morning and I didn't leave until eight p.m."

"What did you after eight?"

"I went down to this Italian restaurant close to where we live and ate some pasta. I probably got home by ten when I went to bed."

"And Lauren wasn't there?"

Perry shook his head.

"She had a concert in the evening. I don't think that was supposed to finish until ten thirty. I can't say what time she got home as I was asleep. I woke up next to her though."

We walked on for a while longer. Talking with Perry he seemed to be a straight shooter. I didn't fancy him as a murderer. Though I'd been fooled before.

"Do you own a gun?" I asked.

Perry looked over at me as we walked on.

"Is that how he was killed?"

I nodded.

"Yes, I have a gun."

"What kind?"

"A Smith & Wesson 4006."

"That's a .40 caliber right?"

Perry looked at me and didn't say anything as a young couple wearing University of New York hoodies walked by.

"Yes," he said. "Is that what caliber was used to shoot him?"

"Don't know yet," I said. "Where is your gun?"

"At home in my safe."

"You sure about that?"

Perry looked at me as we walked on.

"Pretty sure, is there something you want to tell me?"

"You just need to be pretty sure, that's all. When was the last time you took it out?"

"A week ago."

"So you don't know that it's still in your gun safe then?"

Perry sighed.

"I suppose not. But we haven't had any break-ins so I'm assuming that it hasn't gotten lost or grown legs."

"Just be sure when you get home tonight," I said. "If your gun has gone missing and it's the same kind and caliber used to kill Paul, well, you get my meaning."

Perry nodded.

"Doesn't matter if it is my gun anyway, like I've told you a couple of times now, I didn't kill anybody."

"That's good," I said. "Because God knows that innocent men never get sent to jail."

I grinned at him as we walked on. He looked at me and then turned away. We carried on until Perry stood off towards one side of the path, looking into the trees. He pointed at something. I saw what they called a red panda. It looked to me like a furrier ginger cousin of the raccoon. He, could have been a she, was lying in the trees sleeping.

"Funny that animals don't need police and jails to keep themselves in check," said Perry, smiling up at the red panda.

"Maybe that's because there are way less of them than there are of us."

I watched the sleeping red panda, and in the warm vestiges of summer sun I wanted to curl up next to him and take a nap. But that was probably the beer from lunch speaking.

"What else can you tell me about Paul that I might not know about?" I asked.

Perry turned to look at me.

"Not sure there's anything really that I can tell you. He's a self involved philanderer. Though you probably figured that out by now. He had a valuable violin, at least that's what I heard. And he got one of the women pregnant a few years ago. Other than that, I try not to keep abreast of the orchestral gossip."

I nodded at him. It wasn't helpful but I wasn't expecting him to have any news being removed as he was from him.

"What about Kieran? Did he ever share any information with you about Paul?"

"Well, he told me how he'd given Paul a bit of what for, said it made him feel better. But he said Paul hurried off saying he was being followed, and he seemed quite upset about it."

Perry paused for a moment and looked around.

"What is it?" I asked.

"Well, Kieran said, and this was totally in a non-serious manner, that he thought maybe our luck would change and the two guys who were following Paul would solve our problem."

I nodded.

"I heard about them. You don't know anything about that though, do you?"

Perry shook his head and looked down at his watch.

"Listen, I should really get back to my guys if there's nothing else I can do for you."

I shook my head. I was hoping for an easy close. The number of perps who've ended up being jealous husbands and boyfriends stacked the deck this way for me. But on this occasion I was coming up empty. Seemed like maybe Kieran and Perry weren't my Huckleberrys. That meant it could be only one of three things. One of the disgruntled women killed him, these shadowy tails killed him which meant they're real or lastly, it was JJ and his crew, looking to cash in on the value of the violin.

"If you think of anything else," I said, "please let me know. You can reach me through the musical director, Frank."

Perry shook my hand. He had a good, firm honest man's handshake.

"Will do," he said. "And I hope you catch the guy who did it. Not that he meant much to me. I still think he's an ass but that doesn't mean he deserved to die for it."

Perry smiled at me and looked me in the eyes for a moment. He was sincere, and I admired his magnanimity. With more men like that, there'd be less work for the likes of me. I liked the idea of that.

I watched Perry turn back the way we'd come. When he was gone from sight, I looked back up the panda. He was yawning. It was coming on two. He was as cute as a baby but furrier, and I wondered if he'd made his mama proud. I wondered if Paul had too.

## Thirteen

Flushing Meadows holds the U.S. Open tennis tournament every year. I was just vaguely familiar with it. I'm not one of those chumps that thinks a man hitting a ball a few times a year is worth millions. But many do, and that's why they get paid so much for hitting all sorts of balls. White ones, yellow ones, hard ones, soft ones, big ones and small ones. And we watch millionaires do this ad nauseum. There's gotta be some sociologist who's studied this weird behavior.

Anyway, what am I trying to say? Not much worth listening to. Only that I'd sooner do the hitting of the balls than the watching. I'm only telling you about Flushing Meadows because that's where I was heading. Not to play tennis. Not really to Flushing Meadows, but to a coffee shop in Queens called Frangelico's that's in Flushing. Not far from the botanical gardens. The U.S. Open was over. The traffic was light and Terry was driving me the scenic route.

I was heading out to see Stephanie Yerkes née Perkins. She's the one that Paul got pregnant. She lives in Queens and was quite happy to have me come around for coffee. At the local coffee shop that is. Not her home.

Terry dropped me off and said he'd wait. I wasn't going to bitch about it. I was getting used to driving around in the Maybach. Maybe I was getting soft, maybe I was getting sentimental or maybe I was just trying to save Sonia some money. That's how I am... sometimes.

Queens, like much of the island, is full of hardworking middle class folks. You might find some doctors and lawyers out here, but mostly you'll find the trades, office ants and lower management. As such, Frangelico's represented the community quite well. It wasn't fancy. The couple of comfortable chairs might have come out from the owner's basement when he set up his business. The floor was fake tile and patterned so you couldn't tell if it was dirty or not.

The lights were dim but the atmosphere wasn't cozy. It was just around four in the afternoon. The place was mostly empty and the woman I was going to meet was in one of the comfy chairs. I knew that because when I'd called her up she said she'd be wearing a New York Yankees ball cap and she was the only one in here wearing a ball cap. I took off my fedora and tossed it on the empty chair. Stephanie stood up and smiled awkwardly. She was shy or coy. I couldn't tell which.

"Stephanie Yerkes?" I asked, offering her my hand. She took and we shook. She nodded and looked down. I noticed she had a cup of tea on the table by the wall that was between the two chairs.

"Can I get you anything else?" I asked.

She shook her head.

"No, thank you."

I nodded and went to the front counter. An Italian looking fellow asked me what I wanted. He was slim and young. Maybe in his early twenties with brown eyes and wavy Italian black hair that makes men envious and women weak at the knees. I ordered a coffee. He asked me what kind. I said the kind made from coffee beans. He laughed. He thought I was a kidder. He said they had a dark roast or a light roast. I said the darker the better.

He brought me a paper cup. I said I was having it to stay. He poured it into a yellow mug that had a blue smiley face on it. I took it from the counter where it had stained the surface after he'd spilled some from decanting it. I put down two bills. He said it was two fifty seven. I put down another bill and walked away.

This coffee had better taste like gold. I went over to the dumb waiter and put in sugar and cream. Then I walked over and took a seat by Stephanie. She'd been watching me this whole time. I smiled at her as I sat down. I took a sip of coffee. It was good, but not three bucks good.

"Some places I know, you can get a glass of Scotch for the price of this coffee."

"Not here," she said.

"I can see that."

She picked up her mug of tea and took a sip. Stephanie was a plump woman of average height. From what I could tell she had short black hair under the ball cap. She wore a purple windbreaker over a yoga top that was zippered up just above her chest. She wore black spandex pants that weren't becoming. There ought to be rules about who can wear black spandex yoga pants. Not men, and only fit women between about twenty and forty'ish. There's nothing more of an eyesore than two fat black sausages dangling from saggy blimps all encased in black.

Her face was cute though and she didn't wear much makeup. On a plate next to her was some sort of square that she had managed to eat half of. I was thinking of advising her to leave the rest. God knew she didn't need it. But I've learned that my mouth sometimes gets me in trouble.

Looking at her I was trying to figure out how she got Paul's interest. I didn't see how she would have been attractive to him. But maybe she was in better shape before the kids.

"Thanks for taking the time to meet me," I said.

"Not at all. I want to help if I can. When I heard on the news last night about Paul, well, I was quite upset by it."

"Not many people were," I said, grinning.

Stephanie looked down and fiddled with her fingers. She was very self conscious. She took her fork and put another piece of square into her mouth.

"I understand that you and Paul had a relationship for a time," I said, trying to be delicate.

I drank more creamy coffee. A guy carrying a bale of a stomach held up by overalls that were dusty walked in and up to the counter. He had gray stubble that matched the thin curls on his head. Stephanie looked over at me.

"I don't think it was much of a relationship. Or if it was, it was more one sided."

"On your side," I said.

Stephanie nodded.

"I've heard things have worked out for you since then," I said.

"What do you mean?"

"You have a couple of kids and a family. I'm assuming things are well."

Stephanie nodded and reached for her tea. She took a sip and kept the mug in her hands, cradling it. It was a bumpy mug, the color of a blue sky in anger. It was one of those self made clay models. The kind that might have been a first attempt.

"I'm just gonna come out and ask, Stephanie, because I'm sometimes insensitive and mostly because I just hate beating around the bush. Did you kill Paul?"

She looked up at me and frowned.

"God no!" she said.

She said it with some force and I believed her. She seemed genuinely surprised that I'd be so bold as to ask such a question so early in our chat.

"Why would I be here talking to you if I had?" she said. "I just don't think that makes any sense."

"It doesn't," I agreed, "but sometimes murderers, thieves and the like think they can get away with it."

"Maybe I'll ask a more sensitive question then. Have you seen Paul recently?"

"No."

"When was the last time you saw him?"

I took a sip out of my bright yellow mug. The blue smiley face was smiling at Stephanie. She looked off for a moment before replying.

"Quite a long time ago. Probably just before they kicked me out of Lincoln Center."

I nodded.

"Look, I'll admit that Paul broke my heart. He did. But that's been about three or so years now. I've moved on. I have a husband who treats me much better than Paul ever did. I have a good life now. I'm happy, and I'm glad that Paul never kept in touch."

"So he didn't wish you a bon voyage?"

"No, after he heard that I'd gotten pregnant he wouldn't take my calls. He would barely acknowledge me if we passed and then a few months later I was fired."

"With a good severance package, right?"

"You probably already know this, yes, they, or I should say Sonia paid me off with half a million dollars."

I was never good at math. If I was, I wouldn't have become a gumshoe. But this math right here, I think I could figure it out. Stephanie was fired around three years ago and her son is about three. Seems to me she kept the child.

"How old is your son?" I asked.

She looked at me with a frown again. If she kept that up she'd be needing Botox. Though she didn't strike me as the kind that did that to herself.

"He'll be three in a month," she said. "Why do you ask?"

"I'm just doing some math in my head. I'm told that you were given some money for an abortion."

Stephanie nodded.

"But you didn't have it," I said.

She looked up at me and shook her head.

"I couldn't," she said, tearing up but holding it together. "They expected me to, but I didn't. No one knows except Donald, my husband."

"I see," I said.

She darted a hot look at me, that missed. I wasn't injured.

"Look, you don't know what it's like. I couldn't kill my baby. I just couldn't do it."

"I'm not judging," I said. "But how did you keep it from them?"

"Well, I don't really see any of them. Sometimes Sonia and I visit. Probably no more than once or twice a year. During those first six or seven months I pretended that I was depressed and didn't want anything to do with any of them. It wasn't far from the truth. Now, I've told them that Jayden is Donald's son from before."

"Sonia still sends you money I understand?"

"She does. I think she feels guilty about forcing me into the situation she did. I think in her mind it's blood money. Anyway, it's not much but with Donald's salary it helps us from getting into debt."

"And the half mil?"

"We used most of that to buy our house and fund the kids' college education. We also put a little away for our retirement."

I sipped my coffee and Stephanie took another bite of her square. From her lips to her hips. But I kept my mouth shut. She had another bite left.

"Where are your kids now?"

"They're with the neighbor. She babysits once in a while. You know, for a PI, you really ask all sorts of weird questions."

I grinned at her.

"Maybe I'm just not very good at this," I said.

She shook her head.

"No, I don't think so. I get the sense you're pretty good at this, but odd."

I raised my mug at her.

"I'll take that as a compliment then," I said.

Stephanie took a sip of her tea. A young man dressed in a suit came into the coffee shop and walked up to the counter to order something. It was the gray of a banker's suit and his hair was immaculately cropped. Though I wouldn't trust him with my spare change.

"I'm starting to think you had nothing to do with Paul's murder. But maybe you can help me figure out who might have."

"I'll try. But like I said, I haven't kept in touch with anyone there since I left."

"Except Sonia"

"Except Sonia," she repeated.

"Paul was known to have a roving eye," I said. "And from what I've heard, he wasn't very discreet about it."

Stephanie nodded and sipped her tea.

"You might have known about Lauren and Rosanna."

She nodded again.

"I found out towards the end of our… relationship, I guess. Though it just seems farcical to call it that now. But yes, I found out that he'd been sleeping with both Rosanna and Lauren."

"And they're both married."

"I guess Paul wasn't discreet," she said.

"That's what I'm hearing. How did those two get along with each other?"

"Not well once they found out about each other. They turned particularly bitchy. At least that's what I heard. You have to remember that I wasn't in the orchestra, I was part of administration, so I wasn't around them all the time."

"Did you hear about the altercation recently with Paul?" Stephanie shook her head.

"No, I really haven't kept in touch with anyone."

"In the past few months Paul was confronted by both husbands within the same week. Rosanna's husband slapped him around a little bit."

Stephanie put the last piece of square in her mouth. It was a big piece. I might have made it a two bite piece, but I wasn't eating. She chewed it for a while, maybe trying to digest the information I'd just shared. Perhaps that was a big morsel too.

"I'm not surprised by that. Paul could be very charming when he wanted to be, but he also didn't really care about anyone else's feelings. Paul wanted what Paul wanted and he didn't mind stepping on toes to get it."

"I'm getting a fuller picture of him as each meeting passes."

"Maybe," said Stephanie, drinking some tea. "Maybe, one of them did this to him?"

"That's what I thought. I've already spoken with both of them. I don't think they're candidates."

She didn't say anything. She drank more tea. I drank more coffee. The earth spun a little more on its axis and I wasn't getting any closer to the truth.

"I don't know what to suggest then. Paul wasn't very nice once he'd had enough of you or if you couldn't help him anymore, but I don't think that deserved to have him murdered."

I smiled at her.

"In my business you'd be surprised at how little some people think of killing. The man, or woman, capable of murder doesn't think rationally about it like you or I. Why? Because it is an irrational act."

I took the last drink from my coffee and put the smiling-faced mug on the table.

"Did you know much about Paul's drug use?" I asked.

Stephanie nodded.

"A little. He didn't use around me because I wasn't like that. But I knew he liked a bit of cocaine and marijuana now and then."

"Seems to me that now and then turned into more and often."

She looked up at me and frowned.

"I didn't know it was that much of a problem. What I was concerned about when we were together was his drinking."

"He drank a bit then?"

"He drank a lot. Whenever we were out with friends or just out for dinner together, he'd drink more than he should. I always had to drive us around. Looking back now, I'm not sure I would have stayed with him if he hadn't got it under control."

The thing I like about hindsight is how crystal clear it is. But I doubted her sincerity. The number of domestics I went to where alcohol was a factor sometimes gave me the impression I was being paid by the breweries.

"Tell me about his violin?" I asked, hoping to get somewhere with this conversation. His alcoholism wasn't going to help me. It was either his drug use or violin abuse.

"Which one?" she asked.

"The expensive one, the Stradivarius."

"What's there to tell? He had it insured for a lot of money and he got it as a gift from his grandfather," she said.

"How much did he have it insured for?"

"I don't remember, some outrageous number. Ten million maybe."

Ten million exactly.

"Did he tell you how his grandfather got the violin?"

"No, he just said it was a gift from his grandfather."

"So you didn't know his grandfather was a concentration camp guard who stole it from a Jew who ended up under his watch?"

Stephanie frowned most severely this time.

"That's outrageous."

"Maybe, maybe not. John Stampley did some digging and this is what he found."

"That name sounds vaguely familiar."

"He's the guy who was fired so that Paul could get the first violin position when he first arrived."

She nodded.

"If what you're saying is true, that's horrible. Paul might have had many faults, but what he wasn't was a racist."

"I think you mean anti-Semitic."

"Well, yes. But you know what I mean. He didn't hate anyone because of their color or religion."

"Saint Paul Klee," I said.

Stephanie chuckled.

"No, I'm not saying that, I'm just trying to give you a fair impression of him. What I'm saying is that I can't believe that Paul's family was involved in the holocaust."

"We don't know it was his whole family, just his grandfather. In any event, you don't have to be anti-Semitic to enjoy the spoils of hatred."

"I don't understand," she said.

"The Nazis were generally nasty and unpleasant. They did experiments on prisoners, and some of the knowledge obtained by that unethical behavior has proven useful. All I'm saying is that Paul doesn't need to be an anti-Semite in order to keep the violin if he knew his grandfather had obtained it as a result of theft."

"Yes, I suppose you're right. Though it sounds awful."

"That's because it is distasteful. People often find it easy to steal when they're removed from the victims directly."

Stephanie sipped on her tea some more and didn't say anything for a while.

"I don't know what to say about that. All Paul told me was that his grandfather had given him the violin and that it had originally been bought by the English poet, Alexander Pope."

"'What dire offense from am'rous causes springs, what mighty contests rise from trivial things,'"

Stephanie frowned again.

"Those are the first two opening lines of Alexander Popes' The Rape of the Lock," I said.

"I see. You really are quite odd for a PI," she said.

"I paint too," I replied.

She didn't say anything.

"The Rape of the Lock is perhaps a little intriguing regarding this violin that Paul had."

"You'll have to enlighten me," she said.

"The poem is a somewhat satirical recounting of a real event. A suitor of a woman back in the seventeen hundreds cut off a lock of her hair without her permission. It was a theft, plain and simple."

"Hmm, that is interesting. Do you make this stuff up?"

She smiled at me.

"I don't think you could make stuff like this up," I said.

"So there is some parallel in what you're saying. How the first owner of this violin wrote a poem about a theft and Paul's grandfather's theft of the violin itself."

"Well, Alexander Pope, from what I hear, wasn't really the first owner. I understand he bought it, but as a gift for his lover. I find it more ironic than anything else."

"Yes, Paul had told me that Pope had bought if for someone else."

"Martha Blount was her name, hence the violin being called the Blount Stradivarius."

"Right."

"Anyway, we're not here to wax poetical about violins. I don't particularly care to and I imagine you need to be going soon."

Stephanie nodded.

"So I take it then that you have no idea about who Paul used in order to obtain his coke or joints?"

"I do actually," she said. "It was one of his fellow musicians, Gary... Gary Johnson I think his name is."

I nodded.

"That's what I heard. Though Gary tells me that Paul made a deal with Gary's dealer to obtain a large amount of coke and he put his violin up as collateral."

Stephanie shook her head.

"I guess I should be so lucky that I got away from him when I did. Sounds like he became more restless these past few years."

"Sounds like it," I agreed.

"I can't understand why he'd do something like that. That violin meant the world to him. Not only because it was so valuable but because it was given to him by his grandfather. He always spoke well about his grandfather."

"Addicts will do odd things when their addiction is controlling them."

Stephanie looked down at her watch and then drank the last of her tea.

"I don't mean to be rude," she said, "but I need to get going in a minute. Donald will be getting home soon, and we always have dinner together."

I nodded at her.

"No, you've been very helpful," I lied. "I think you've answered everything that I can think of asking."

She picked up her handbag and stood up. I stood up with her. We shook hands.

"I hope you find out who did this," she said. "Paul didn't deserve it."

"That's the idea," I said.

I watched her walk out the coffee shop and then I doffed my fedora. It was a little after five and I needed a drink. Something to oil my thinking cap so I could try and figure out this mess.

## Fourteen

I figured Monday would be a good day to go shopping for drugs. It was the start of the week. A new day for more opportunities for those in the illicit trades. Sonia needed Terry so I was left to my own devices. I decided to make some inquiries around Central Park at some thugs who looked like they might know of a drug dealer or two.

JJ was reasonably well known, though I was assured you couldn't get to see him without an appointment. After some haggling and knocking of heads I got a broad address for him. He hung out mostly in northeast Harlem. That's all I had to go on and that's all I needed.

I was told to head towards some old vacated, crumbling buildings right on Harlem River Drive. That's where he'd likely be. I got a description of him too. I was looking for a short, skinny guy with a lot of tattoos. Sleeves of tattoos they told me. He likes to wear a few gold chains around his neck over his wife beater. He wears black cargo pants and black army boots. He had gold teeth. It's called a grill, so I was told, and he had long dreadlocks that fall to his shoulders.

I took a yellow cab down to the river. I got him to drop me off by some baseball diamonds on the west side of Harlem River

Drive. I paid the cabbie and put on my fedora. It was warm so I was only wearing a white shirt and brown pants. In a corner, huddled like baseball players in a dugout were three black youths. They had the baggie clothes and snarling attitude of gangsters or wannabe gangsters.

I walked up to them full of smiles and warm wishes. Their clothes were baggy enough that they could have easily been carrying some bang bangs. The middle one had a brown bag over a bottle of some kind of liquor. Maybe it was just a big beer. He snarled at me as I came up to them.

His two chums stood up and looked down their noses at me. They could do that. At least the one guy could because he was taller than me. We stared at each other for a short while. All three of us. Then the middle one spoke.

"What you want, Crisco?"

"I want to talk to JJ."

More staring and eyeballing. We were in the shade so I didn't mind it too much. It wasn't hot. I grinned at them.

"You think this is funny coming out here to the hood?" the middle one asked.

"Pretty funny, yeah," I said.

"How so?"

"It's my first time in New York," I said, "and I never would have figured I'd be out in dog shit acres talking to some wannabe bangers."

The two guys standing on either side of me lifted up their sweaters a bit and revealed nice chrome pistols stuck into their pants.

"You haven't shot off your balls, have you?" I asked, looking at each of them.

"I think you better just fuck off, Crisco, go back to the city where you belong," said the middle one. I figured the other two for mutes.

166

"Can't do that," I said. "Not until I've spoken to my boy, JJ."

Like I said. Sometimes I can't help myself, my mouth gets me into trouble. The guy on my left turned to look at the middle guy still sitting down. I knew what was coming, so I decided to surprise them with my wit and charm.

I kneed the guy on my left as he was looking away. He turned back towards me, buckling under the pain of his Charlie horse. I took this opportunity to grab him around the neck and acquaint his nose with my knee. He dropped to his hands and knees as blood rained onto the dusty ground below him.

By this time his buddy on the right was fumbling with his. As he pulled it out I grabbed his wrist with both of my hands and walked right into his outstretched arm, holding it hard across my chest. Then I took my left hand and threw it as a bar up against his throat. My forearm made contact but it wasn't hard enough to break his windpipe. It was enough to lie him flat out on his back. He landed with a hard thump, knocking out whatever air was left in his lungs.

His pistol clattered on the dusty ground and I went to pick it up. I turned and pointed it back at the group. The middle one by this time had stood up. His hands were by his side.

"You packing?" I asked him.

He shook his head. He wasn't looking at me with a snarl anymore.

"Show me," I said.

He lifted up his sweater and there were no gun handles sticking out.

"Turn around."

He turned around and he was clean. Only his posse had been packing. I turned to look at the first guy, the bigger one, still on his hands and knees.

"Throw me your piece," I said to him.

He looked up at me with his nose still bleeding, still a little dazed. He sat back on his knees and pulled out his pistol and threw it in my direction. It was as shiny as the one in my hand that was pointed at his face. His was gold whereas the one I was holding was a shiny silver. I picked it up and slipped it in the back of my pants.

"Good," I said. "Now let's try this again. Where's JJ?"

The second guy was still on the ground struggling to get air into his lungs like a fish out of water.

"He's just across the block."

The middle guy nodded to his left.

"Shit man, are you some kinda ninja?"

"Yeah, something like that," I said. "Now you guys behave."

I backed away from them.

"Can we have our gats back?" asked the middle one.

I shook my head. I walked east and across the road. I tucked the silver pistol into the back of my pants right next to the other one. Each handle pointing away from the other. I wasn't looking for a gun fight.

The next block over was the one with the abandoned building on it. It was reasonably deserted. But I saw my guy. JJ was leaning against the wall on the south side of the building overlooking Harlem River. He had a couple of big lads with him. The one guy was obese, the other was muscled. both were around six and change. Both wore tracksuits, the fat one was in white. I hear folks think it's slimming. It wasn't working for him. The muscle head was wearing a navy tracksuit.

I walked up to them nice and slow so they could see me coming a mile away. I held my hands out in a non-threatening manner. They watched me like steely-eyed hawks. The muscle head opened his jacket a bit to show me his gat. I nodded at him. At about ten to fifteen feet away I stopped in front of them.

"Are you JJ?" I asked. "Jamal Johnson."

The fat black guy dressed in white made a step towards me. JJ held out his hand and the guy relaxed back against the wall.

"Who wants to know?" JJ asked.

"My name's Anthony Carrick," I said. "I'm a friend of Paul Klee's."

JJ looked me up and down.

"Don't look like you're carrying my money. And if you ain't, you best keep on walking."

"That's the thing," I said. "I've come here to talk to you about what's owing."

JJ looked out and around the vicinity for a while. I think he was trying to figure out if I was a cop or not. I don't think he thought I was. Not dressed the way I was and not coming alone to a place like this.

"Paul knows what's owing," said JJ, "and he knows it's due by the end of the week. There's nothing to discuss."

"There is," I said. "Paul's not gonna be able to pay the rest."

That got JJ a little more focused. The muscle head started towards me, but JJ put up his hand to stop him. JJ shook his head at me.

"Man, what kind of fool comes here to tell me I ain't gonna get my money? I should just bust a cap in yo' ass to make a point. I'll get my money by the end of the week and tell Paul he now owes me forty five for this bullshit you've come with."

It sounded to me like JJ didn't know Paul was dead. He was concerned with one thing and one thing only. His money. If he'd killed Paul, I don't see how he could have pulled off this kind of conversation.

"There's only one problem with that," I said.

"Yeah, what's that?"

"Paul's dead."

JJ looked at me steadily for a while without blinking. Everyone was staring at me. I might as well have been a model on a catwalk in next to nothing. Though I didn't feel particularly sexy.

"Is that so?" said JJ.

I nodded.

"You're not fooling?"

I shook my head.

"How can I be sure?"

"Here's the thing," I said. "I'm here today. Maybe tomorrow the cops are going to come on by to have a word. And they're probably gonna come by and have a word because they'll figure that kilo, or whatever is left, of the coke they're gonna find in Paul's apartment looks suspiciously like the stuff you sell. That's not gonna help you, is it?"

JJ looked around. There wasn't much to see. I peered to my left, but I couldn't see the three black musketeers I'd left across the park by the baseball diamonds. Maybe they'd left or maybe they were sulking. I didn't care. Cars drove by on Harlem River Drive but none paid too much attention to us. Maybe because we were a hundred feet or so from them.

"What do you want?" asked JJ.

"I want to know if you did it."

"Did what?"

"Killed him," I said.

"Why do you care?"

"Because I've been hired by the Philharmonic to look into his disappearance. See, Paul disappeared on Friday. Never showed up for practice or the concert. I got a call on Friday evening. I came over from LA on Saturday morning, and I mean to find out what happened to him."

"And you think I'm gonna tell you what you want to know."

I nodded and grinned at him. JJ shook his head and laughed. He looked over at his two boys. They smiled at him.

"Man, you've got balls, I'll tell you that. But why shouldn't I just drop you right here?"

"Because it's easier if you tell me what happened than if you wait until the five oh show up."

"That makes no sense. I'll just have you disappeared and then disappear myself," he said.

"That would be a mistake. You see," I said, "New York's finest are waiting for me this afternoon. I've got a meeting with Detectives Cooper and Simms who are looking into Paul's homicide. If I don't show up they know who I was with. That's you."

I was hoping this wasn't going to turn sideways on me. I figured JJ didn't have anything to lose. At this stage I didn't think he was good for it. I just wanted to get his side of the story. It might shed some light in some dark corners about what's going on with this mess.

"Alright," he said. "I'm feeling magnanimous."

"That's a big word for a gangster," I said.

JJ smiled at me.

"I went to college. But this pays better than office work, and it's more exciting."

I nodded my head.

"So what can you tell me?" I asked.

"I can tell you I didn't have that punk killed."

"And yet he owed you forty large," I said.

JJ nodded. He had his one foot resting against the back of the wall. He pulled out a joint and lit it. He inhaled deeply and held the breath for a moment.

"Dead men don't pay no rent," he said. "Besides, he told me he had a violin that was insured for ten million."

"That's nice," I said. "But how were you gonna get that money?"

"You're not a business man, so I'm gonna help you with this. He told me where he kept the violin. He said if he couldn't pay up I could keep the violin and he'd get the insurance money and we'd split it."

"And you believed him? Everyone else tells me he kept the violin with him at all times."

"And you're gonna tell me they were with him twenty-four seven?"

I shook my head.

"How did you know you could trust him?"

"Because we were in business together."

"Really? He buys fifty grand worth of coke off you and puts up a violin worth ten mil as collateral? I'm not buying it."

"That's because you ain't getting it, Crisco," said JJ.

"Then help me."

"This drug deal was just a front. A front for him to get a hold of that ten mil. He came to me with the idea a few weeks ago. Said he needed to start looking out for himself. He thought he was going to be fired from his musical job soon and he wanted to cash in before then."

"So he was going to pull an insurance fraud?"

JJ shook his head.

"I ain't saying that."

JJ was smart. He wasn't going to indict himself even if he knew I wasn't a cop.

"All I'm saying is that he had a situation he wanted my help with. It was going to be win win."

"Fifty fifty?" I asked.

JJ nodded and took another puff of his joint. He handed it over to the fat guy who took a puff.

"Fifty fifty seemed fair. He was gonna get five mil and he was gonna get to keep the violin."

"How's that?"

"I was gonna make it look like it was stolen and when all the dust settled he'd get it back."

"And he was gonna trust you?"

"He had no choice. I might deal in black market goods, but my word is solid."

"Why you?"

JJ took another toke and then passed it on to muscle head. He grinned at me like he was going to share a secret.

"Why not me?"

"Because I wouldn't trust you."

JJ laughed.

"I'll tell you why. Because that cracker didn't have nobody else to turn to, that's why. You think a white boy like that, all privileged and shit is gonna know folks like me. He's lucky because he knew me through Gary. Without me he wouldn't have any chance of pulling off something like this."

I nodded. It did make sense. It was risky, but I had the feeling that Paul being the spoiled kid he was didn't care about risk. He was probably arrogant about it.

"So tell me how this worked. You just took Paul on his word that he would hand over the violin when he was ready to do the insurance fraud?"

"I hardly knew him. Gary said he was a'ight. But that didn't go far. No man, Paul gave me a key to the kingdom so to speak."

"What do you mean?" I asked.

"Like I said. Paul didn't have that violin with him every night. When he came to talk to me about this arrangement, I needed some reassurances. He said he'd keep the violin in a locker from midnight to eight every night."

"How do you know he did that?"

"Because I've got a key."

"Did he tell you why he was carrying such an expensive violin around?"

"Sure did, 'cos I told him he could just leave the violin locked up all the time, but he said he was worried about that, because he was getting followed."

"So why did he feel safer at night?"

"He said they didn't tail him overnight, just during the day. Shit man, I don't really give a shit. The thing is he was good to his word."

"So you've seen the violin?"

JJ nodded and looked at fatty next to him.

"My nigger here, checked on Friday night just after midnight. Didn't you?"

JJ looked at the fat man and he nodded at JJ, not looking away from me.

"And since then?"

"It stays in the locker until Monday morning."

"Only now he's dead," I said.

JJ nodded.

"So you say."

"Who else has a key to this locker?"

"Only him and me," said JJ.

"Where is this locker?"

"Shit, you think I'm gonna tell you?"

"Doesn't matter, you said only you and him have a key. Why do you care?"

"I suppose it doesn't hurt. You don't know the number. Besides you could probably figure it out. Since nine eleven lockers have become real hard to find. Paul was using a place called The Glovebox."

I nodded.

"Did you notice anyone following him?" I asked.

JJ shrugged.

"I dunno, but when he got his coke about three weeks ago he was real nervous. He kept looking around. He nodded his head at this one car that was parked over there."

JJ cocked his head towards the park across the block where the baseball diamonds were. This is where I'd been dropped off by my cabbie.

"He said those were the same guys who had been following him. I had one of my guys take him home from the other side of this building."

"What happened then?"

"Well as soon as Paul disappeared into this tenement the car took off."

"What kind of car was it?"

"Black Mercedes."

"Did you get the plate?"

JJ frowned at me and grinned.

"Shit, man, do I look like I'm the cops to you."

I didn't say anything. Fatty leaned in and whispered something to JJ. JJ nodded at him.

"DLW0403," said the fat guy.

"It wasn't a New York plate neither," said JJ.

"I figured."

"How did you know when you first met him that he had a valuable violin?"

"He showed it to me."

"Right, like you know the insides of violins like you know the insides of a hooker's bra," I said.

"Man, you're a lippy mothafucka coming into my turf and talking to me like that."

"I'm just asking. How did you know the violin was valuable?"

"He showed it to me like I said, and he showed me the insurance papers on it. Gave me copies as a matter of fact."

"Seems to me like there are a lot of people looking to get that violin."

"How do you figure that?" asked JJ.

"Because it was stolen. His grandfather stole it from a woman in a German concentration camp. At least that's the story I heard."

"Is that a fact?"

"Not yet, but it's sounding more reasonable the more I get along on this case."

JJ looked down, took a last puff from his joint and then threw it on the ground where he ground it out with his foot.

"You've been helpful," I said. "I hope business picks up for you."

I started to back away from them towards the corner of the street.

"Don't go looking for that violin," I said. "Cops will be all over that place by the time you get there."

I backed my way all the way to the corner of the street. I crossed over and started walking south alongside Harlem River Drive. I fished out my phone and made a call.

"Terry," I said. "Are you free... I need a ride... I'm heading south on Harlem River Drive, not far from West 143rd... It's not such a bad place, if you're looking for gang bangers."

I hung up and pulled out my cigarette pack. I lit one up and kept up my pace heading south. This part of Harlem wasn't all that busy. The traffic was heavy but not many folk around here liked to walk around much. I felt safer with shiny gats nestled snugly against my butt cheeks.

I was just coming up on Park Avenue when Terry found me. It wasn't the Park Avenue that tourists would come to see, but I figured it was still filled with robbers. Just not of the Robber Baron sort. Those folks, the respectable robbers that got away with the biggest heist of the millennium lived down closer to the park. Some called them Captains of Industry, I much preferred the term Robber Barons, and I was employed by one.

And as I got into one of their cars I got to thinking about the class system in this country of mine that was once great. Now it was like an old mansion. It looked great on the outside but its insides were rotten having been eaten out by termites and their pals. Not that you're asking, but the American Dream seems to have turned into a nightmare for some.

# Fifteen

I had gone back to my hotel for a nap. After that I headed down to the restaurant for a steak. I was feeling fresh and vigorous. I had called Detective George Simms and he had offered to meet me at the Central Park Precinct.

Simms told me that the precinct was inside Central Park. Down by the Jacqueline Kennedy Onassis Reservoir on the south side. I was going to walk. I had a full belly and the sun was shining. I started out towards the middle of the park. Even some women looked my way and smiled. I was feeling invincible. But I needed to take a look inside the crime scene and figure out who had done what and why they'd done it. Simms had been a real mensch over the phone. Even more helpful than the first time I'd met him. It sounded to me like Sonia had reached out to the police commissioner. With deep pockets there's lots of space to keep your pawns.

Central Park Precinct is a mix of old and new. To me it looked like a turtle with feet and head stretching out from its shell. It was a weird architectural hodgepodge. I'd told Simms to meet me outside by the baseball diamonds. I told him I had a couple of presents that he might like to unwrap before we had our sit down.

Just south of the precinct was a place called The Great Lawn. That's something else that didn't make sense to me. A lawn is a lush field of immaculate grass. Almost like a putting green. This lawn was just a grouping of eight baseball diamonds.

Simms was waiting at the far end of this lawn. By the very first diamond by the precinct. He was standing around idly smoking a cigarette and with one hand stuck in his pocket. He nodded at me as I came up to him.

"Good to see you again," he said, offering his hand.

We shook, and I looked him in the eye. I figured he was sincere. I put my soft suitcase down. It was actually my carryon. It had nothing in it except for two blinged out bang bangs. I fished out my pack of cigarettes. Simms offered a light and I accepted. I inhaled as he looked at me.

"You've got some clout," he said. "Knowing people in high places helps, doesn't it?"

He grinned and I nodded at him. There was no one else on this lawn within a hundred feet of us.

"Better than knowing people in low places," I said. "So did the commish speak to your people?"

Simms nodded and puffed on his cigarette.

"Sure did. We've been told to offer you all the help that you need."

"How nice," I said.

Simms grinned.

"Truth though, is that we could use your help. We're bringing in the husbands this evening for interviews. I'm betting you've travelled further afield."

"I've been doing some sightseeing in this fair city."

Simms nodded and flicked his cigarette out onto the baseball diamond and then ground it out with his shoe. He pulled out a small baggie from his pocket and picked up the stub.

"We've gotta set the right example," he said.

I nodded.

"So what have you got for me that can't wait until we're inside."

I looked down at my bag.

"Take a look inside," I said. "I didn't want to push the generosity of NY's finest."

Simms kneeled down and unzipped my bag. He took a peek inside.

"Jesus," he said. "Where did you get these?"

He didn't pick them up, but he looked into the bag for a while.

"I got them off a couple of bangers down in Harlem. Figured they weren't licensed so I kept them to give to you."

Simms looked up and grinned at me.

"You're right. A gold Beretta 92 9mm, and a silver Remington 1911 .45 Auto. That's good work."

"Well, I figured you scratched my back I'd scratch yours."

Simms stood up.

"Let's not waste any time," he said, and he picked up my suitcase and headed towards the precinct.

I followed him, smoking my cigarette until we got into the main outside courtyard where I put it out. Simms explained to me that originally most of the older buildings were stables which had been renovated for police use. It started to make a lot more sense to me.

We walked inside and through the main lobby. There weren't any metal detectors which I found weird. I could've walked in with my bling bling and lit the place up. I asked Simms about that but he said they weren't worried. The glass was bullet resistant and there was only one way in. They were thinking of putting in screeners, but he said that most of the traffic was police and not civilian.

He led me up some stairs and off to the left. Then down a hall a ways and we entered his office. He put my bag behind his desk.

"I'll need that back," I said.

"Yeah, let me just get some evidence bags and grab Cooper."

He walked out again and I stood looking around the sparse office. The floor was a golden yellow of polished wood and his desk and chairs in the room were the same modular furniture like you'd find in pretty much any government building anywhere. From municipal up to federal. It didn't inspire confidence. It spoke loudly of bean counters and budget men.

I took a seat. Simms didn't have much on his desk. A couple of folders, some pens in a coffee mug, a three level mail tray and a computer monitor. There was also a metal cabinet on the floor on the left side as you walked in. I took off my hat and put it on the corner of his desk. There was a picture frame with its black back to me. I picked it up and turned it around. It was his wedding day. Didn't look all that old. His wife was slim and attractive. But wedding photographs always put your best side forward.

Simms came back in with an even more disheveled Cooper. His face was as sullen and gray as the moon. He took the seat next to me but pulled it a bit further away. Maybe he didn't like the smell of my cologne. Simms sat behind his desk.

"I just want you to know that this isn't my choice," said Cooper, looking at me.

"I figured that out a couple of days ago at the Philharmonic," I said.

"So long as we're on the same page."

"We're not on the same page," I said. "The people who hired me have more clout than good sense and they could have you riding desk for the rest of your career if they wanted."

"Is that a threat?"

"If you want it to be. I can make one phone call, Cooper, and have you off this case and Simms and I can wrap it up by supper time."

Cooper stared me down for a while, his mustache twitching like a nervous caterpillar slipping off his lip.

"Let's just get to work on this together," said Simms, putting on his blue beret of the peacekeepers.

"It's no goddamn surprise you were kicked off the job," said Cooper. "I looked into it."

"Then you don't know the half of it," I said.

Cooper shrugged, and looked over at Simms.

"Carrick here brought us a present this morning," said Simms.

"Yeah, what's that?" asked Cooper.

Simms fished out my bag from behind him and put it on the table. Then he unzipped it and pulled out each gun, holding it with the plastic evidence bag. He put them down in front of Cooper.

"That looks like the Park Avenue Pimps firepower," said Cooper.

"That's what I was thinking," said Simms.

Cooper looked over at me. He nodded towards the desk where the guns were.

"How did you get those?"

"I found them on a couple of bangers who didn't want to dance."

Cooper shook his head.

"You're lucky," he said. "These gang bangers don't have any compulsion about killing."

"Luck had nothing to do with it," I said.

"I didn't tell you this," said Simms, "but Carrick here won the ninety-eight middleweight boxing title against Steve Little."

Cooper looked over at me again and sized me up.

"That's impressive," he said. "Little was unbeaten to that point."

"I still am," I said.

"Still what?" asked Cooper.

"Unbeaten."

Cooper shook his head.

"You're an asshole," he said.

"That's because I don't like you."

Simms grinned at me. I had a feeling he liked what Cooper was getting.

"Whatever happened to Little?" I asked.

"He's the captain over at the 104th in Queens," said Simms.

"Good," I said, "he's done well for himself. Seemed like a good guy."

"Listen," said Simms, looking at Cooper. "Carrick has a lot of respect for Little. I think he just gets a kick out of riling you up. He told me that the Little fight was the toughest he had."

Cooper shrugged his shoulders.

"Who did you get these from?" he asked, cocking his head over at the guns again.

"I don't know. We didn't exchange personal details. I was on my way to see Jamal Johnson, and at about West 145th down by the river I found these chumps drinking liquor by some baseball diamonds. Figured they could help me get a line on where JJ was."

"And I guess they were helpful?" asked Simms.

"After some polite banter," I said.

Simms grinned.

"Shit, we need more guys like you on the job," he said.

"Guys like me wouldn't last very long. There's a reason I'm no longer with LAPD. Like your partner Coop says, I couldn't adjust my attitude very well. Being a civilian allows me more discretion. I like that."

"True. The law can handcuff us sometimes."

"That's why I want us to help each other on this."

"You know you could be up on assault charges," said Cooper.

"Who said anything about assault?" I asked.

"I'm thinking those gang bangers didn't just hand over their guns because you asked nicely."

"A gentleman never tells," I said, grinning at him like a wolf that smells dinner. I didn't like him. If I wasn't in such a magnanimous mood and if he wasn't a cop and I wasn't on a case I might have thought about cleaning his clock for him. His timing seemed off.

"Jamal Johnson," said Simms. "How's he involved in this?"

"He's not, but I had to check him out."

"Why did you have to check him out?" asked Cooper.

I looked back at him.

"You've done some interviews with the musicians right?" Cooper nodded. "So you know Klee was a coke head, right?" Cooper nodded again. "And you've been working this city longer than I have so you might also know that Jamal is a coke dealer."

"Yeah, we know that," said Cooper, "but that's not our precinct."

"Fair enough," I said, "but you know. Anyway, I heard from Gary Johnson, the trombone player at the Phil, that he used to get coke for Klee."

Cooper looked over at Simms and raised his eyebrows.

"See how helpful it is when we all work together," said Simms.

"Right," I said. "Gary probably didn't tell you that part, did he?"

Simms shook his head.

"Okay. So Gary gets drugs for Klee. But a few weeks ago he tells me that Klee, coming unbuckled decides he wants to go straight to the source. Gary tells me that Klee buys a kilo of coke from Jamal on layaway."

Simms laughed out loud.

"No way," he said, "these guys don't do layaway."

"I guess they thought Klee was a swell guy. The kind they could trust."

I smiled at Simms.

"You're shitting us. Tell us what really happened." Simms said.

"He went and got a kilo of coke from Jamal. He put ten grand down on fifty grand worth of coke. Gary thinks he's gonna try and sell it to his upscale friends and clients he's met through the Philharmonic."

"That's an interesting idea, but I'm not buying the idea that Jamal is going to front him forty grand," said Cooper. "That's not how those guys typically do business."

I nodded at him.

"I thought it was sketchy so I went to talk to Jamal about it," I said.

"And I suppose he told you everything. I bet you had a real heart to heart," said Cooper.

He looked at me smirking. I smiled at him.

"As a matter of fact, we did. See, when you're not a cop, it's funny what people will tell you when they know they can't be arrested."

Cooper didn't say anything.

"What did he say?" asked Simms.

I looked over at Simms. My black bag was still on the table. The guns were still on the table on top of their bags. They hadn't been made safe. It was a good thing I'd taken the bullets out and put them in a side pocket.

"Jamal said he had in fact fronted Klee the kilo of coke for ten grand. I mean, he didn't say it exactly like that, but that was the understanding. But it was a business arrangement."

"A business arrangement," said Cooper, shaking his head. "Please."

"Is he always this open minded?" I asked Simms.

"Not usually, but he's a good cop."

"A business arrangement," I said again, looking at Cooper. "You must have known about Klee's violin. The expensive one?"

Cooper nodded.

"Had it insured for ten mil."

"That's right," I said. "Now imagine a violin like that gets stolen or lost. Imagine that Klee collects the ten mil for it."

"But he loved that violin, so everyone said," said Simms.

"Right, like I love the last cigarette in my pack."

"So what are you saying?" asked Cooper.

"I'm saying that Klee had help to pull this insurance fraud."

"Bullshit," said Cooper.

I pulled out my phone and started to dial a number.

"I wonder how fast I can have you riding desk?" I asked, looking at Cooper.

Simms put his hand out towards me.

"C'mon," he said. "Carrick, we're all on the same team. Let's start working together. Cooper, please, stop being a dick."

Cooper and I had a staring contest. I felt so junior high, so I looked over at Simms and grinned at him.

"If walrus here will show he's on the same team, I'm game. Otherwise I'm gonna make this call and get the hell out of here and solve this homicide and embarrass the both of you."

Simms looked at Cooper and raised his eyebrows and bumped his head in Cooper's direction.

"Alright," said Cooper, looking at me. "I'll play ball."

I looked at Cooper. I gave him a stony stare. Mostly because I didn't care for him much, and some because I didn't really give a shit about him. I wanted into the crime scene and these guys were my ticket.

"Like I was saying," I said. "Klee was fixing to set up an insurance fraud."

"That's pretty ballsy," said Simms.

"You guys didn't get a flavor for him from his interviews?" I asked.

"Some," said Simms.

"Let me paint a picture for you. I'm not crying over him. Seems he was an arrogant SOB who figured he was owed everything. You heard how he got his positions in the orchestra, right?"

Cooper and Simms nodded at me.

"Right, so here's a guy who figures he can get away with whatever strikes his fancy. As Jamal tells it, he was fixing to cash in the insurance on the violin. He was on his last good graces with the Philharmonic. You must know that, they were gonna get rid of him if he didn't buckle up, and by all accounts he wasn't gonna buckle up."

Simms nodded.

"So he came up with this genius idea whereby Jamal and his lads steal the violin and Klee cashes in on the insurance. They split the ten mil fifty fifty. Then after the dust has settled, Klee gets his violin back. Like Jamal told me, it was win win."

Simms shook his head.

"That son of a bitch," he said. "So you think this worry about a couple of thugs following him was all bullshit?"

"That's what I thought originally," I said. "I figured it'd make a good cover for why he's carrying his violin around all the time. But I spoke to Jamal about that and he told me he saw the guys that were following Klee. So I think that's pretty legit."

Simms nodded.

"So where did he keep the violin?"

"I thought so," I said.

"Thought what?" asked Simms.

"You guys haven't found the Strad, have you?" I asked.

Simms shook his head.

"Found a bunch of other violins at his place, but no Strad," Simms acknowledged.

"Jamal tells me he kept it in a locker at The Glovebox overnight from around midnight to eight in the morning. Though I'm thinking it's likely not there."

"How do you figure that?" asked Cooper.

"Because only he and Jamal have a key. If he didn't have the violin with him it's either been stolen from him when he was murdered, which is unlikely..."

"Why?" asked Cooper.

"Because Jamal tells me he kept the violin in the locker over the weekend until Monday around eight in the morning. He only used the Strad on special occasions so I don't figure he was planning to use it for Saturday's performance."

"How so?" asked Cooper, he was becoming more chatty as the time wiled away.

"Because it's Vivaldi's Four Seasons. Everybody does that all the time. It's not special. In any event when was he murdered?" I asked.

"Coroner puts TOD at between eight and noon on Friday," said Simms.

I nodded.

"Okay, so he puts the violin away on Thursday evening. Come Friday morning I don't think he's gone to fetch it from the locker when he's surprised by whoever killed him. I don't think he had a chance to get it yet."

"That's quite the supposition," said Cooper.

"Maybe, but then Jamal also tells me that his guy checked in on the violin late Friday night and it was still there. Now you're saying Klee was dead by Friday morning. That means he hadn't picked it up since he put it away on Thursday evening."

"Why didn't you just say that?" asked Cooper, starting to get a little testy with me.

"Where's the fun in that. Deductive reasoning, my dear Cooper."

That was cheesy, I admit it. But Cooper could use some cheese. I think he wanted to start rolling eyeballs at me but he caught himself. He did a weird tilt of his head, like a dog might when he's trying to understand you.

"We might want to get some guys out there to check it out?" said Simms, looking at Cooper. Cooper nodded. Simms picked up the phone. He spoke to the other end and ordered some unis to make it out to The Glovebox. He covered the mouthpiece and looked up at me.

"What's the locker number?"

I shrugged.

"I dunno and I don't think it's important," I said.

Simms cursed under his breath. He told the other end just to send the unis and make sure they take note of anything taken out of the locker and if it's a violin to detain them. He hung up and looked at me.

"I thought you knew where the violin was located?"

"I did," I said.

"You don't. You just told me you don't know the locker number."

"I don't."

"Jesus, what is it? Do you know it or not?" Simms was getting a little riled up.

"I know that the locker is located at The Glovebox. Why do you think Jamal would give me the locker number?"

"Because you had a heart to heart."

"Yeah, but he's not stupid. Anyway, I reckon it doesn't matter now anyway."

"How do you figure that?" asked Cooper, as Simms looked forlorn, looking at his desk.

"In between meeting you and Jamal I had a nice steak lunch. Jamal has probably sent his guys to find the violin in the locker. I'm gonna go out on a limb and say that the violin was likely swiped sometime Friday or Saturday. Sunday at the very latest. It hasn't been at The Glovebox for at least a day."

"You think?" asked Cooper.

"I do. Let me spell it out for you. Jamal desperately needs the violin now. With Klee dead, he's not gonna get any insurance money, so his scam is up. The only thing he can leverage is the violin. So he checks up on it on Friday night, and it's still there. But he doesn't take it. Why not? Because he doesn't know that Klee is dead. Ergo, he didn't have Klee killed. It wouldn't have made sense for him in any event. With Klee dead, Jamal's losing out on five mil."

"Okay, so Jamal didn't kill Klee and he didn't take the violin on Friday night, so he says," said Cooper.

"So I believe him."

"And that's what you're gonna go on?" asked Cooper.

"It's all I have to go on, but he seemed sincere."

"Okay," said Cooper, "I'll play. Let's pretend you're right. What's happened to the violin?"

"Somebody else got to it."

"Like who?"

"Like the men who killed him," I said.

"And who are they?" asked Simms, rejoining the conversation.

"Can't share that right now."

Simms frowned at me.

"I thought we were working on this together?" he said.

"I thought you guys were giving me all the help I needed, not vice versa."

"You're an ass," said Simms. We weren't so pally pally anymore.

"I'm not trying to be difficult," I said. "I just need to get my arrows straight and I'll give you everything. Listen, I'm not gonna arrest anyone, you guys are gonna get that glory. I just don't want anything fucked up before then."

Cooper looked over at Simms and raised his eyebrows.

"Alright," he said, "you wanna do all the work and give us the glory, I can live with that. What can you tell us?"

"I'm thinking it all comes down to the violin."

"What comes down to the violin?" asked Cooper.

"Everything, particularly the murder," I said.

"I still like one of the husbands for it," said Cooper.

"So did I until I spoke with them. They've both got alibis."

"We'll be the judge of that," said Cooper.

"What kind of bullet was Klee shot with?" I asked.

"Two bullets and they were both .40 caliber," said Cooper.

"Have you got any further analysis on them?" I asked.

Simms looked up at me and then over at Cooper. Cooper nodded.

"Ballistics figures they're a match for a Heckler & Koch USP, but obviously we don't know which specific gun until we test them."

I nodded. It was all starting to fall into place.

"Just as I thought."

"This helps you?" asked Simms.

"Yeah it does. I'll throw you a bone. Figure out who likes to use that kind of handgun regularly. Who issues it to their department and you'll be well on your way."

"And I suppose you know?" asked Cooper.

"As easy as a search on the internets," I said, smiling at them. "And if I'm right we're gonna have a helluva time getting justice. Might even turn relations sour."

"You like talking in riddles, don't you?" asked Simms, looking at me with a grin. I was starting to think all was forgiven.

"Well, we appreciate the tips, but we've still gotta bring in the husbands to make sure," said Cooper.

"No doubt," I said. "I'll give you another leg up. Kieran doesn't have a gun, so far as he told me, and I figure he was being honest. We had an understanding you see. As for Perry, he tells me he has a Smith & Wesson 4006. That's a .40 caliber but not the kind you're looking for."

I looked at them. Simms was making notes.

"Don't say I didn't do anything for you."

"You're a real pal," said Simms, looking up and smiling at me.

"Listen," I said. "I'd like to take a look at the crime scene. There might be something there that will shed further light on the situation."

"You've been given clearance," said Simms.

"So I can just rock up and the uni will be good with that?"

"No," said Cooper. "You need to rock up and tell him who you are and give him some ID. Then you'll be good."

"However," added Simms, "if you wait until five we'll be clearing out of the crime scene. We've got everything we need, so the uni will be locking and leaving it then."

"What about a key?" I asked.

"Speak to the super," said Simms.

"And where am I going?"

"To the crime scenes," said Simms not realizing what I was asking.

"What's the address?"

"It's the Bon Vivant Views on Central Park South. Apartment nine oh five," said Simms.

I looked at my watch, it was well past two. I looked at Cooper and Simms. They looked ready to take an afternoon nap.

"I've done a lot of talking. You guys have done a lot of listening. What can I get from you?" I said.

"Probably not much that you don't already know," said Simms.

"Yeah, seems like you've done your homework already," agreed Cooper. "Something we didn't know was the vic's involvement with Jamal. That's not something you easily get from interviews. Not when you're the police."

I nodded.

"Gary wasn't very cooperative at first, not until we told him we were gonna haul him in for an interview. Then suddenly he became a lot more chatty. But he didn't give us Klee," said Cooper.

"You heard about John Stampley?" I asked.

Simms nodded.

"Yeah," he said, "but to hold a grudge like that for that long. I'm not thinking he did it."

"Me neither," I said. "But I like him more for what he found out about the violin."

"That it's been stolen?" asked Simms.

I nodded.

"That's hearsay, and I'm not that interested in hearsay until we find out that it might be relevant to the case," said Cooper.

"I just told you it might be relevant to the case," I said.

"Yeah, but you didn't give us much."

"Well, I'm gonna go pay him a visit tonight or tomorrow and verify the information he supposedly got."

"You do that," said Cooper. "In the meantime, we're gonna bring in the husbands. Nine times out of ten in cases like this, it's a jealous lover. Simple as that."

"I thought it was eight times out of ten," I said, being as sarcastic as possible. Cooper didn't pick up on it.

"Whatever, eighty percent, ninety percent, it's still just percentages."

"NASA wasn't hiring when you applied with your advanced mathematics degree?" I asked.

Cooper frowned at me but didn't say anything. I stood up to go. I put on my hat and grabbed my bag. I opened the side zipper pocket and scooped out the bullets. I rolled them out onto the table. Some rolled to Simms, others rolled towards Cooper who was too slow or maybe too lazy to stop them from rolling onto the floor. I didn't give a shit.

"You guys might like these too," I said.

Simms caught the few that were rolling down the end of his desk.

"I'm outta here. By tomorrow I'll tell you exactly how this went down, while you're still figuring out who next to interview."

I was looking at Cooper. I liked Simms, but I figured he was probably better on his own.

## Sixteen

I had pissed away my afternoon after leaving the Central Park Precinct and Detectives Cooper and Simms. It was a nice day in New York. The sun was shining and it was warm. I decided to walk around the park for a few hours and watch the world go by. Or at least watch New York go by.

In the middle of the day I was astonished to see just how many people enjoy the park. I knew that employment was at an all time low, but to me it looked like half of New Yorkers were either taking a personal day or were unemployed.

Central Park sits on over eight hundred and forty acres so the Internet tells me. Very few of those acres are not being inhabited by people. Even within the innermost center of the park there was still noise and people milling around. I saw several green Martians, which I learned later were actually Parks' Enforcement Patrol. The men in green.

I took a walk around the reservoir which is over one and a half miles. That was as far north as I headed. I spent most of my time down in the lower half of the park enjoying the view of tight bums in yoga pants strutting on by.

In such a large city filled with so many people, I found more lonely souls in that green space than I'd encountered in my life.

With activity abounding and the jostling of bodies, you could still be lonely in the middle of a torrent of people.

That got me to thinking about Klee. I wondered if he was lonely too. I've only seen empty shells do the things that he did. The womanizing, the boozing and drugs. The screwing around. Looking for things to fill the emptiness. All the while, like a ship adrift in choppy seas, taking on more water and drowning all the quicker.

I sat on a bench and watched nature for a while. I saw an old woman with a wire basket on wheels leaning towards a fat gray squirrel and offering him shelled peanuts. She seemed to get more delight out of the transaction than the squirrel did. She kept leaning in over and over. Each time with a new peanut. She had a whole brown paper, crumpled bag of them in her lap.

Her clothes were old and disheveled. She had on a light cardigan over a floral print dress. The elbows of the cardigan were frayed and faded. She was thin. A skeleton covered by a thin, loose layer of skin. I got to thinking that most of her pension however small it might have been, probably went to feed the wildlife around here. Didn't matter, it clearly gave her unbounded joy.

There was a dance between her and the squirrel. She'd reach out with bony fingers, clutching a shelled peanut and the squirrel would scurry away. Then it'd come back again, slowly, nervously, creeping like a thief in the night. In the last few inches it'd hurry up and grab the peanut and then back off a foot or two. Those little hands and small fingers and sharp teeth would make short work of the shell. It'd shovel the peanut into its mouth. This went on for a while. Once he'd had his fill he scurried away up a tree to stash his bounty for the coming winter.

When the squirrel left and before the next one came, the old woman with big rimmed glasses would eat a peanut herself. Looking out across the green space. I followed her gaze, but there wasn't anything there that caught my eye. Perhaps those rheumy eyes were looking inward instead.

I left around dinner time and decided I'd let Sonia pay for a very expensive steak. The best steak that money could by, so the concierge at the hotel told me was at Haystack. Haystack was a pretentious joint that required a jacket and tie, so I put one on. I wore the fedora too which they didn't mind.

The ambiance was dark and yellow. Dark woods and warm yellow lights. It was clean and immaculate with high backed, comfortable chairs. They put me in a corner in a two seater which in most other places would have fit four.

In LA, I ate for a week on what my filet mignon cost at this joint, and I'm no vegetarian eating beans and rice when I'm at home. I asked the waiter who was a short guy about my age if it was worth it. He laughed a rolling, bubbling laugh like I'd just shared a private joke. Then he got real serious really quick and told me I was about to enjoy the best steak of my life.

The place was full when I got there and with furrowed brows I was informed there were no cancellations. I told them I had promised to meet Sonia Varnier here. In that case, right this way they said. And here I was, sitting by myself in a corner of an overpriced steak joint waiting for the best steak of my life.

I admire hyperbole as much as the next guy, but not when it comes to my food. I figured the steer my steak came from was probably the same ranch in Texas that sent Denny's theirs.

I waited a long time. I was on my second beer by the time the steak came. Seems to me, the bigger the price, the longer the wait for the food. The steak was big and served on its own plate. The potato had it's own plate and the asparagus also sat all alone.

No fancy sauces, the only flavor enhancements for the steak the waiter assured me were its own natural juices and proprietary house rub. I looked at it and it looked good. I dug in and tasted it. It wasn't the best steak I'd ever had in my life but it would have been in the top hundred. That's a feat, I've eaten a lot of steak.

Still the pretentiousness of the patrons was nauseating and almost ruined my meal. I'm a simple guy. I come in for a meal, not a world tour of gastronomic excess. I like one meal. Seldom appetizers and dessert. Sometimes I'll have a coffee. But this place was making me feel uncomfortable. I figured a coffee could wait until after the crime scene. I got my check and looked at it.

After all was said and done I managed to crack three figures. I put Benjamin down on the table. Looked to me like he was frowning. Poor Richard wasn't happy at the expense. I figured he'd rather I go to bed hungry than rise the next morning in debt. Thing is, this was on Sonia. To shut him up I gave him the company of a couple of Honest Abes. They could philosophize about it all night long. I was trying to work for a living.

I kept the receipt and decided to walk to The Glovebox. It wasn't far and I wanted to see if the cops had spied anyone coming in to open it up. I had my doubts, but I wanted confirmation. It wasn't far. A fifteen minute walk took me there, through the darkening sky pregnant with bulbous clouds that threatened rain but were full of hot air.

The Glovebox is a small thin business that goes down deep. It's on one level, but I quickly found out it has a basement. It's not really a storage place. The biggest lockers are about three feet wide by four feet tall. The smallest the size of a mailbox.

I looked around for a while. The place had steady business, mostly tourists coming in and out fetching backpacks and luggage on wheels. In the far corner, underneath two dull black eyes of cameras was the counter with a Goth girl chewing bubble gum and leaning over a magazine.

I walked up to her. There were no cops hanging around inside or even outside. Maybe there was in the basement but I didn't think so. The Goth girl looked up at me and rolled her pink bubblegum around on a pink tongue that I could see bracketed between purple painted lips.

"I'm looking for Officer Philip Marlowe," I said. "He was here earlier."

"You his boss?" she asked, chewing her gum like cud.

"I am," I said.

She looked down at her magazine and turned a page.

"He left a couple of hours ago," she said, not looking at me.

She went to turn the page of her magazine again. I put my hand on it and the page tore a little.

"Hey," she said, looking at me with a frown on her face. She stopped chewing her gum.

"Listen, darling," I said. "We're investigating a murder, and the guy who rented that locker from you might have something to do with it. Now I want you to take me to that locker so I can go and have a look. Otherwise I'm gonna get a warrant and shut this place down while I look inside every locker. I'll bring drug sniffing dogs and if I find just a whiff of anything this place will be closed down for good. How do you think that'll look to your boss?"

I gave her a hard stare. I might have been Mount Rushmore for all she knew. Her eyelids fluttered.

"Geez, mister, you don't have to be such a hard ass," she said.

"It's detective," I said to her.

"I can't leave my desk," she said, "but the guy's locker is in the basement. Zero zero seven. But there's nothing to see. It's already been broken into."

I nodded at her and walked past her counter to the back of the room where stairs wound down into the basement of this place. Zero zero seven was towards the front of The Glovebox. It was in a bank of similar sized lockers, all about two feet square that went two feet deep. These lockers had locks that required a key. Zero zero seven didn't require a key anymore. Looked to me like somebody had taken a crowbar to the locker and opened it up that way. The edge of it by the lock was bent in.

I opened the locker and saw that it was empty. I turned around and looked back down towards the stairs. There were no cameras in this part of the building. The light was stingy too, and other than the lockers there was nothing of note in the room.

I went back upstairs to see my Goth girl. She hadn't moved. She was still leaning on the counter and reading her magazine. I walked up to her.

"Who busted the locker?" I asked.

She shrugged and straightened up.

"I dunno," she said. "We don't spy on our customers." She said that like it was a compliment."

"Do you check out your lockers to make sure none of them have been damaged?" I asked.

She nodded.

"At midnight and noon. Every twelve hours we have to check them. We charge our customers if they damage or deface the lockers."

"So when was the first time you noticed that zero zero seven was broken into?"

She moved to the side of her counter where a computer screen was located. She sat down and tapped onto a keyboard for a bit.

"Charlene said she saw double oh seven was broken when she checked on Saturday at midnight. At noon it was still fine."

She giggled.

"What's so funny?"

"I just realized the locker is double oh seven. You know, like that James Bond guy?"

I nodded at her and smiled. It was a painful smile that had no reason to live so it died right there, limply, on my face.

"Listen," I said. "I need to see your video footage from Saturday between noon and midnight. There might be more people at risk because of what was stolen from that locker."

"I can get it for you," she said.

I smiled at her. This time it had more staying power.

"You're being very helpful," I replied. "I'll be sure to remember that."

She liked that. She smiled at me. She tapped away at her keyboard with more vigor.

"Here it is," she said. "I'm not supposed to do this, but you can come in here."

She got up and opened the swinging door and lifted the counter for me to get into her small office space. She closed up the door after me and then sat back down on the chair.

"Just use these arrows to go back and forth," she said. "If you want to stop just click here, and if you want to go super slow, just click here. You're lucky. We only keep the video for seventy-two hours. Tomorrow it'll get erased."

"I live under a horseshoe," I said.

She didn't get that.

"Thanks," I offered. She got that one and then got up from the chair and went to help someone at the counter.

"I wanna rent a locker for a couple of hours," he said.

Goth girl started going on about their policy, how they need fifty dollars cash deposit if not paying by credit card and that it's cheaper to rent for a day. At that point I zoned out and started zooming through the video in front of me.

The video was in black and white and not in high def. Goth girl had stopped it at eleven forty-seven on Saturday morning. I zoomed through for several minutes until at one fifty-six I saw someone leaving with what looked like a hard violin case. I froze the video. The person was wearing a dark hoody and they looked small and feminine. The hand was slender and delicate wrapped around the violin case's handle. There was a small bulge on the back of the head towards the top of the hoody.

I had a feeling I knew who this was, but I couldn't be sure. I started scrolling back. This took a little longer. Several minutes went by before I found what I was looking for. At one fifty-two this same person came in wearing the hoody. Their hands were thrust into jean pockets and they kept their head down. You couldn't get a good look at the face, but I could see the nose. It was cute and shaped like a ski jump. It belonged to Christina Tedder. I was pretty sure of that. Along the side of her right leg inside the jeans you could just make out what looked like it could have been a crowbar.

Seemed to me like she'd stolen the violin. Did that mean she'd also popped Klee twice in the chest? I wasn't sure, but it seemed odd that if she had, she'd wait twenty four hours to collect her prize.

I closed the program I was in. I didn't want anyone else taking a look by chance. I got up and walked over to Goth girl who had started back on her magazine.

"Thanks," I said. "That was very helpful."

"So you won't need to be closing us down?" she asked.

I shook my head.

"I've got another question for you though."

"What's that?"

"Did you see any big guys, I'm talking six feet and then some, come in while you've been here?"

She shook her head.

"No. I only started at one. But nobody like that's been in here."

Not that you'd see them anyway, I thought, with your nose stuck in a magazine. I didn't feel like going through more video just on the off chance. If those two goons were here, they didn't

204

know what they were looking for, or they came too late. I knew who took the violin. What I needed to know now was why.

"Don't discuss this with anyone," I said, as I got myself out from the counter I was in.

"Even the boss?" she asked.

"Especially the boss," I said. "We need to be focusing on this case. When it's all cleared up we'll let you know."

I found it easy to lie to some people some of the time. Maybe it was my years as a cop. Whatever, it came naturally, like slipping on a comfy pair of loafers.

I walked out into the night. I caught a tide of pedestrians and rode it back towards the Ritz and from there it wasn't far to the Bon Vivant Views. The scene of the crime.

I marveled at how busy New York was. Not like LA. At least the Santa Monica area where I lived. Folks slept in LA. New York seemed filled with the walking dead. Insomniacs and zombies. It was the kind of place that would run me dry if I stayed too long. A man needs time for quiet reflection if he's going to build character, and solve crimes.

I walked passed the Ritz and carried on towards Bon Vivant. The evening was warm enough and my slacks and shirt and hat were all I needed. I didn't have a permit to carry in New York and so I hadn't bought my gun. Not that I felt like I needed it. The crime scene had been cleared by now and I was just gonna nose around and see if anything spoke to me. Knowing New York as well as I did, which was not well, I didn't figure a guy like me would qualify for a carry permit. Though having met Sonia, I had the sense she might have managed it for me if I'd wanted it. I didn't want it and I hadn't thought of it so it was moot.

The Bon Vivant Views is a high rise apartment building that had forty-four stories. Its limestone exterior gives it a clean and old look. The doorman opened the door for me. Seems these parts of New York I was spending most of my time in are catered to the old and handicapped. They open doors, push elevator buttons and maybe even dress you. I didn't need help with any of that.

I approached the main concierge desk. A smartly dressed young man looked up at me and smiled with fake teeth. He was dressed in a black suit with a red tie. His hair was blond and straight and thin and parted to the right.

"I'd like to take a look at the crime scene," I said.

He looked around nervously hoping that nobody could hear us. There was nobody around to hear us.

"Certainly, sir, can I get your name please?"

I gave him my name. He smiled and nodded. Told me he was just going to call maintenance, and they'd show me up. I waited at the desk. He told me it would only be a few minutes, and it was.

A big burly guy in blue work pants and a short blue work shirt walked towards me. "Hank" was embroidered on his shirt, just above his left chest. His forearms were as thick and hairy as a gorilla's. He wore a bushy mustache and his head carried a curly mess of brown hair. He looked like he could have been in a cheesy seventies porn flick, if he wasn't so ugly. He grunted at me. Might have been words but I wasn't sure.

He went over to the main desk where the refined young blond man gave him a keycard. He walked towards a bank of elevators and I followed him. The elevator opened and swallowed us both. There was an elevator attendant standing in the elevator. He asked Hank where we were going. Hank told him the ninth floor. The elevator attendant put in a key and turned it. The elevator doors closed and he pushed the button that had a black nine on it.

We took the elevator up in silence. Nobody talked to anyone. I didn't care. I didn't have much to say. The elevator doors opened on the ninth floor and I walked out after Hank. We turned right and a couple of doors down from the elevator on the left side was nine zero five. The carpet along the hall was beige and thick. It felt like I was walking along a soft forest floor. It had lots of give. Hank put in the keycard and opened the door. He stepped into the main foyer. I stepped in after him.

"Do you need me?" he asked. His voice was gruff and throaty like he spoke from one of New York's sewers.

I shook my head. Hank started to leave.

"Just close the door when you're done. It'll lock itself."

I turned and watched Hank leave. Then I took a few steps into the main hall of the apartment. There were closets on the right. Up ahead was the kitchen which I walked towards. The sink was first and then off to the right was the rest of the kitchen. It was a good size for the apartment. It was uncluttered. There was nothing on the fridge. No photographs or magnets. I opened it up. There were some beers inside and an opened bottle of white wine. Some wrinkled apples were in the crisper like the bald heads of old ladies. A couple of boxes of Chinese takeout stood on the shelves like white bricks. There was a bottle of milk but not much else worth mentioning. The freezer was half empty. But what was in it were a variety of frozen dinners, a loaf of sliced bread and two ice trays with ice. The one was half empty.

I closed the freezer and looked around. I had the feeling that Klee ate out most days and didn't do much entertaining in his apartment except for screwing the women that came by. The sink was empty and as parched as the desert. Didn't look like it had seen water for days. I opened the cupboards below the sink and garbage was half empty too. Everything about Klee's life seemed to me like it was half empty. What was in the garbage was empty takeout boxes and paper plates and plastic cutlery.

I looked around in some of the other cupboards. Most of them were mostly empty. There were some glasses, mugs, plates and those sorts of things but nothing that interested me. I walked out of the kitchen and went around to the other side of the counter opposite the sink. There were two bar stools there that looked as if they hadn't moved since they'd been introduced to the place.

I was now practically in the living room. In front of me was a large L-shaped sofa. It was facing towards the far wall where a large flat screen TV hung like a square of black night. On my right as I looked at it was a tall comfy leather chair. I walked around it and faced the sofa. That must have been the sofa he'd been shot in. I looked at it more closely. The left side of it, from my perspective, away from the corner of the L seemed more worn. I figured that's where he was seated when he was shot. There was an ottoman in front of that cushion too.

I walked up to it and bent down over it. There was no blood, not telltale signs that any violence had occurred there. It obviously wasn't a through and through, and it looked like he hadn't bled much at all.

The smell was still terrible in the place, most acutely in this living room. It smelled like someone had put shit and meat out in the hot sun to go putrid. I'd smelled it many times before and I never got used to it. The smell of death warmed up could gag a horse.

I stepped away and took off my hat and brought it up to my nose. That helped a bit. I looked around but couldn't see any windows to open. In front of the sofa was a large rectangular glass coffee table that had the Friday Times on it. It also had a couple of men's magazines, and a cup of coffee that wasn't finished.

I took a moment to think. What I was hoping to find was some evidence that someone had swiped his key for the locker at The Glovebox. I didn't know where he'd keep it. If it was me, I'd keep it on me. I'd likely have the key in my wallet. But Cooper and Simms hadn't found it, or they would have told me about it and already have gone to The Glovebox before I'd spoken to them.

That meant he kept it at his apartment. The most common places for something like that would be underwear drawers or in a book case or a drawer of his nightstand. I'm thinking he was paranoid because he thought he was being followed, and he was. So I reckon he'd hide the key somewhere he thought was safe. That meant it wouldn't be in plain sight.

I had a suspicion it would be in his room somewhere. His room was off to my right as I still stood looking at the couch. I moved around it and then went towards the bedroom. The door was slightly ajar. I pushed it open and looked in. It was dark, so I turned on the light. To the left was the door to what was probably the closet. Just beyond that was a door to what most likely was the en suite. To my right was a large chest of drawers. I walked up to the chest of drawers and opened up the first drawer. It was filled with clean boxers and boxer briefs. I rifled through them but couldn't find anything that was interesting to me.

I closed the drawer and as it clicked there seemed to be a similar click just after. Like it had echoed. My ears pricked up and the hair on the back of my neck stood to attention. I listened quietly. My hat was on the top of the chest of drawers.

I had an eerie sense someone was in the room with me. I spun around fast bringing my fists up to my face. Just as I did, this tall concrete fella threw a hook that glanced off my wrists and smacked me upside the left temple. He was huge and his weight through that fist felt like a wrecking ball.

I staggered along the front of the drawer. He was a brawler, though he didn't feel like a boxer. He had an unorthodox style that was probably a mix of all sorts of nasty arts. I sent a jab to feel for distance and it caught him on the cheek. He was in close.

Closer than he needed to be. He had over half a foot of height on me, and probably fifty or more pounds on me.

My head started to clear as he threw a left-handed hook my way. I saw this one coming and ducked underneath it while bringing an uppercut up against his jaw. My only advantage seemed to be speed. I made a good connection with his chin. The problem was it was made of lead. It didn't seem to move him much.

He backed off and swiveled around my right side. I was now facing the door though it was a distance beyond me. We were now closer to the far wall. He was standing near the bedside table. He had short dirty blond hair in a buzz cut. His nose was used to handling fists and his ears were cauliflowers.

I sent another jab to feel him out. He leaned away from it and sent one back which kissed me on the right cheek. Even his jabs had mustard behind them.

I was out of my weight class and I was in an enclosed space. None of these were going to help me. Not against a brawler. I was also concerned by who this was. I knew he had a friend, but I didn't know where his friend was. I couldn't focus enough on him without trying to figure out if I was about to be blindsided.

I took a quick look over my left shoulder. This wasn't just a rookie mistake, it was catastrophic. He sent another left hook to visit my right jaw. It dazed me. I staggered back a step, and pulled up my hands higher. He sent a right hook around like a slamming iron ball. There were stars in my peripheral vision but I managed to duck and the fist glanced off the top of my head. I don't have a glass chin. In fact I'd never been knocked out, but I could see it coming if the ref didn't step in within the next few minutes.

There was no ref. I had to help myself. The right hook had left an opening and I planned on taking it. As the right bounced off the top of my head I came up with an overhand which landed square on the left temple of this giant. My vision started to clear and I could see that I had dazed him.

I came up as he staggered towards the bed. I sent a jab which touched him on the mouth and he staggered back more, almost falling onto the bed. I sent another quick jab, but I knew I needed to act quick. He was slowly sliding along the side of the bed. I set up a hook which was heading right towards his left cheek when a blur of motion caught my attention on my left and I looked at it.

I saw a blackjack like a dark gray fish coming. It slapped against the side of my head. It was lights out. I fell to my knees, my hook as impotent as a eunuch's desire. I fell towards the wall behind me and my head landed between it and the bedside table.

My field of vision narrowed. There was a long dark path in front of me. Everything was distorted. I looked down the tunnel of my vision at the barrel of a gun. Behind it was a tall skinny giant. He looked over to his left.

"Niklas, we must go. He's not worth it."

The guy who said it was the one who had used me as a punching bag. The gun was withdrawn from my face and the lights were turned off. Not the lights in the room. The lights in my head.

Days later it seemed like someone was slapping me with another fish. I opened my eyes. Slowly the face came into my field of vision. It looked like a walrus. After a few seconds I realized it was the mustachioed Hank. He was slapping me with his gorilla hands.

"That's enough," I said to him, putting my hands up to block his blows.

I went to stand up. I put my hand on the side table but it missed and slid down the wall catching on a loose outlet cover. I cursed. It had scraped my small finger.

I got up more carefully this time. I put my fingers gingerly to my temple. It was wet. When I looked at them there was a small amount of blood. But the bump was as large as an ostrich's egg. I winced. It still hurt like a hot stone against my head.

"Are you alright?" asked Hank, and not waiting for my reply, "I'm gonna call the cops."

I shook my head.

"How long was I out?"

"Dunno. I came in and saw you out on the floor, but not before being threatened by those two who were in here with you."

"Did you let them in?" I asked.

Hank shook his head.

"No, I dunno how they got in. I was down the hall waiting for the elevator when I remembered I had something for you, so I came back. The tall skinny one came out of the bedroom followed by the heavy one. The skinny one had a gun and looked at his friend and said 'keep going Sven'. The heavy one said 'don't do it'. I think he was telling the skinny one not to shoot me. He kept the gun on me all the way until he got into the hall and then he told me not to call the cops. I nodded at him."

"So the big guy was called Sven?"

Hank nodded.

"What did they want?" he asked.

"To use me as a punching bag I guess."

"I'm calling the cops," said Hank, not asking, telling.

"Before you do. What did you come back to tell me?"

"Detective Simms had left a message asking me to tell you not to mess with the crime scene just in case they weren't finished with it."

I nodded. Sounded like a stupid message. I've been around crime scenes before, but perhaps I should be grateful. Maybe Hank coming back here like that saved my life.

"I'm going to call the cops," said Hank for the third time.

He left and I sat down on the side of the bed and rubbed my head. Then I shook my head and tried to shake out the cobwebs. I looked around and thought I should go back to rifling through the chest of drawers. But I wasn't up to the task. Then I realized there was a bedside table right next to me. Being lazy and discombobulated, glad I could still say the word, I figured I'd start there. I opened the drawer. There wasn't much in it. A bottle of lube, a few condoms in their packets and a small screwdriver. That was a weird item to keep in your bedside table. Not the best self defense weapon but I guess each to his own.

That was it. There were no other drawers. The bottom only had a shelf on which were some books. They all looked like thrillers from what I could tell of their titles.

I sat back and thought for a minute. Where would Klee keep the key for his Glovebox locker? Maybe it was in the chest of drawers still. I steeled myself to get up and have a look. I glanced down at my finger and noticed a curl of loose skin like a split bulb of garlic. I pulled it off, and looked at the outlet cover that had done it. It dawned on me then. Why was an outlet loose? Then I realized I'd just seen the screwdriver. I pulled it out again and knelt down by the outlet cover. I unscrewed the screws and pulled the cover off.

There was nothing on the wall side of the outlet except for the two female plugs. I looked at the inside of the cover and there it was, hidden in plain sight. Written in black felt were the words "The Glovebox #007". Just below it was a piece of torn clear plastic tape. That's where the key must have been for the locker. And I knew exactly who took it.

But I needed to know when she took it and how. How did she get past the uni at the door once this had become a crime scene? And I realized she didn't need to get in after the cops were here, she could have gotten in before.

## Seventeen

I left the apartment with Hank still on the phone looking after me with a frown. I headed down to the lobby and went straight to the front desk. The same blond was still there. He smiled at me but his smile was strained. Perhaps it was my swollen lip, cheek and temple.

"You must have cameras of the lobby right?" I asked.

He nodded.

"I'd like to see the footage from last Friday morning."

He pinched his lips together. The news wasn't going to be good.

"We only keep recorded digital for seventy-two hours. It's automatically erased," he said with a genuinely glum look.

"Shit," I cursed under my breath, "that doesn't help me. You might want to consider upping your retention policy."

He smiled good-naturedly and nodded. I turned to go but stopped in my tracks. I turned back to look at him.

"Did you happen to see two big men with dirty blond hair here on Friday morning?" I asked.

It was a gamble, but I was betting red was gonna come up. It did.

"Like the two who just left?" he asked.

I looked around. There was no sign of them.

"What two?"

"You just missed them," he said. "They were about six five. The one was stocky, the other was thin. Very well dressed."

I nodded vigorously.

"Yes, them," I said, "were they here on Friday morning?"

More nodding of the head.

"Yes, I saw them. They came in just after nine. Said they had important business with Mr. Klee. They told me they were from the German Consulate on a very important case of national security."

"And?" I asked.

"Well, I told them which apartment Mr. Klee was in and they went right up."

"How long did they stay for?"

"Not long, ten, maybe fifteen minutes. They came back down, thanked me and said that everything had been sorted out. Though they didn't look too happy, especially the stocky one."

No doubt, I thought. Mr. Double-Tap-Niklas probably didn't give Mr. Hammer-And-Anvil-Sven time to beat the information out of Klee.

"Did you tell this to the police?" I asked.

"No, why?"

"Because it's related to Klee's homicide is why."

Blond bobblehead frowned at me, trying to put it all together. I figured him for a natural blond.

"Was there a woman who came in shortly after them?" I asked.

"We have lots of women who live here," he said.

I nodded.

"Right, but she wouldn't have lived here. Attractive woman with black hair. Probably in a pony tail, slim and about five five? Piercing blue eyes?"

Blond boy smiled and grinned at me.

"Yeah, I remember her now. Had a slight accent. She came in just before I was getting off shift. Just before noon. Very nice lady. Asked me the same questions you're asking me. Wanted to know if those two Germans had been in. I told her they had. She said she was from Homeland Security, so I let her up too."

"How long did she stay?"

"I don't know, she didn't come down by the time I was off shift which was about ten minutes later.

"Have you seen her since?"

He shook his head.

"Everything alright?" he asked.

"Why shouldn't it be? I got tenderized by two Germans in the very same apartment that your tenant was murdered."

"I'm sorry to hear that," he said.

He was as oily as a fifties haircut and just as smooth. I walked away, and just as I left the Bon Vivant Views a couple of cruisers pulled up outside and four cops walked in. Sometimes a fedora and the dark of night can hide a beating better than sunglasses.

I walked the streets of Manhattan for a while looking for a well in which to drown my sorrows. Somewhere off of East 86th and Park Avenue I found a bar dark enough to match my moods and liquid enough to drown my sorrows. I pulled up to the bar and had the barkeep bring the bottle of Scotch to me. I spent the rest of the night meeting it half way.

By two in the morning I was out of money and out of sobriety. I made my way back to the Ritz with a fuzzy head that was warm and thick without a twinge of pain and a belly that huddled around the ebbing coals of Johnny Walker's fire.

## Eighteen

Drinking always seems like a fine idea at the time. The next morning I spend the first hour cursing my stupidity. But once the aspirin has wrestled my headache to submission I'm feeling right with the world once again. It was Tuesday morning. Late in the morning, just after ten.

I was still arguing with myself about how much I shouldn't have drunk as much as I did. Meanwhile the aspirin was taking its time sauntering up to the goliath of my headache. I decided to take a shower and count my blessings. That took all of a few seconds so I started thinking about the case.

I'd been in New York three days. I was entering into my fourth. That meant I'd made two grand already, plus expenses. Not bad. I wouldn't be homeless for another month or two at least. I could also buy some paints and paintbrushes. . Ain't life swell? I figured I'd have this case wrapped up by the end of the day or the next day latest. I knew who killed Klee and I figured I knew why they killed him, but I needed to find out where the violin was. That was the missing piece.

I got out of the shower and called a guy I knew in the CIA. It wasn't the Culinary Institute of America which wasn't far from where I was. Though bacon and eggs sounded pretty good to me.

No, I called my guy in the intelligence agency. We went back to the days I was on the job in LA. We scratched each other's backs from time to time. My back was itchy. I asked him to get me anything he could on Christina Tedder, if that was her real name. You might be wondering why I was asking a guy from the CIA when Tedder told the Bon Vivant's bon vivant that she was from Homeland Security? The quick answer is that I didn't believe her, and my guy at the CIA could find that out.

I made another couple of phone calls to reach out to John Stampley. He was as cold and hard as the bottle of vodka in the back of my freezer. But I warmed him over with my charm, personality and Dale Carnegie's winning strategies.

You might imagine I used some erudite wit. On the contrary. I simply told him that he was being investigated for the murder of Klee and that I was there to help him. Either that, or the coppers were gonna be all over him like maggots on a cadaver. He preferred the first option.

I dressed in new clothes. Dark charcoal gray pants, a navy blue shirt and my black fedora. I put on a dark gray sports coat and I looked better than I felt. I added a dash of cologne for old time's sake and headed out the door. I was ravenous and I was on the prowl for bacon and eggs.

I didn't want to give another try to an uppity overpriced establishment so I went to a local diner. Concierge at the Ritz recommended Viand Cafe up on Broadway. He was a big strapping lad who looked like he knew his food. So I trusted him.

I headed up there. Viand wasn't too far from the Lincoln Center. It looked like a nice upscale joint. Clean, new blue awnings on the outside with nice wood paneling around the booths which had thick comfy mustard colored cushions. I found a booth and sat down. I put my hat down next to me. A friendly waitress came up and offered a menu. She was fat like a hippo with dimples in each cheek. I ordered a coffee and looked at the prices. The prices were right. The kinda place I felt at home at.

She came back with the coffee and I asked her about the bacon and egg sandwich. She said it was amazing. So I ordered it and waited. The diner was less than half full. It was coming on eleven anyway, and I was just ahead of the lunch crowd.

I had a big appetite and a long way to go after brunch. Stampley was up in Union City in Jersey which was just across the river. It was a working class neighborhood from what I could figure, and I was trying to decide if I should take the Maybach or the yellow limo. The Maybach would get some lookie-loos. I was trying to figure if that was something I wanted. I figured it couldn't hurt. It would tell Stampley I knew people. Powerful people. That might get him trusting me easier. Better than having to win him over in the laboratory of sweet science. I was getting tired of feeding the mute my knuckle sandwiches.

I took out my phone and called Terry. He answered as cordially as he always had. But he was sad he couldn't help me out. Not until later in the day. Said that his employer, I think he meant Sonia, needed the car for a meeting with the banker. I hung up just as the egg sandwich came by.

It sat like two eyebrows on the plate above a spidered nose of coleslaw. I could take it or leave it. I'd make up my mind after I'd eaten the sandwich. A green pickle lay just below the one half of the sandwich like a tear. The egg was fried and the white toast looked like it might have kissed the griddle too. Crispy bacon was thick on the egg's face like a wet scab. I know this because I picked up the slice of toast facing me and had a look.

It smelled good and rich and savory. I could feel the saliva pool in my mouth. I was just about to take a bite when the waitress came by and refilled my coffee. That's what I like about places like this. The coffee never runs dry or tastes burnt.

I ate my sandwich and drank my coffee. I took a bite of the pickle when I was done and tried the coleslaw. I decided to leave it. The sandwich had put a smile on my face and a plug in my gut. I was happy as a kid full of cotton candy at the carnival. For less than a dime I'd had my fill of food and coffee. I left a fin too, because I'm not a cheap bastard. I understand and appreciate hard work. And working on your feet all day slinging for dollars ain't exactly Wall Street.

I picked up my hat and put it back on. I rubbed my knuckles, first my left hand and then my right. They were still slightly red and tender. I preferred boxing in gloves, and I preferred not doing any more while I was here in New York.

But without the Maybach, I couldn't see a way to make Stampley chatty. Though I was gonna try and use my charm. I stepped up to the end of the sidewalk and hailed a cab. My driver was a Jamaican with a colorful knitted cap over dreadlocks. He had an air freshener hung from the mirror that was shaped like a marijuana leaf. It didn't smell like it.

I gave him the address and he took me down through Lincoln Tunnel. He offered me some idle chit chat. I was full, but I nibbled a bit anyway. He told me how he wanted to head on over to LA. How he didn't like the cold winters in New York. I told him I didn't like the cold winters of LA. He laughed at that.

He dropped me outside Stampley's small house on Fulton Street. It was a small box crammed up against other small boxes. It looked nice though. The red brick was clean, the steps up to the front door were clean and there were bright flowers bobbing at me from the small green garden he had on the right under the windows.

I saw an older man behind the windows in the living room. He got up as I came up the front of his house. I rapped on the front door. The door opened moments later. I'd forgotten the kind of guy I was meeting. In front of me was a man in his mid seventies. Thin and frail and stooped over with a cigarette in his right hand. He wore gray slacks and a white shirt that was leaning towards gray.

I rubbed my hands again. No way was I gonna be giving an old man a class in the sweet science. It was gonna have to be old school charm or bust. I smiled at him like he was my grandpa I hadn't seen in years. I offered my hand and he took it with his. It was a cold and dry hand, fragile as an autumn leaf.

"Anthony Carrick?" he asked, the voice coming up creaking like old barnyard doors.

"Yes," I said, "you must be Mr. Stampley."

I was using my undusted charm.

"John, just call me John," he said. "Come in."

"Sure will," I replied.

He turned around and walked up the hall a bit and then turned right into the living room. He was wearing worn gray slippers that matched his pants. He left me with the door wide open. I closed it after the both of us. The neighborhood was quiet. Nobody was around walking or snooping. I liked that.

I followed him into the living room. He was bowed over his recliner and side table. He coughed a good throaty one that must have dislodged a slug. But I never saw it.

"I'm going to make tea. Will you have some?" he asked, not turning around to look at me.

"Sounds good," I said. "Do you need a hand?"

"No."

He picked up a white mug that had UCHS on it with a big blue eagle with wings flared upwards clinging to the letters. If I were a betting man I'd bet that was a mug from Union City High School. Stampley shuffled into the dining room that was behind the living room and then he went left into the kitchen.

I looked around the living room. It was pretty sparse. There was a tube TV in one corner on a wooden TV stand with a VCR below it. On a separate stand in the middle of the room by the windows was a turntable on top with vinyl records all piled underneath, leaning towards the left. There was a couch along the wall that separated the hall from the living room. A wooden coffee table stood in front of it with an ashtray on it that hadn't been used. There were a couple of National Geographic magazines on it. I looked down at them. They were three years old. The couch was showing signs of wear. It was covered by a Salvation Army blanket but not all of its bald spots were hidden. On the wall across from the couch was a picture of a violinist. Looked like Stampley from about a couple of decades earlier. He was in the midst of some sort of crescendo. At least that's what it looked like. The only other frame hanging on the wall was of a Van Gogh print, Starry Night.

I looked back towards the dining room. His recliner was black leather that was wrinkled as much as he was. It was showing extreme wear. To the right of the recliner was a small round wooden table. On it was an ashtray that had half a dozen or more crippled cigarette butts. A packet of cigarettes was next to the ashtray and on top of it lay a silver lighter.

Stampley came back in to the living room carrying a plastic tray that looked like it was printed with a map of the New York City Subway system. He put the tray down on the coffee table in front of the couch. He waved at the couch with a limp hand. I sat down in it. Stampley picked up his mug which was already filled with creamy tea.

"It's probably ready," he said.

I helped myself. I poured the orange colored tea into a blue mug which had "World's Greatest Grandpa" written on it in white child's lettering. I didn't feel that old. It was signed by "Samantha" with a couple of hearts after the name. I added cream and sugar and stirred for a bit while Stampley coughed some more and sat down slowly in his recliner.

"You have grandkids," I said, looking over at him.

He looked at me through eyes topped by sagging lids. The corner of them drooped like jowls over the eye. He nodded and reached for his pack of cigarettes. He lit one up. I decided I'd join him. I fished out my own packet. He offered me a light, but I already had one. I showed him my cheap plastic lighter. I lit my cigarette and blew smoke towards the far wall.

"How old would Samantha be now?" I asked.

He looked at the blue mug in my hand and thought for a moment.

"Nine in November," he said.

I smiled at him. He wasn't looking at me. He blew smoke at the ceiling and looked at the tip of his cigarette.

"So you're a PI," he said.

He still didn't look at me. I nodded.

"Sounds like dangerous work."

"Can be," I said.

I sipped my tea. He smoked his cigarette.

"How many grandkids you got?" I asked.

"Just Samantha," he said.

"How many kids you got?" I asked.

He looked at me and took a puff on his cigarette. He blew smoke in my direction but he was too far for it to reach me. I inhaled on my cigarette and blew circles around him.

"You probably know that," he said.

"I do."

"Then why you asking?"

"I'm being polite."

He shrugged and took a sip of tea. He put the mug back down by the ashtray and tipped off his ash.

"No need," he said. "I'll tell you what you want to know."

"Tell me about your kid," I said.

He looked back at me.

"Maggie's unhappily married. Has been for years. It's only Sam that keeps them together. That and the money."

I nodded. I knew all about unhappy marriages.

"Sam's coming over after school. I'd rather this was finished by then."

"It will be," I said.

He nodded and smoked some more. I did the same. Above us the gray clouds gathered and huddled together by the stippled ceiling like Greek gods pondering the fate of men.

"And your wife died some years back," I said.

He nodded.

"Breast cancer that metastasized to her lung. Drowned to death real slow. Horrible thing."

I nodded again and drank some tea.

"Thanks for the tea."

Stampley nodded at me.

"You're a miserable son of a bitch," he said in his monotone, crackling voice.

"I get that a lot," I said. "Don't mean to be."

"You sit there and talk to me about the sadness in my life like we're discussing the paint on my wall."

"Would you rather I lie, pretend like it really eats me up inside to hear about your crap life."

Stampley kept his eye on me for a bit. We stared at each other for some time. Seems that happens a lot.

"No," he finally said.

"The life of man can be solitary, poor, nasty, brutish and short," I said.

"Hobbes was talking about war."

Stampley drank more tea and offered me more of his hairy eyeball. I took a helping and offered him one of mine.

"Seems to me that you've been at war for a long time."

I was talking about an internal conflict. Stampley didn't look so good. He sat there, thin and frail and jaundiced, enjoying his cancer sticks while he waited for the Grim Reaper. Looked to me like he had nothing left to live for.

"The only joy in my life was stolen from me," he said.

"Family or music?" I asked, knowing the answer.

"Music."

"Tell me about it."

"What's to tell? You know all about it probably."

"I know what others have told. I haven't heard it from you."

Stampley puffed on his cigarette some more. I drank tea and then inhaled. I blew rings across the coffee table and looked at The Starry Night.

"It's probably what you heard," he said. "I was kicked out of first violin so that sniveling son of a bitch could get in. Spent the rest of the best of my life teaching whiny teens music. None of them interested in violin or classical music. All they want to learn is the riffs to their favorite rock songs."

"But you got a pension," I offered.

"I would have had a lot more if I'd made concertmaster like I should've."

"What were you doing on Friday morning between eight and noon?" I asked.

"That's when he was done in?" asked Stampley.

I smiled at him.

"Good," he said, and his lips curled at the corners. It was the first sign of emotion I'd seen in him. "I was at my doctor's from nine until ten. Then I was getting my blood taken. I only got home a little after eleven. You think I killed him?"

I shook my head and puffed on my cigarette.

"I'll take it if you have no one else good for it," he said.

"I know who did it."

"How?" he asked.

"Good old fashioned detective work."

Stampley shook his head.

"No, I meant, how did he die?"

"Shot in the chest."

"Good."

"Do you own any guns?"

Stampley shook his head again.

"Did he suffer?"

"Probably not," I said. "Seemed like the killers knew what they were doing."

"Pity."

Stampley looked down the living room and out the window. He seemed far away. He smoked his cigarette and then put it out in the ashtray. He picked up his mug and took a sip. He cradled it in both hands and they shook every so slightly.

"I take it you and him didn't see eye to eye."

"I hated the asshole."

Stampley took another sip of tea and then looked at me.

"He stole everything from me. Everything that was good in my life. Everything I was good at. Everything I loved."

Stampley looked away and visited faraway places in his mind for a while. I watched him and finished my cigarette.

"Even tried to bed my wife and daughter," he said, looking out the far windows.

I followed his gaze but there was nothing there. He was deep inside his own troubled mind. I drank my tea.

"I wanted to talk to you about his violin."

That caught Stampley's interest. He looked at me.

"The Blount Strad?"

I nodded.

"He didn't deserve it."

"Because it was stolen?"

"Because he didn't deserve it. He didn't treat it right. Didn't play it right. And yes, because it was stolen."

"How did you find out it was stolen?"

"Good old fashioned detective work."

I thought he was trying to be funny but he wasn't smiling.

"Do you have proof?"

"Yes I have proof. I sent it to the Israelis, I thought they would be interested in it."

"And were they?"

"Never heard from them."

"When did you send them the proof?" I asked.

"About six months ago."

"Did you keep copies?"

Stampley nodded and put his mug back down on the table. He stood up and shuffled into the dining room. There was a small desk in the one corner. He opened up the top drawer and pulled out a couple of documents. He came back into the living room and handed me the two documents before sitting back down.

"Cost me twenty-five thousand dollars to get this twenty years ago."

I looked at the papers. They were both official looking Nazi records. The first one was signed by an SS Scharführer Eric Kaufmann. The second one was signed by an SS-TV Standartenführer Swen Boehm. I looked up at Stampley.

"This doesn't mean much to me," I said.

He nodded.

"It's in German."

"I can see that."

"The top one is signed by Scharführer Kaufmann. That's like a squad leader. The important thing is that this is a copy of itemized possessions for Anke Mueller and family that Kaufmann's squad took when they arrested them."

I nodded as I looked down at the sheet. One item jumped up to me immediately. Stradivari-Geige.

"You'll see the Blount violin on that sheet about halfway down. It's called 'Stradivari-Geige', and next to it is the serial number."

I nodded.

"Look at the date of this form."

It was dated the seventh of September nineteen forty-two.

"Look at the date of the next form."

I shuffled the first paper behind the second. The second was dated on the eighth of September nineteen forty-two.

"Look at them closely."

I looked at them closely. They looked identical. They were the same kind of form.

"I don't see a difference other than the date and the signature."

Stampley shook his head.

"Do you see 'Stradivari-Geige'?"

I scanned the page. That seemed to be the only item missing. I nodded my head.

"You see what happened. Ms. Mueller gets captured by Kaufmann and a detailed itemized list is created of her belongings. But when she's brought into the concentration camp there's no sign of it."

"Maybe Kaufmann took it," I offered.

Stampley shook his head again.

"No, it was Swen Boehm. And you know who he is right?"

I nodded.

"The very same Ryszard or Richard Kucharski. Klee's grandfather."

"Exactly, and I checked the serial number on Klee's Stradivarius and it matched the serial number that Kaufmann took down when Mueller was arrested."

"I see, so what did you do with all that information?"

"I threatened the asshole with it. At first he didn't believe me. But the Germans are disciplined and detailed, they kept great records. When I showed him the papers he begged me not to tell anyone."

"But all you wanted was your violin position back right?"

He nodded.

"But Klee never gave it up."

Stampley nodded some more and drank some tea.

"Right, but he eventually paid me over a hundred grand to keep quiet over the next five years."

"Then how come you had a change of mind six months ago."

"It looked like Klee was getting too big for his britches. He was on TV selling one of his CDs and bragging about how good it was. He just kept pissing me off over the years and I'd finally had enough. So I sent it to the Israelis. I figured if Mueller still had any family, then they deserved the violin back."

"Magnanimous of you."

Stampley shot me a look. When it suited him, twenty years later he was feeling all big hearted about it.

"What did you do with the money?" I asked.

He looked at me like I was an idiot.

"A hundred grand over five years. You know how easy that is to spend?"

I shrugged.

"I spent it all. I should have saved some for Sam, but I was young and bitter and didn't think I'd have any grandkids."

I put out my cigarette and drank the rest of my tea. Seemed to me I knew everything I needed to know about this case now. The hard part was about getting justice. Maybe Klee got what he deserved, but I figured he got it for the wrong reasons. I knew Sonia wouldn't be satisfied if his killers weren't brought in for justice. But that took reach beyond my pay grade. I knew a couple of guys who might be able reach that far, and I was gonna pay them a visit later.

"And the Israelis never got back to you about it?"

Stampley shook his head. I drank the rest of my tea and put the empty mug on the coffee table.

"No. All I got from them was a letter thanking me for taking the time to write to them. Didn't even acknowledge what it was about."

"How did you get it to the Israelis?" I asked.

"I just mailed it to the Israeli consulate here."

I nodded.

"And nobody got in touch with you? You've never heard from a woman called Christina Tedder?"

Stampley shook his head.

"Should I have?"

I shrugged.

"I guess not."

I looked at him for a while and at the papers in my hand.

"Can I get some copies of these?"

"You can have them. They are copies. Not that I care anymore. The bastard is dead. Justice has been done."

I got up to leave. I looked around the room but it didn't seem like a musician's room anymore.

"You still play?"

Stampley looked up at me.

"The violin?"

I nodded. He took another cigarette out of his pack and lit it. Then he looked up at me.

"I quit when I retired some years back," he said.

I nodded at him. My charm was wearing thin. My phone started to vibrate. It was my guy from the CIA. I was gonna take his call. I started to leave but hesitated a moment. Stampley made no effort to show me out. So I did it myself.

I closed the door behind myself and walked down the steps and out onto the sidewalk. I didn't look back and I didn't think he'd be looking after me either. I missed the call but decided to make another one for a cab. They weren't as plentiful around here as they were in the city.

## Nineteen

I phoned my guy back from the CIA and he gave me the information I had requested. It was as I'd suspected, and I was going to follow up on it as soon as I'd seen a couple of New York's finest.

It was after three and I was taking a stroll in the park. I was on my way to see Simms and Cooper. I didn't think they'd had much luck with their investigation, but I wanted to find out what they knew. I figured I could give them a helping hand. Point them in the right direction as a concerned citizen.

I was walking through the Great Lawn. Simms wasn't at the other end to meet me. I wasn't expecting him either. A few of the baseball diamonds were being played. One of them had bases loaded. I watched for a few minutes but no runs made it home. I was starting to think this case might not be a home run either.

I told the uniform at the front desk of the Central Park Station who I was. He made a phone call and sent me on my way. I found Simms in his office by himself. I walked in and sat down as he looked up at me. He was filling out some paperwork.

"Anthony, good to see you," he said.

"Likewise."

Though I didn't feel it. I was in a bad mood. Stampley seemed to have that effect on people. Or maybe it was the useless hitters not being able to get runs in with bases loaded. Could be I just hadn't slept enough. I couldn't even muster a smile.

"Where's Cooper?" I asked.

"He's gone to get coffee. Should be back in a couple of minutes."

"Swell."

Simms smiled at me.

"He's getting you one too."

"Swell," I said again.

"You're not having a great day are you?"

"I've had better."

"Tell me about it?"

So I did.

"This case is a dog's breakfast. This murder is going to go down unsolved."

"How so?"

"Because you guys ain't got jurisdiction over the killers."

"Is that so?" said a voice behind me.

Simms looked up at him and I looked behind me. Cooper came in carrying a cardboard tray with three coffees in it. He handed them out like medals. I took a couple of creams and couple of sugars from a brown bag he put on Simms' table and stirred my coffee with a plastic straw.

"Sure is," I said after a while.

"What is?" asked Cooper, sitting down next to me.

"You're gonna have to close this case as unsolved."

"The hell we are," said Cooper.

"I like your spirit," I said.

"We'll get him," said Cooper. "We're closing in on leads."

"Right," I said, "like a fat man's belt around his trousers."

Simms laughed. Cooper didn't.

"You're mighty cocky for a man who ain't got no jurisdiction in these parts."

"Just in a bad mood," I said. "My employer is not gonna be happy that there's no resolution."

"You're not getting any further in the case then?" asked Simms.

"No, I've figured it out and I know who's got the violin. At least I'm pretty certain. Did you speak to the husbands yet?"

I wanted to hear what Simms and Cooper had rather than give them my news. I'd done a lot of sharing earlier and I figured it was now time for them to give me some love.

"Yeah, we spoke to both husbands and they don't look good for it," admitted Simms.

"I could have saved you some time on that," I said.

"You're bragging now? Telling us you told us so," said Cooper.

"I guess so. I'm in that kind of a mood. So where to now?" I asked.

"We're gonna look into the gun like you said. See which agencies use the H&K USP," said Simms.

"I'll give you a head's up with that," I said.

"How kind," said Cooper sarcastically. "You really think you know who did this? You're gonna come in here and tell us our business."

"Something like that," I said.

I grinned at Cooper and took a sip of coffee. I was being an ass. I couldn't help it.

"Good coffee," I said, trying to be nice.

Cooper didn't say anything.

"Did your man at The Glovebox find anything?" I asked, knowing the answer.

"No. The locker was already broken open and the contents stolen. We verified it was Klee's but don't know who took it. Videotape showed someone in a hoodie," said Simms.

"When was this?" I asked.

"When was what?"

"When the locker was busted into?"

"Looks like Saturday afternoon," said Simms.

I nodded.

"That's something then," I said, trying to be encouraging.

"Sure is," said Cooper. "Like I said, we're following up leads. The person leaving in the hoodie like Simms said was carrying a violin case."

"Maybe it had a Tommy gun in it," I said, cheerfully.

Cooper frowned at me.

"So now you're saying we're looking for Al Capone," he said.

Sarcasm suited him well. He wore it like cheap cologne. It lingered on him like a stench.

"Why not? If not Al Capone, maybe fairies or jilted husbands."

Simms was smirking. I could see it out of the corner of my eye. Cooper was getting hot under the color. His skin was pinking.

"Why'd I even get this joker a coffee?" Cooper asked, looking at Simms. Simms shrugged.

"You take him too seriously," said Simms. "He's playing with you like a cat with a ball of yarn."

That was closer to the truth than anything else I'd heard in the last few days. I grinned at Simms. He winked at me.

"Alright," I said, "let's cut the crap. Have you spoken to everyone at the Philharmonic?"

Simms nodded.

"Did you speak to the caretaker?" I asked.

Simms shook his head.

"Really?"

He nodded.

"What about it?" asked Cooper. "He's only been there a couple of months and he has nothing to do with the musicians."

"Three months," I corrected him.

Cooper shrugged and looked at Simms and then nodded his head towards me. Simms nodded at me.

"What's this about?" he asked.

"It's about the killers of Klee," I said.

"That'd make a good title for a murder mystery, I reckon," said Simms.

"You're a regular couple of clowns. Is the circus in town?" I asked.

Simms laughed.

"Seriously, stop beating around the bush and tell us what we're missing," said Simms.

"The new caretaker is Martin Maurer. That sounds German to me. Moody confirms he is German, tells me that the first caretaker, a guy by the name of Wit Walczak, stops showing up for work a few months ago. So they have to hire someone new. This new guy Maurer just happens to come in at the right time. Coincidence? I don't think so."

"Now you've got something against Germans?" asked Cooper.

"Their cars," I said, "they're stealing the market from GM and Ford."

Cooper frowns, he takes me too seriously. Simms smiles though, so I look at him.

"It's the German connection. Let me put it out there really simply for you. This violin, this Blount violin as it's called, is worth north of ten million. That's not pocket change. But more than that, it's one of kind. The detail is something else, that's what I'm told. And it's old. So this violin belongs to a Jew named Anke Mueller. A German Jew. She gets sent to Mittelsteine where she dies. What happens to the violin?"

"We know what happens to the violin," said Cooper, "it belongs to Klee."

"Before that?"

Cooper was still frowning like French bulldog with a gray mustache. I reach into my shirt pocket and pull out the two folded pieces of paper. I hand them to Simms.

"I spoke to Stampley earlier in the day. He gave me these. Stampley is the guy who was kicked off the orchestra twenty some years ago so Klee could get a first violin spot."

Simms nodded.

"So I asked him if he really did put a PI on Klee back in the day. He said he did, got some really juicy intel on him at a cost. Said it cost him twenty-five grand. Those two pieces of paper you're holding are worth twenty-five grand. Not because they're old Nazi papers, but because that's the effort it took for Stampley's PI to get this info."

Simms handed the papers over to Cooper. Cooper shuffled them around and looked at them with his permanent frown.

"Tell us about these." asked Simms.

I nodded at him.

"Mueller was picked up by a squad of Germans, probably just on routine patrol looking to ferret out Jews. This squad leader, Scharführer Kaufmann, finds her and her family. This piece of paper you have there is the itemized collection of her and her families belongings when they're arrested. There's one item of interest on there. 'Stradivari-Geige'. That's the Blount violin. How do we know? Because Stampley verified the serial number on Klee's violin with the serial number on that paper."

Cooper shrugged.

"Still not sure what this violin has got to do with anything," he said.

"You want to look at the second paper," I said. "This one lists the belongings when Mueller is taken to Mittelsteine. It's dated the next day. No violin listed right?"

Cooper shrugged. I look at Simms he shrugs too.

"So you're saying someone stole the violin from Mueller?" asked Simms.

"That's exactly what I'm saying."

"Who?" asked Cooper.

"The guy whose signature is on that second paper."

Cooper looked at it and his eyes moved down to the bottom of it.

"Standartenführer Swen Boehm," said Cooper.

"Exactly."

"Exactly what? So the guy takes it and then it gets back to Klee's grandfather who is probably related to this Mueller woman," said Cooper.

"Standartenführer," I said, "is like the regiment leader. This guy Boehm, is the leader of those guards presiding over Mittelsteine. He was part of the Death's-Head Units. The guys in charge of the concentration camps."

I might as well be speaking German to Cooper and Simms.

"Right, and after the war, like I said," said Cooper, "the violin gets back to its rightful owner. I don't understand what this has to do with Klee's death and the missing violin. Someone stole it because it was valuable, that's all."

"Oh, ye of little faith," I said, biting my tongue on stronger words.

"Let's hear him out," said Simms, looking at Cooper. "I think Anthony has more."

I nodded at Simms.

"There's lots more. You're thinking Klee got killed because he was an asshole. There were a lot of people who didn't like him. I'll give you that. That was my first impression, that he was killed by someone because he was an asshole. But that's not what got him killed."

"You're saying he was killed because of a violin?" asked Simms.

I nodded. Cooper frowns even more. Soon his eyebrows are going to be over his eyes.

"That's right. Klee was killed over a violin, because he didn't want to give it up or couldn't for whatever reason."

"So who took it then?" asked Cooper.

"The Germans," I said.

Cooper frowned and tossed his head up in the air slightly like I'm being an idiot.

"The Germans, really?"

"Yes, really. Klee wasn't a Jew. I checked."

"Then they took it to get it back to the right people," said Cooper.

"How charming," I said. "I wish I'd managed to keep my innocence through all the years I was on the job."

"Stop baiting the old man," said Simms. "Just tell us your story."

I looked at him and grinned.

"Right. Klee was killed for the violin. He was murdered by a couple of Germans who want to bring it back to the motherland where they think it belongs."

"And who are these Germans?" asked Cooper.

"They're with the German Consulate. I only know their first names."

"What are they?" asked Simms.

Simms had turned to his computer and was getting ready to type them in.

"Sven and Niklas. They're both big. Over six five the pair of them. Sven's heavy with a buzz cut and a nose like squashed pear. Niklas doesn't use his fists as much as his gun. He's got a full head of hair and he's thin."

"We can cross check this info with the DHS," said Simms. "Shouldn't take long."

"While we're waiting I'll tell you the rest of my tale. Swen Boehm, with a W this time, was Klee's grandfather. He stole the violin from Mueller when he found it in her possession when she was brought into the concentration camp. He later gave it to Klee. The thing is, it's not Klee's, and it doesn't belong to the Germans either."

"Are you saying they got it?" asked Simms.

"No, but that's why they killed him. They were looking for it and probably startled Klee when they barged into his apartment on Friday morning. I think Sven wanted to let his fists do the talking but instead Niklas uses his H&K before they can get the info out of him. This is the same Niklas who almost shot me if it wasn't for the maintenance guy at the Bon Vivant Views. Anyway, they had come back looking for the whereabouts of the violin. They didn't know by then that it had been stolen. That's how I know they didn't get it."

"Who did get it then?" asked Cooper.

"Can't say at the moment. But I'll let you know when I can."

"What do you mean you can't say?" asked Cooper.

"I'm okay with the violin finding its rightful home."

"Which is?" asked Cooper.

"The relatives of Anke Mueller. When I'm certain it'll get to them safely I'll let you know who got it. Doesn't matter anyway. Like I said, this is gonna be unsolved in your books."

Simms looked up at the computer screen and then swiveled it towards me. The pictures of Sven and Niklas looked at me like mug shots.

"These the guys?" asked Simms.

I nodded.

"Sven Blau and Nikolas Austerlitz, security attachés to the German diplomat," said Simms.

Cooper leaned in to take a look at the two men.

"Jesus, they do have immunity," he said.

"That's what I told you."

"You've told us a lot of things," said Cooper. "How do you know it's them?"

"Because they tried to kill me and they match the description of anyone who saw the two men who were following Klee over the last several weeks. I bet the caretaker is linked to them too. Figured he could easily get the violin out of the safe in the orchestral basement where Klee kept it up until Klee started getting followed. So they had to use other means."

"So they killed him just to get his violin?" asked Cooper.

"Didn't send their best guys to do it. Maybe they got interrupted, maybe they didn't want the collateral. I don't know. But dollars for strippers they did it. Though you'll probably never know for certain."

"How so?" asked Cooper.

"Because I doubt you'll get a warrant for their guns to test them, and that'll prove it. And no doubt the GSR is no longer on their hands if you can get them to consent to that even."

"Maybe it wasn't them," said Cooper.

"Yeah, and maybe Santa's gonna leave me a present all wrapped up in lingerie this season," I said. "Who else do you think did it? The husbands as you figure it out didn't do it."

"Maybe this Stampley guy. He had a lot to lose," said Cooper.

"And maybe you'll spend the next few weeks exhausting all your leads and come up bupkis. That's alright with me. You knock yourself out. But you won't find anyone to put it on."

Cooper looked at Simms and Simms shrugged.

"I think he's right. I like it," said Simms.

"In any event I'm pretty sure I can get justice to prevail," I said.

"How so?" asked Simms.

"The people who got a hold of the violin owe me a solid," I said.

"How do you figure that?" asked Simms.

"Because I haven't told you who they are. If I did you could likely stop the violin from being shipped out of here. From where I sit, sometimes when you can't get legal justice you can get street justice. And in my books that works out just as good."

"I dunno," said Cooper, "maybe I'll have a go at them. Bring them in for questioning and see what I can get them to say."

I smiled at him.

"Always the optimist," I said.

"Could be done," he answered.

"Could be, if that's how you want to play it. But you've got no proof."

"Got enough for a warrant," he said.

"How do you figure that?" I asked.

"Like you said, they match the descriptions of the guys who've been following Klee around for the last while. I reckon I can bring in someone who'll recognize these mug shots, and put them at the Bon Vivant Views around the time of Klee's death. That should be enough to bring them."

"And if they don't want to, then what? You can't get a warrant," I said.

Simms nodded.

"It's true, Coop. I don't see how we're gonna get them to turn on each other or even admit to anything. They're probably pros and even if they're not, they're not gonna come in and answer questions. Especially if they did it," said Simms.

"What he said," I said.

"Then we keep digging and we keep looking for evidence until we find enough to convince a DA to lay charges," said Cooper.

I chuckled. Cooper looked at me out of a hairy eyeball.

"I doubt you'll find anything else you haven't found already, and even if you do good luck with finding a DA who'll do that for you. And likely by then, they'll be long gone out of the country," I said.

Simms nodded at Cooper and then shrugged. He turned to look at me.

"How did you know these guys were with the German Consulate?" he asked.

"That wasn't too hard," I said. "Jamal told me he saw a couple of guys sticking out like sore thumbs when he last met Klee. Even got a partial plate on it. I knew the plate was on a consular vehicle by the first bit, and it included the country code."

Simms upturned his mouth and nodded.

"That's good work," he said.

I laughed.

"Yeah, it would have been, until I spoke to the guy at Klee's apartment and he told me these two clowns came in and said they were from the German Consulate on national security issues. That sort of gave it away."

"Still," said Simms, "you knew before then."

I nodded. I had.

"So what now?" Simms asked.

"Now I leave you gentle detectives to figure out how you're gonna close this mess. As for me, my work is done. I've gotta go collect my paycheck and give Ms. Varnier the bad news that she might not get the justice she wants."

"It doesn't bother you that these two are gonna get away with it?" asked Cooper.

I looked over at him. He wasn't frowning. He looked tired, like a man who'd just woken up after a bender.

"No, for a couple of reasons. Firstly, this guy Klee was an ass. Not that he deserved to get killed for it, but still, it's hard to have a lot of empathy for such a huge asshole. Secondly, and more importantly, I think I can get justice served, street style, and that'll suit me just fine."

"But Varnier won't like it then?" asked Simms.

"We'll see. I don't think it's the kinda justice she was hoping for. But even billionaires can't be choosers in a case like this. You can keep the papers for your records."

Cooper still had them folded in his hand like a used hankie he didn't know what to do with.

Simms got up.

"I'll walk you out," he said.

I put on my hat and followed him out of the office. Cooper sat there looking at the papers in his hand. He didn't say anything to me, and I didn't care.

"Don't mind Coop," said Simms, when we were out in the main courtyard, "he takes losses like these pretty hard and we've had a few too many lately."

I nodded. I didn't hold it against him. I knew what it was like even though I'd never lost a case, but sometimes the DA had dropped the ball. It hurt like a scraped knuckle across an oil filter.

"Hey," said Simms, "if you ever want back on the job. Think about us."

I grinned at him.

"Thanks, Simms, a guy like you could make a guy like me change my mind about that. But here's the thing. I don't play well with others, especially brass and cop shops got too much brass and not enough leather."

Simms nodded.

"I know what you mean. The politics is brutal."

We shook hands and I left him standing there watching my back as I left. I walked back the same way I came. Only this time I saw a small stringy kid hit a home run and run through four bases in a baseball diamond on the Great Lawn. Ain't life grand?

## Twenty

The walk through the park put things in perspective. Murder Inc. was at an all time low in the city. That still put about one point one five New Yorkers dead every day. A guy in my line of work could make a killing in this city. Not that I was thinking of moving. LA had more than enough to keep me busy. Less in real number but more as percentages.

Still it always got me to thinking about why people kill each other. Not for good reasons. The good murders, if I can call them that, are rare. I'm talking about saving your own life or the life of someone you love. No, I'm talking about the everyday murders. The ones I get tied up in. The ones for no good reasons, or no reason at all.

Like this one. No reason at all to kill Klee. Really, I think a spoiled brat like that would have given up the key to the locker with just a slap on the cheek. Instead they send Niklas, probably a psychopath to do a bully's job. Hell, he almost killed me if it wasn't for Sven.

I scrub away at the edges of this social mold, but it still spreads, staining enough lives everyday to make a good man weary.

But I was getting maudlin and that's not how I wanted to remember my last days in the Big Apple. People were out in the park, playing and watching over kids. Some were on their way home from a day's grind. I was hoping to catch someone before they got off work. I was gonna call in that favor I figured I was owed.

I walked up West 65th Street against the traffic. I found the administration building I had first visited at Lincoln Center and I took the flights to get to Moody's office. I walked into the reception area. Christina Tedder was there behind her desk shuffling some papers. She looked up and smiled at me.

It was a smile could make you forget what you knew. But I wasn't in the forgetting kind of mood. I smiled back.

"Mr. Carrick, nice to see you again," she said.

"Likewise."

"Frank's not in at the moment," she said. "You can probably find him in the hall."

"It's not Frank I'm here to see," I said, still smiling.

"Then who is it?"

"You."

She frowned and put her right hand to her chest.

"Me? Really?"

"Really."

She seemed a little more nervous than she should be if she had nothing to hide.

"Then how can I help?" she said trying to recover her composure.

"You know I was brought in to investigate Klee going missing. Then it turned into a homicide."

"I know, terrible that happened."

"Some wouldn't think so."

She furrowed her brow some more. It was cute. But cute had long before been put to bed.

SECOND FIDDLE (AN ANTHONY CARRICK MYSTERY)

"There were a lot of folks around who had a lot of reasons to do an unkindness to Klee, maybe even kill him."

Christina's mouth got hard and sharp like a mouth carved from marble.

"I hope you're not suggesting I killed him," she said.

I waved my hand in front of me as if that was the silliest idea I'd ever heard in my life.

"Good heavens no," I said. "Though I think you're quite capable of that sort of thing."

More squinting and furrowing. I was planting bushelfuls of the seeds of doubt. I figured they'd start yielding a bountiful crop any minute now.

"As I said, how can I help you?"

"You want to get down to brass tacks. I like that. Where's the violin?"

"I don't know what you're talking about."

That wasn't the response I thought I'd get from someone who knew nothing about the violin. An appropriate response might have been to inquire over which violin.

"The violin you took from The Glovebox," I said. "The Blount violin that belonged to Klee."

"Didn't belong to him," she said.

That's what I was looking for.

"I know," I said. "In fact, I'm glad it'll get back to the family that should have it."

She looked up at me and searched for a while. Feeling for any tell tale signs of lies. She wouldn't find any, because there were none.

"I still don't know how I can help you."

"I'll get to that. Christina Tedder isn't your real name, is it?"

A blank stare. I smiled at her.

"Okay," I said. "I'll make this easy. I think we're on the same side. I don't care about the violin, but I'd like some closure on this case for those who did care about Klee, even though many, and I'd include you in it, didn't. The way I see it is you haven't shipped that violin off. No, you're gonna personally deliver it back to Israel and the family it belongs to. It's valuable and that's what it deserves. Now here's what I can do. I can be an asshole when I want to be. Everybody knows that, it's just in my nature. You help me and I won't tell NYPD that you've got the violin. They'll put unis on you and tail you. Heck I might even swear to an affidavit that I saw you personally take it. That'll get them a warrant..."

"Okay, Mr. Carrick," she said, "I get what you're saying."

"It's Anthony, friends and business associates call me Anthony. We're doing business here."

"What do you want, Anthony?" she asked.

It was an accent I could get used to waking up next to every morning. But it wasn't gonna happen. Like they say. If wishes were kisses everybody would get laid.

"I'd like to see some justice for my client. I had a run in with those Germans you've been working against. You can see the rouge and other makeup they applied to my face. Niklas Austerlitz would've killed me if it wasn't for his colleague and the maintenance guy coming back into the apartment. I figure there's no love lost between the three of you."

"I know who they are," she said.

"And I figure you're probably with Mossad, right?"

Christina nodded.

"Good. I thought as much. That means you have ways of getting things done. Subtle ways. I'd like to see Niklas and Sven get their just desserts. In return you get my everlasting gratitude and silence."

Christina had stood up and was standing across the counter from me. She looked at me steadily with trained eyes that tried to bore into my soul. It wasn't working, I'd been round the block too many times.

"What sort of justice are thinking of?" she asked.

"The biblical kind, emphasis on the Old Testament. An eye for an eye sort of thing."

"This might not be easy," she said. "Those two have diplomatic immunity, but more than that, I'm not sure they're going to be around much longer having messed this task up."

"I have every faith in you," I said.

She rested her chin between her thumb and forefinger and thought for a moment.

"I'll see what I can do," she said. "Are you only concerned about justice for your client?"

I grinned at her.

"Not really. I like to see the world in balance. But seeing how friendly we're being, even if you can't do anything for me, there's justice to be had by returning what rightfully belongs to Mueller's family."

Christina nodded and smiled at me.

"I assume you've located the relatives?"

She nodded.

"Anke has a granddaughter who'll get the violin. She's married with a family, but she's the oldest living descendant."

"Good," I said. "Tell me something. I know how you came to learn about the violin, from Stampley. But how did the Germans find out?"

"There's a secretive branch in the German government that is combing through old records from the war and looking to hijack any items they believe belong to the German people. Anke was a German citizen at the time of her death. I think some in the German government think that the violin belongs to Germany then."

I nodded and tipped my hat.

"Good work, Christina, or whatever your name is." I grinned at her. "Better you than them."

Christina extended her hand out to me and we shook. She had a strong firm grip and she looked straight in the eye. I liked that.

"Chava Kaplan, Anthony, that's my name," she said, smiling from once more, full soft lips.

"Chava, I like it. It's unusual."

"It means life. Israel appreciates your discretion."

"To hell with Israel," I said smiling, "what about you?"

"Me too."

I turned and walked out of the office and back down onto the street. Sometimes discretion is the better part of valor. And sometimes valor is its own reward.

## Twenty-One

I'd left Lincoln Center just before five. It had been a full day to be sure. Things were falling into place. It was only Tuesday and the week lay ahead of me like a naked concubine upon satin sheets. I thought I might stay the week in Modern Gomorrah and enjoy her company. See some sights, eat some apples and maybe take in a show.

But this day, this Tuesday, the fourth day here was still needed to wrap up loose ends. I needed to collect my paycheck and deliver the mixed news about this case. I wasn't sure Sonia was going to like the ungainliness of it all. It was an awkward teenage stepchild of a murder. The kind that just won't tuck its loose frayed ends away.

I got back to the Ritz and made a phone call. Sonia picked up and I told her that my job here was done. She sounded cautiously optimistic. I told her I'd like to see her at her earliest convenience to explain my findings in person. She sounded fine with that. I always prefer to deliver my messages in person. She told me that Terry would come around at seven. She wanted to have me over for dinner.

She asked what I might like to eat. I told her steak, a big one, would be right up my alley. That was it. I showered and shaved and made myself presentable. I watched the news for a while which just depressed me so I flipped over to a crime drama. In the first five minutes I already knew who'd done it. If only it was that easy in real life.

With a few minutes left before seven, and after the drama had confirmed my suspicion about the identity of the killer I went downstairs to wait for my ride. The lobby was mostly empty. Some guests coming back from dinner. Others heading out for a show. All dressed impeccably, making me look like a schlump in just slacks and a shirt with a windbreaker over top.

I didn't have to feel awkward for long. Terry was nothing if he wasn't punctual. At exactly seven he pulled up outside the front doors. If I didn't know any better I might be forgiven for thinking I was in Switzerland.

I walked out as he was getting out of the driver's side. He opened my door and I stepped into the luxury I had become accustomed to. But not too accustomed.

We made idle chit chat on the leisurely drive to Sonia's opulent mansion. Terry was nothing if not discreet. Not once did he ask me about the case, but I had a feeling that he was itching to find out. So I teased him with it. Told him I was meeting with his employer to wrap up the case. He politely said how delighted Ms. Varnier would be.

I nodded and smiled to myself. Perhaps not as delighted as he might think. He said all the right things. How awful it was for such a young talent to be snatched in the prime of his life. I nodded and we commiserated. We knitted polite yarns the rest of the way.

Terry let me out of the car and tipped his hat to me. I did the same at him. I walked into Varnier's apartment building and introduced myself to Jeremiah like I had the first time. His enthusiasm was just as grand as the first time he had met me. He seemed genuinely pleased to see me again. He even said so. Told me that Ms. Varnier was looking forward to seeing me again.

I followed him all the way to her front door, just like I had done a few days before. Sonia opened it up and thanked Jeremiah. He headed back from where he had come. Sonia smiled at me and opened the door wider. I walked in, but the place still didn't feel like home. Maybe because it was too big, or maybe because it wasn't home. But mostly because it felt to me clinical and without heart.

I followed Sonia into the large open living room as we had done the first time. She sat in her chair and I sat down on the couch again. Alfred was all over me like a swarm of flies on a filet mignon. I asked for the Scotch again. He smiled knowingly and moved away quietly. Sonia had in her hand another glass of wine. Red. I had the feeling of déjà vu.

We didn't say anything as I waited for my drink. After Alfred had delivered it and Sonia had nodded him away, and I'd had a drink we started chatting.

"Great views you have," I said, starting off nice and slow.

"Thank you," she said.

"I just came back from seeing the detectives in charge of this case."

It was a lie, but a harmless one.

"That's what you said you wanted to talk to me about. Klee was buried today," she said.

She looked away from me as her eyes misted over.

"You should have told me. I would have been there."

"That's kind of you, but I wanted you to focus on finding out who did this. I'm assuming you know who it was."

"Who being plural in this case," I said.

Sonia nodded just a small nod of understanding.

"You might not be happy with the resolution."

I looked at her to get a read. She looked at me for a while and then smiled the unhappiest smile I'd seen in New York, and I'd seen a lot of them. She nodded her head again too.

"I don't see how. You did say you know who did it."

"Yes, but you're not going to get the justice that I think you were hoping for."

"I see."

She looked down at her wine glass and swirled it around a bit. Then she took a sip. I drank some Scotch. After a while she looked at me and held her gaze steady.

"You might as well tell me about it then. I hate all of this beating around the bush."

I nodded.

"It's easy to tell. Two attachés from the German Consulate killed Klee. I should say only one of them did, but they conspired together."

Sonia's gaze started to falter. Her eyes watered up. She looked down again but that didn't help. The tears dripped out of each eye like shards of glass. Alfred was there with a tissue as if by magic. She took one and dabbed at her eyes. She looked at him with a small, brave smile. He left the tissues on a side table by her chair. She looked back at me.

"You say it with such coldness," she said.

I couldn't figure out if that was a barb or just her interpretation of the facts.

"Didn't mean to," I said. "Those are just the facts. I work in facts mostly. That's what you hired me to do. I try not to get emotionally involved in my cases. It doesn't help."

She nodded and dabbed at her eyes again. Then she tucked the tissue up into her cardigan sleeve.

"He was shot twice in the chest," I said. "That's usually a sign of a pro hit. He wouldn't have suffered."

I was trying to layer a blanket of kindness over this ugly business. I didn't know for a fact that getting shot twice in the chest was painless, I'd never had the misfortune. Maybe as painless as death can be I guess. But people like to hear that. They like to hear that the riverboat over Styx is a quiet smooth ride. Maybe it is. Maybe Klee didn't have time to think about the pain. Maybe the brain was dead before the neurons had a chance to fire. Maybe these are questions that don't need asking.

Sonia looked up at me and smiled again. The smiles were getting warmer.

"Is that what made you realize who did it?" she asked.

I shook my head.

"Not really," I said. "It's not uncommon for people to shoot more than once in the heat of anger. It could have easily been one of the husbands of the women he was sleeping with. What started to put it all together were these two mystery men I kept hearing about who had been following him. At first it was easy to dismiss, but having met a couple of people who actually saw them was the first clue. Then learning about the value of the violin and the way it was obtained helped me narrow in."

"What happened to the violin?" she asked. "Have the police found it?"

I shook my head again.

"No. But I have."

"Where is it?"

"I can't say. It is going back to the rightful owners."

"And who do you believe to be the rightful owners?"

I didn't know if that was a pointed question at me or if Sonia was really asking for my opinion. Sometimes I like to think the best of people, so I gave her my opinion.

"The relatives of Anke Mueller who was killed in Mittelsteine. They'll get it."

Sonia nodded and sipped her wine.

"That seems fair," she said. "I like to think that Paul never knew how the violin was obtained by his grandfather."

And I like to think that most people aren't that idiotic. But I bit my tongue and instead drank my Scotch. Maybe Paul didn't know for most of his life. But Stampley told him all about it. And then he knew. People just like to disbelieve. Disbelief is as dangerous as belief sometimes. Like the disbelieving wife who doesn't think her husband is diddling the kids. But that's another story.

I looked at Sonia as she looked down pensively, swirling her wine. She had a small smile on her face, and when she looked up at me she smiled bigger.

"He was a good man," she said. "Even for all his faults he was good and kind."

She bracketed her comment with a smile and then looked down. I drank more Scotch, and I didn't say anything. People are always good when they're dead. Hell, we're all saints once we're gone. The Klee I never met was a womanizer, pedant and entitled son of a bitch. But now, he's Saint Klee to those who knew him. Maybe we just like to think better of people than they sometimes are. Loss always turns the blind eye.

Sonia looked back up at me and her face had hardened. It had taken the color and texture of stone.

"Why won't there be any justice?" she asked.

"Because they have diplomatic immunity. But more than that, the cops won't even be able to get as far as gathering the evidence they need."

"What do you mean?"

"Well, for one thing, they'll never give up their guns for ballistic testing. And by now the gunshot residue is long gone."

"That's not what they make you believe on television."

She wasn't smiling.

"TV makes everything look so easy," I said. "Fact is, most times you'll have no chance of finding GSR after about six hours. Even less if the shooter washes his hands and changes his clothes."

Sonia frowned at me. She didn't like them apples. I didn't either, but that's the barrel we'd been given.

"When you're dealing with pros," I continued. "It can be extremely hard to fix a murder on them. You usually have to wait for them to mess up. And we don't have the time to wait for these two. I bet within the week they'll be back in Germany."

Sonia's frown furrowed deeper. The farmer of her mind was planting seeds of disgust at a furious rate.

"So there's nothing that can be done?"

She looked at me through stony eyes. From where I was sitting they had the color of granite. The tears had been stemmed. The anger had come galloping in.

"Nothing the cops can do?"

Sonia stared at me for a while. Trying to read what was on my mind. What was on my mind was getting my money.

"And there's nothing you can do?" she asked.

"There's lots I can do," I said.

"Like what?"

"Well, like get paid and head back to LA and forget about this whole tragedy."

She pinched her eyebrows back together again. She didn't like that.

"I mean, what could you do to help get justice for Paul... and for me in this situation."

I had a feeling I knew what she was asking. But I wasn't a hit man. At least not usually.

"What do you want me to do, Sonia?" I asked. "Paul was an asshole from most accounts I've heard from those who knew him. Not saying he deserved what he got, but sometimes we have to make do with the hands we've been dealt."

Sonia swirled her wine and took a sip and then stared into the slowly disappearing red liquid. After some time she looked up at me.

"I'd like justice," she said. "I'd be willing to pay anything really. I don't want them getting away with it."

"So an eye for an eye. Is that what you're suggesting?"

I had never had someone so carefully ask me to murder someone before, and this was the feeling I was getting. She looked down and didn't say anything.

"You want me to assassinate them?"

I used that word purposefully. I figured she'd like the sound of it better than 'murder' or 'kill'. She looked up at me.

"Not necessarily, though it wouldn't hurt me if that happened. I just want them to be made aware of what they've done. I want them to understand the pain they've caused me."

I looked at her steadily for a while. She couldn't hold my gaze. I get that. It's hard to ask someone to murder on your behalf and think you're doing God's work. I've never seen it act as the salve that folks think it'll be.

"I'm not an assassin, Sonia. Certainly not under these circumstances."

Not to say I couldn't see circumstances where I might seek vengeance. But not only would this task be difficult, it'd be pointless.

Sonia nodded her head and stood up.

"I understand," she said, trying to smile. "I don't know what I was thinking. Nothing's going to bring Paul back. I'll get my checkbook."

I watched her walk away and sipped on my Scotch. She wasn't gone long. She came back and sat in her chair again.

"How much do I owe you?"

"Twenty five hundred is my minimum rate. This didn't go over the minimum, so it's twenty five hundred plus expenses. I haven't added them all up yet."

"An estimate," she said. "I trust you."

I cocked my head to one side and thought for a moment.

"I reckon two fifty ought to cover most of my expenses or thereabouts."

She nodded and started scribbling on her check. She tore it off when she was done and handed it over to me. I leaned across the table between us and took it. It was for twenty thousand dollars. I had to look twice.

"Thank you," I said, "but this isn't necessary."

"You've earned it, Anthony," she said. "And in a way I admire your blunt forthright attitude. I can tell you're a man of strong moral principle, and I appreciate the work you've done."

I nodded, folded up the check and put it in my shirt pocket. I took the last swig of my Scotch and put the tumbler on the table. I stood up and grabbed my fedora. Sonia stood up too.

"Thanks again, Anthony," she said.

"Sure," I said. "For a rich lady, I like you, so I want to give you a bit of advice. Vengeance isn't the way to mitigate the pain. Only time will do that. Sometimes I don't know why bad things happen, but those are questions that don't help by asking."

I put on my hat and turned to go when she came up to me and embraced me. She held me tight for a while and tucked her head into my shoulder. I patted her back. After a while she pulled away and smiled shyly.

"Sorry," she said, "this whole thing has just been so difficult and I feel so alone."

I didn't know what to say to that. A woman with her means wouldn't be alone for long. And maybe that was the problem. The jackals would be circling soon enough. I put on my hat.

"Keep an eye on the news over the next few days. You might still get that justice you're seeking."

"What do you mean?" she asked.

"I might not be an assassin but there are others who might like to see the two who murdered Paul erased."

I thought I saw the smallest curl of a genuine smile on the corners of her lips as I turned to leave.

## Twenty-Two

Sonia had paid for my stay at the Ritz for a week. That meant check out only had to happen on Saturday at eleven. I spent Saturday night at the Ritz on my own dime. I had earned it. Sonia had made sure of that.

The Big Apple was a fun place to visit but I wouldn't want to live there. It'd keep a man like me too busy. Besides, I like the beach and the warm sand and the smog of LA. It might give it a dour face but the tourists always remind you of happier times.

Sunday I was going home. I had been expecting Christina Tedder to have done me a favor already. But she hadn't. Maybe she'd gotten cold feet or maybe Mossad wasn't as good as I'd been told. It didn't matter anymore anyway. I had enough money for the next six months and maybe if my next art show in the fall was a success, I might be able to take the year off. Put all this blood letting behind me.

I was comforted that I was able to tell Sonia who'd done it. That was something, right? Though there was a weight in my belly, like a small cold stone that just didn't sit right. Those two German killers deserved their comeuppance. But I wasn't sure it was coming.

Hell, if I could have summoned the motivation I might have delivered justice myself. But it would have been a tough job, they'd probably have remained holed up in the consulate and I would have had a helluva time getting in. And I didn't really see myself stretching that far for Paul Klee. I never met him, but still I didn't like him. No way was I gonna break a sweat for him.

So I sat in the waiting lounge of the airport for my flight back to The Big Orange. I was feeling a little maudlin. Maybe I'd been too hard on Sonia. Maybe I'd judged her too harshly for being rich. Maybe she'd come from humble beginnings. Most likely though, I was getting too sentimental for this kind of work.

I figured I needed to head back into the ring and spend a few more days studying the sweet science. I was getting soft. Not so much physically, but emotionally. And that can be deadly.

Let the dead bury the dead. The living have enough strife to contend with.

A part of me had hoped that Christina or Chava would have been good to her word. Maybe there was still time. Maybe they were still in town. Right, and maybe I believe in unicorns and fairies.

As I sat worrying about things beyond my control boarding was called. I was in business class and that had the privilege of boarding first. It got me thinking about other things. For instance, it got me understanding how the rich come to think of themselves as better than us.

For instance, if you give a fella a million dollars a year for running a company he'll soon figure he's worth it. Despite the fact that the guys actually making the product on the floor are lucky to make fifty thou. Then after a while he'll see his buddy at Acme making five million and soon that's what he figures he's worth.

Then they get catered to, like boarding first. Being treated differently by restaurants, hotels, airlines. It's no wonder they start to feel entitled. Like maybe they're paying too much taxes to keep single moms on welfare.

I smiled at the gate attendant as I walked down the jet bridge to the plane. If there's anything I've learned staring into the barrel of human suffering and vice it's this. The deadly sins can quickly run amok if not checked by virtues, whether self imposed or otherwise.

The plane filled up quick and I was served a Scotch before we had even started to taxi down the runway. Nobody was sitting next to me. I had the aisle to myself.

The captain came on and the flight attendants did their mime at the front. I didn't mind that part. Not with the flight attendant I was looking at. She had light brown hair in a pony tail that danced at the back of her head like a tail as she walked up and down the aisle. Her calves were bare below her knee length dress and as shapely as tear drops. Her bum was as tight as two bubbles about to burst and her white teeth like piano keys that played sad songs with my heart.

I was thinking of flirting with her as she came by offering me all manner of tasty morsels, but then I thought of Emily back in LA. I wanted to play that long ball out and see if she'd intercept it. So I bit my tongue and drank my whisky.

At around thirty-five thousand feet someplace over the Midwest I got bored with the inflight movie. I flicked over to CNN to see if anything interesting had been happening in the world.

I didn't have to wait long to see the angels smiling down upon me. At around the time of takeoff a German consular vehicle had exploded on its way to the airport. The reporter identified the three men who had died at the scene as the German ambassador's chauffeur Mr. Markus Wolf as well as two attachés with the consulate, Mr. Niklas Austerlitz and Mr. Sven Blau. These were the same two faces I'd come to know at Paul Klee's apartment the other day.

The reporter was suggesting that it was the work of terrorists. Perhaps Islamist extremists. Why not? They're the current bogey man, I suppose. Though I knew different. I knew who had done it, and if they were worth their salt the truth would never come out.

I expected to feel better about the news but I didn't. And it wasn't because a third party had died needlessly. It just didn't bring me the peace and tranquility I'd been hoping for. Maybe it had for Sonia. If she'd been watching.

## About Jason Blacker

Jason Blacker was born in Cape Town but spent most of his first 18 years in Johannesburg. When not grinding his fingers down to stubs at the keyboard he enjoys drinking tea, calisthenics and running. Currently he lives in Canada.

Under his own name he writes hard boiled as well as cozy mysteries, action adventure, thrillers, literary fiction and anything else that tickles his muse. Jason Blacker also writes poetry and daily haikus at his haiku blog.

You can find his haikus and other poetry at his website **www.haiqueue.com**.

To stay up to date and learn about new releases be sure to visit **www.jasonblacker.com** where you can find more information about his writing and upcoming projects.

If you enjoy space opera in the tradition of Star Trek then take a look at Jason Blacker's pen name "Sylynt Storme". It is under the name Sylynt Storme where you can find both sci-fi and vampire fiction written by Jason Blacker.

"Star Sails" is the space opera series and "The Misgivings of the Vampire Lucius Lafayette" is his vampire series.